NEVER EVER

EVA RAE THOMAS MYSTERY - BOOK 3

WILLOW ROSE

Books by the Author

HARRY HUNTER MYSTERY SERIES

- ALL THE GOOD GIRLS
- RUN GIRL RUN
- NO OTHER WAY
- NEVER WALK ALONE

MARY MILLS MYSTERY SERIES

- WHAT HURTS THE MOST
- YOU CAN RUN
- YOU CAN'T HIDE
- CAREFUL LITTLE EYES

EVA RAE THOMAS MYSTERY SERIES

- DON'T LIE TO ME
- WHAT YOU DID
- NEVER EVER
- SAY YOU LOVE ME
- LET ME GO
- IT'S NOT OVER
- NOT DEAD YET
- TO DIE FOR

EMMA FROST SERIES

- ITSY BITSY SPIDER
- MISS DOLLY HAD A DOLLY
- RUN, RUN AS FAST AS YOU CAN
- CROSS YOUR HEART AND HOPE TO DIE
- PEEK-A-BOO I SEE YOU

- Tweedledum and Tweedledee
- Easy as One, Two, Three
- There's No Place like Home
- Slenderman
- Where the Wild Roses Grow
- Waltzing Mathilda
- Drip Drop Dead
- Black Frost

JACK RYDER SERIES

- Hit the Road Jack
- Slip out the Back Jack
- The House that Jack Built
- Black Jack
- Girl Next Door
- Her Final Word
- Don't Tell

REBEKKA FRANCK SERIES

- One, Two...He is Coming for You
- Three, Four...Better Lock Your Door
- Five, Six...Grab your Crucifix
- Seven, Eight...Gonna Stay up Late
- Nine, Ten...Never Sleep Again
- Eleven, Twelve...Dig and Delve
- Thirteen, Fourteen...Little Boy Unseen
- Better Not Cry
- Ten Little Girls
- It Ends Here

MYSTERY/THRILLER/HORROR NOVELS

- Sorry Can't Save You
- In One Fell Swoop

- Umbrella Man
- Blackbird Fly
- To Hell in a Handbasket
- Edwina

HORROR SHORT-STORIES

- Mommy Dearest
- The Bird
- Better watch out
- Eenie, Meenie
- Rock-a-Bye Baby
- Nibble, Nibble, Crunch
- Humpty Dumpty
- Chain Letter

PARANORMAL SUSPENSE/ROMANCE NOVELS

- In Cold Blood
- The Surge
- Girl Divided

THE VAMPIRES OF SHADOW HILLS SERIES

- Flesh and Blood
- Blood and Fire
- Fire and Beauty
- Beauty and Beasts
- Beasts and Magic
- Magic and Witchcraft
- Witchcraft and War
- War and Order
- Order and Chaos
- Chaos and Courage

THE AFTERLIFE SERIES

- BEYOND
- SERENITY
- ENDURANCE
- COURAGEOUS

THE WOLFBOY CHRONICLES

- A GYPSY SONG
- I AM WOLF

DAUGHTERS OF THE JAGUAR

- SAVAGE
- BROKEN

Prologue

Earlington Heights Metrorail Station
Orange Line
Southbound

Chapter 1

He got in through the third door after the train pulled in at 7:58 a.m. as usual. Ryan Scott was holding his Starbucks coffee in one hand and had his backpack slung over his shoulder. Once inside, he spotted a free seat and moved toward it, then sat down. The train departed and rattled along while Ryan sipped his coffee and went through the news headlines on his phone.

Ryan had just landed a summer internship at *The Miami Times* and had to make sure he was updated before today's editorial meeting. The dream was to become a reporter, but the road was long. As a part of his Master of Journalism program at the University of Washington, he was required to do a six-week-long internship. He was still going through training but needed ideas to pitch so he could one day do his own story. Ryan knew he needed to stand out from the crowd, and he had learned that, in order to do so, he needed a good story. The newsroom was always on the hunt for the next big breaking news story, and he needed to pitch some original ideas and demonstrate initiative. He desperately wanted to see his name in the paper.

Of course, he did.

The train came to a stop at Allapattah and some of the passengers left while new ones boarded. A black woman sat next to Ryan, and he moved his backpack to make room for her. The train was getting more crowded now, as usual, as they headed south toward downtown Miami.

Ryan smiled politely at the woman who sat down next to him with a heavy sigh. A poster on the wall across from them asked if they suffered from schizophrenia in both English and Spanish. The woman wore striped pants and sat with her big green purse in her lap. Across from them sat an old man, and next to him, a young teenage girl, holding a bag. Ryan smiled at her as their eyes met, but she didn't smile back.

Santa Clara station came and went, and more people came onboard wearing light clothes and sunglasses. The AC on the train wasn't very good, and it was hot. Ryan felt his hands getting clammy as more people came on board. The train moved along next to the road below, and Ryan looked down at the rows of cars that were stuck in a jam, while the train shot through town nice and smoothly. A man about Ryan's age was reading a book in the corner, while another man was holding his briefcase close like he was afraid that someone might steal it. A Hispanic-looking teenage girl at the other end of the train seemed lost in her own thoughts. The window behind the old man had been tagged with graffiti, blocking the view.

Ryan looked at his phone again when the train approached the Civic Center. Ryan stared at the old texts from Susan and wondered if he would ever see her again. She had been ignoring him for days now, and he feared she was moving on. Ryan had liked Susan and wanted there to be more. But she wasn't answering any of his texts anymore, and the last time he took her for dinner at the Olive Garden, she had been distant and continuously on her phone.

Ryan closed the phone with a deep sigh and looked up as the train's brakes screeched loudly, and they came to a halt. At the Civic Center, a lot of people got up, including the young girl in front of him. Ryan still had two stops left, and he leaned his head back when his eyes landed on something underneath one of the seats. Some liquid of some sort was slowly seeping across the floor. Ryan felt his eyes stinging and rubbed them, then felt an unease in the pit of his stomach.

In a sudden attack of inexplicable panic, he rose to his feet and elbowed his way out through the crowd. The doors were about to close as he jumped out at the last second and into the car behind him, heart beating fast in his chest as the train took off once again.

Chapter 2

As the Orange Line southbound arrived at Government Station and opened the doors, the crowd waiting to get on board didn't realize at first what was going on. As usual, they approached the doors, waiting for them to open, so people could get out and then they could get in.

Evelyn Edwards was one of those waiting for the train. As always, she took the train from Government to Douglas Road, where she worked at Nordstrom in Merrick Park. Evelyn had her driver's license revoked after a DUI and had found that taking the train was actually a lot easier than being stuck in traffic every day.

On this particular day, Evelyn was lost in her own thoughts, thinking about her grown daughter, who she hadn't seen in four months. She had called her the night before to apologize once again, but she hadn't picked up. Evelyn felt shameful and wanted to tell her just how sorry she was for the things she had said. She also wanted to tell her daughter that the drinking had stopped now and she was doing AA, this time really doing the program with all the steps and not just sitting there because she had to. She wanted to tell her that she was better and that things had changed. Really changed this time. She wanted to tell her all those things, but her daughter wouldn't even answer her darn phone.

Don't you know you're all I've got?

Evelyn was so lost in her thoughts that she didn't even notice the passengers behind the doors. She didn't see their crying and strained faces as they were pressed against the glass, nor did she hear the hammering on the doors or the desperate cries for them to open.

When the doors did slide open simultaneously, and the passengers inside, screaming and gasping for air, tumbled out, Evelyn didn't even look up from her phone. She was looking at her background photo, a picture of her daughter taken on the beach when she was only five, the day she remembered as one of the best in her life.

Before everything turned bad. Before she started to drink. Before Juan died. Before she lost Pablo while eight months pregnant. Before the clouds darkened above them. Before she cried in bed all day. Before the fog of grief made her a prisoner in her own mind and destroyed everything.

Before all that.

We can go back, can't we? Can we find ourselves again?

Evelyn lifted her gaze and realized that the crowd in front of her had dispersed and an entire flock of passengers staggered toward her. Several of them collapsed in front of her feet. One woman came toward her, and Evelyn didn't notice her before it was too late, and she collapsed in Evelyn's arms. Blood was gushing from her nose and eyes, and she was gasping for air, choking and wheezing.

Evelyn shrieked tearfully and pushed her away, just as a man sank to the ground in front of her, his rag-doll-limp body falling to the platform with a thud. Evelyn stood, paralyzed, and watched this, blood smeared on her clothes and hands, while hundreds of people lay gasping on the ground, reminding her of the fish on her father's boat when she was a child.

A man in front of her lifted his head and looked her straight in the eyes, then breathed his last breath with a deep sigh. Seeing this,

Evelyn whimpered, then turned around, wanting to get away from there, fast, when she suddenly stood face to face with a soldier. He, and the rest of his troop coming up behind him were wearing gas masks and clothes that to Evelyn looked like spacesuits.

ONE MONTH LATER

Chapter 3

"We're here for your annual inspection."

I showed the small woman behind the front desk my identification card from Florida Department of Health, moving it very quickly to make sure she didn't get a proper look at it and realize it wasn't me on the picture, but someone who looked remotely like me. The woman had told me she was the manager of the spa.

"We need full access to the premises, please," I said.

We were me and my sister, Sydney. I called her that even though it wasn't the name she went by these days, and no one had called her that since she was seven years old. She was known publicly as Kelly Stone, the Hollywood actress. Still, I insisted on calling her Sydney, which was her birth name before our biological father stole her in a Wal-Mart and kidnapped her to London, where she grew up apart from me. I, on the other hand, grew up on the Space Coast in Florida with our mother, believing my sister was dead and gone. We had recently found one another after thirty-six years apart. It wasn't easy to reconnect after all this time, especially not after her scumbag of a boyfriend had kidnapped my daughter, Olivia, and sold her to an even worse scumbag on the

10

Internet. Sydney, naturally, felt terrible about it, and that was why she had insisted on helping me find her again. As a former FBI agent, I had told her I was capable of doing this myself, but still, she had shown up at my house, ready to go on the day I had decided to leave. There wasn't anything I could say to talk her out of coming.

So, here we were — two sisters on a road trip through Hell.

We had been on the road for three months now, following my daughter's tracks, searching for the man they call the Iron Fist. Our search had led us to this place, The Orient Spa in Leisure City. The badge, I had stolen from a real health inspector in Palm Bay. It granted me access to places like these, where I could do my search. It wasn't exactly legal, any of it, but I was way beyond playing by the rules. My daughter was missing, and I was getting her back. No matter what it took. There was no way I was going to give up on finding her.

Never. Ever.

Sydney stood behind me, still wearing sunglasses so no one would recognize her. She had dyed her hair black and wore fake colored contacts whenever we went anywhere. I was naturally terrified that she would end up drawing attention to us, but I had to admit, she was doing pretty well at hiding her identity. I guess it came in handy that she was an actress. She even spoke completely different, hiding her British accent with a heavy American one.

The small Asian woman in front of me nodded. I saw her eyes grow weary.

"Yes, yes, of course. Go ahead."

We were pretending to be looking for roaches and rats in a routine inspection, so Sydney and I walked around the lobby and soon spotted a door leading to the back.

"What's behind that door?" I asked.

"Just the office in the back," the woman said, shifting on her feet, clearly feeling uneasy.

I smiled. "We're going to need to check that as well."

Her eyes grew big. "Oh, really? It's messy back there. There's nothing there. Costumer never come there."

"Doesn't matter," I said. "It can still pose a health hazard. We need to check everything."

"But old health inspector never went in there," she said. "He says it not necessary."

I smiled again. "Well, that's probably why he isn't here, but I am. Open the door, ma'am."

Chapter 4

T he manager fumbled with the keys as she opened the door. The two other women who were introduced as massage therapists stayed behind, while Sydney stayed with them.

"We are up to date on all licenses," the manager said.

"That's good," I said indifferently and rushed in as soon as she had pulled the door open. The small woman hurried ahead of me. She ran into a room to our right, and I went in after her. As we entered and I spotted the mattresses on the floor, she tried to cover them up with a blanket. I still managed to see clothing and personal hygiene items before she covered it all up. Seeing this made me feel uneasy. The manager was visibly nervous while trying to cover up the items.

I continued down the hall and found another room — same thing. Mattresses spread on the floor, bedding, clothes, stuff for personal hygiene. There was a small refrigerator in the corner. I opened it and found it filled with food and drinks. A trash can had empty personal care items in it, mouthwash and shampoo.

It didn't take a genius to figure out what was going on here.

I rushed out the door back into the hallway, the small woman getting nervous now.

"Where you going, huh?"

Not answering her, I walked down the hall and tried to open a third door. It was locked.

"Open this," I said, my pulse quickening.

The woman stared at me. "I can't. No key."

I didn't think about it twice. I gave the door a violent kick, and it slammed open.

Just as I thought. Behind it, staring back at me sat eight young girls. Their eyes glared at me anxiously; their arms were wrapped around each other. Some were crying. All were dressed in barely any clothes.

The sight made me sick to my stomach. I turned on my heel, walked back in the hallway, and spotted the manager. She was backing up toward the exit when I pulled my gun from the holster and pointed it at her.

"You're not going anywhere. Get back here, now."

Sydney came up behind her, blocking her way out. The manager stared at the gun, then up at me.

"We're going to have a little chat," Sydney said and grabbed her by the neck. "In your office."

Sydney pushed her into the office, and I came in, then grabbed her and pressed my gun to the back of her head, pressing her down onto her desk. My hands were shaking when imagining one of these girls being Olivia. This was the fifth of these types of joints we had hit just in the past month, and everywhere it was the same — girls dressed in nothing, malnourished, confused, and scared. They would tell us stories of being taken and of many men coming to them at night, of being raped by hundreds of them a day, and of being shipped from one spa parlor to another during the day, enter- taining more men than you'd want to think about.

It was beyond disgusting.

And one of them, somewhere out there, could be my daughter.

I couldn't finish the thought.

"I have money," the manager began. "I pay, you…"

"Shut up, lady. Shut up and listen to me. The way I see it, this can go two ways. Either I call the cops right now, and all of you end up in jail for many, many years."

"Or...?" the woman asked, her voice filling with hope.

"Or you give me what I want."

Chapter 5

J ust like the rest of them, she opted for the second solution. Of course, she did. I let go of her neck and let her sit down in a chair. Her hair was a mess as it had come out of her tight bun, and her eyes were anxious. She was broken. Just the way I needed her to be.

"What you want?" she asked.

I sat down in front of her; the gun still lingering in my hand.

"There's a man they call the Iron Fist," I said. "I need to get to him. I need to know where to find him. The last place we busted told us you might know."

The woman's eyes went from anxious to terrified as she looked up at me. She shook her head.

"I don't know no Iron Fist."

"And we're back to lying again," I said with a deep sigh. "You have a tell, do you know that? I'm sort of an expert in people and profiling them, and I can see straight through you. You wanna know how? You roll your lips back when you tell a lie, and you gesture with both hands after you have given me your answer. Both are 'tells.' So, do you want to tell me the truth, or should I call my friends at the sheriff's office?"

The woman's nostrils flared a couple of times, and her eyes lingered on me. I placed a picture of Olivia in front of her.

"I am looking for this girl," I said. "Have you seen her?"

The woman looked at it, then shook her head. "No."

I studied her. There were no signs that she was lying this time. *Dang it!*

"All right, back to the Iron Fist. What do you know about him?"

The woman's lips quivered as she opened them to speak. "He buy girls," she said.

I nodded. "And where does he get those girls?"

She shrugged. "Wherever he can. Internet mostly."

"Has he bought any girls from you?"

The woman looked at me, then swallowed. She answered with nearly a whisper.

"Yes."

"And where does he take those girls?"

She shook her head. "I don't know."

"You're doing it again, the lip thing," I said and looked at Sydney. "She's doing it again."

Sydney nodded. "I saw it."

The woman exhaled. "Okay, he take them to Miami. That's all I know."

"Miami, huh? Where in Miami?" I asked, feeling relieved that we were finally getting somewhere.

"I don't know."

I could see no sign that she was lying, unfortunately. Miami was a big city to look for one man. But it was better than nothing. I was closing in, and that, at least, was something. I just hoped the guy still had my girl and hadn't sold her to someone else. With the stories I had heard from most of these girls, I wasn't too confident that she had remained in the same place for all this time. But it was the only lead I had, and I knew from experience that if you kept digging in the same place, at some point, you'd find something.

I rose to my feet and looked at my sister. "I guess we're going to Miami, then."

The Asian woman nodded, probably just happy at the prospect

of us leaving. I glared at her, anger rising inside of me as I thought about her and people like her who lived by keeping these girls in slavery. What I had seen in the past three months had broken my heart to pieces.

The woman got up too. "So… no police?"

I stopped in my tracks, then leaned over and slammed my fist into her face so hard I heard her nose break.

"Yeah, about that. Turns out I have a tell too. When I knock out scumbags like you right after telling you that I won't report you to the police, then I'm actually lying. Guess you should have known that."

Chapter 6

W e left the three women in the back office, tied up with strips. As soon as we were in the parking lot, in the mini-van that Sydney had bought for us when we decided to leave my old car because we knew it would be tracked after our first bust, I tapped the number of the local police enforcement.

I told them the address and what they would find when they got there. I also advised them to bring someone from a local shelter. I usually recommended a place called *No More Tears* since they seemed to be doing a good job of taking care of victims of human trafficking. I then threw the burner phone in the trash and got into the car, where Sydney had kept the engine running. I looked at her, then smiled, exhausted, before we took off, tires screeching across the asphalt while leaving the small strip mall.

This was the ninth of these types of spas that we had turned over to the police somewhere in Florida over the past three months. I couldn't believe how easy they were to find. Just a simple Google search had led me to the first one not far from my own home in Cocoa Beach. In a forum on the Internet, the all-male customers discussed vividly what you could expect to get there, what services they provided. They didn't even try to hide it. And so, I went to check it out. In the back, I found about ten girls, ages twelve to seventeen, ready to entertain the men who came as customers. To imagine that this was going on right beneath our noses, was terrifying. These girls came from all over the world, and some even from right here in Florida. And they were being held captive right here, right under our noses.

The only issue was that what I had done made me a criminal in the eyes of the law, and now they had put out a warrant for my arrest. Aggravated assault. I had lost it in the first place we took down and beat the crap out of the owner. If Sydney hadn't stopped me, I was certain I would have killed the guy. Still, I wasn't sorry I had hurt him. I was just sad that a surveillance camera had taken my picture as I left the shop.

Sydney looked briefly at me as she hit I-95 toward Miami. I held back my tears and tried hard to erase the images of those young girls in that room, and their big eyes staring back at me, pleading for my help. Hopefully, they would at least be liberated from their hell now. I could only pray that those who pulled the strings would be prosecuted as well, but I wasn't getting my hopes up. Those sleaze bags had a way of keeping themselves out of jail.

Meanwhile, we were going for one of the big guns. The man they called the Iron Fist. We didn't know much about him, but the little we knew made the hairs stand up on the back of my neck.

"You wanna grab a coffee and something to eat before we continue?" Sydney asked.

I gave her a look. She had been so amazing through all this, constantly taking care of me. I didn't know she had this side to her; I had to admit. This was very far from the entitled drama queen and Hollywood actress that I had taken her for, and I felt so thankful, yet I had no way of showing her. I was still so angry at her because of what had happened to Olivia. I knew it wasn't her fault. There was no way she could have known who her boyfriend was, yet I couldn't help myself. I needed someone to blame; I needed someone to take the fall, and she was the closest.

"I'm not hungry," I said and glanced out the window. "Although, coffee sounds about right."

She nodded. "Okay. I'll stop at the next rest area, and we can take a break."

"We should probably ditch the car too," I said.

"Again?" she asked tiredly. "I thought you said it looked like the strip mall had no cameras?"

I nodded with a sigh. "I could be wrong. Besides, there's always a witness; there's always someone who will have seen it and who will call the cops. We need to get rid of it."

Sydney nodded again. "Okay. We'll do that after we get our coffee."

Chapter 7

Matt stared at his screen. In front of him smiled Eva Rae in a picture taken four months earlier on the beach. It was a great day, he remembered. They had brought all the kids together, her three and his Elijah. Matt had hoped that Alex and Elijah would bond if they spent the entire day together, but that hadn't happened. Elijah had sat underneath the gazebo all day, grumbling because he wasn't allowed to play on his computer. Matt remembered how hard Eva Rae had tried to get him to play with the other kids. She had even built the biggest sandcastle with Alex and kept asking Elijah if he didn't want to help. It wasn't until she pulled out Alex's kite and put it up, running down the beach holding it, that Elijah had suddenly gotten interested. He had crawled out and played with them, laughing when it fell down, and Eva Rae fell flat on her face in the sand.

Eva Rae was the only one in the world who had made Elijah laugh. Matt didn't know how she did it. But that was just her.

That's how amazing she was.

Gosh, I miss you.

She had been gone for three months now, and he had no idea where she was. It was probably for his own sake that she didn't contact him, but boy, it hurt. Matt had followed the investigation into what happened at The Bridge Spa in Rockledge after she beat a guy half to death in there. And he knew that the two detectives at the sheriff's office who had put out a warrant for her arrest had no idea where she was either. He also knew it was good that he didn't know because that would put him a dilemma if they came to question him. Eva Rae had known that, and that's why she had left without telling him where she went.

He had seen it in her eyes on the day he last saw her. It was at the CBPD station when they were questioning Anthony Piatkowski, the man who had targeted Eva Rae and then kidnapped her daughter, Olivia, who was only fifteen years old. They had grilled him for days on end, but he kept saying that he didn't know where Olivia was, only that he had taken her to the airport where the Iron Fist's men had picked up the girl. After that, he had no idea where she went. It was out of his hands.

Unfortunately, it turned out he was speaking the truth.

After weeks of going through his affairs, all they had found on his computer were the brief coded messages where they had agreed to the details. There was no trace of this Iron Fist or Olivia since.

That was when Eva Rae decided to take matters into her own hands, and once Matt heard about the manager at the spa getting attacked, and then how the police had received a call telling them where to find ten trafficked girls, he immediately knew in his heart that this had Eva Rae written all over it. He also knew there was no going back for her now, and that it would be a long time before he saw her again. If he ever saw her again.

Matt didn't know for certain, but he assumed that her sister had gone along with her since she had been nowhere near her house since. He hoped he was right in his assumption that the two of them were in this together since he didn't like for Eva Rae to be alone. She had to be feeling awful, and he was so frustrated that he wasn't able to be there with her to comfort her and hold her close. It tormented him not to know how she was feeling or to be able to help her. He wanted to fix this so badly.

There had been silent calls to his landline late at night that he suspected might be her. He believed it was her way of letting him know that she was okay and that she was still around.

But now that another month had passed, he was beginning to get anxious. What was her plan? And would she ever be able to come back?

Sgt. Mason pulled him out of his thoughts as he approached his desk.

"Chief wants to see you," he said. "Asap."

Chapter 8

S he slept on a stained mattress in a room with six other girls. There was no furniture in the house she was kept in and only one toilet.

Every night, she was taken out of the house and put into a van. They then drove for about an hour till they reached a factory, where they cleaned dead chicken and put them into a liquid that killed all bacteria before they were packaged and sent away.

They had given them no gloves to protect their skin, and now Olivia had gotten a rash and was itching all the way up her arm. The night before, she had complained about it to one of the men guarding them, but he had pulled her outside the factory and slapped her till she couldn't stand on her feet anymore, then yelled at her that she wouldn't get any toilet breaks for the rest of the night.

Now, as she lay on her stinky mattress, Olivia kept crying. She was thinking about her mother and her siblings and missed them terribly. It was daytime out, and the other girls were asleep, but Olivia couldn't find any rest. She was so scared, and she felt so hopeless. She hated the house, and she hated the factory even more. It stunk of rotten meat. There were chicken blood and innards all over the floors. But that wasn't the worst part. The worst part was that she never got to see the sun. There were no windows in the factory, nor in the house where they were kept. Armed men guarded the doors, and if they tried to escape, they were beaten. On one of the first days Olivia had been there, there had been a girl, Mya, who had tried to crawl out of the small window under the ceiling in the toilet. The guards had caught her in the yard, and Olivia had heard them as they beat her up all night. They had never seen Mya again.

Some of the girls had been to many other places before this, and they talked about being raped over and over again. They liked it better where they were now because at least they weren't raped. They were beaten again and again, but they'd take that any day over being raped by *so many men you couldn't even count them.*

The thought made Olivia cry even harder. Was that what was in store for her next? Would they sell her to some pimp? Would they move her out of state?

Mom, where are you? Are you looking for me? I am here, Mom. I am right here. I just don't know where here is.

One of the girls lying next to her, Juanita, was crying in her sleep. Olivia looked at her, then placed a hand on her shoulder to calm her down.

It worked. The girl stopped whimpering and continued to sleep. Olivia exhaled and looked at the other girls in the sparse light from the small lightbulb dangling from the ceiling. She wished she could sleep like these girls. She wished she could just disappear into a world of dreams and forget where she was for a few hours. She would dream of a day on the beach with her family. She would even want her dad to be there, even though she was so angry with him for leaving them and finding another woman, one who didn't want his kids around.

Still, she wanted him to be there with her because she missed him. She missed the life she had, with everything it contained, even the problems of high school and going through a divorce. At least that was all normal stuff. What she was living through now wasn't normal.

It was Hell on Earth.

Chapter 9

THEN

They hadn't seen each other in five years. Helen Wellington looked at her old friend Angela, who smiled and waved at her from her seat at the restaurant Ariete. Helen waved back, then walked to her, a sense of dread in her stomach.

Was it a mistake for her to come?

"Helen," Angela said and rose to her feet. She reached out her arms and pulled Helen into a hug. "Let me look at you. Dear Lord, it's been forever."

"Not since Kylie's wedding," Helen said and sat down.

Angela was still smiling. "Has it really been that long?"

"You look amazing," Helen said, then looked down at herself. She was underdressed compared to her old friend, who was wearing a gorgeous yellow pencil dress and had impeccably styled hair. Helen used to be like that; she used to be the best dressed anywhere she went, and the one to radiate in a crowd, but not anymore. The past two years had been a struggle.

A waiter arrived, and they ordered lobster, pasta, and white wine.

"So, how have you been?" Angela asked.

Helen sighed. Angela had contacted her on Instagram and told her she was back in town and asked her if she had time for lunch.

"To be honest, I'm going through a rough time right now," she said.

Helen was surprised at her own openness; she hadn't expected to want to be since she wasn't usually, but this was her old best friend. They had known each other since third grade, and there was just something about Angela that made her want to open up.

"Really?" Angela said. "How so?"

Helen bit her cheek. She felt the sadness inside of her. It was like this monster that never slept but was constantly looking for a way to show its ugly face. Helen didn't know how to keep it down anymore.

"I've recently discovered that I can't have children," she said.

"Brian and I tried for years, and then we finally got checked out, and lo and behold, I was infertile. Having children was the biggest dream for Brian, so he left, and so, well... here I am. Probably going to be alone for the rest of my life. To be honest, I feel like I have nothing much left to get out of bed for."

Angela put a hand to her chest. "That's awful, Helen. I am so sorry."

The wine arrived, and Helen took a long deep sip. She still hadn't quite gotten used to telling her story yet, and it was a lot harder than she had thought it would be.

"Yeah, well, that's life, right?" she said.

Angela tilted her head. "It doesn't have to be."

Helen sipped more wine, then looked at her old friend suspiciously and a little offended.

"What is that supposed to mean?"

Angela drank too, then exhaled. "Nothing. It's just... well, I used to be miserable like you — two years of depression and anxiety. I was popping all the pills you can imagine, and nothing helped. I could barely get out of bed. So, let's just say I know how you feel."

Helen scrutinized her friend when the food arrived. She looked down at the seafood but didn't have much appetite. She had lost a lot of weight over the past several months because she didn't feel like eating.

"But you're better now?" she asked as she had swallowed the first bite anyway. "I mean you look great and you seem really happy? How did you get out of it?"

Angela sipped her wine, and a smile spread across her lips as she put the glass down.

"I thought you'd never ask," she said and leaned forward. "If you want to, I can get you what I have. I can help you."

Chapter 10

"*So far no one has claimed responsibility for the July 9th attack on the Metrorail, and the authorities are still asking for help from the public. If anyone has seen anything that might help progress the investigation, then please come forward and call the number on the screen.*"

I stared at the TV in our hotel room. Sydney had gotten us a room at the Ritz Carlton Hotel in Coconut Grove, Miami. I thought it was silly to stay in these expensive surroundings, but she insisted that she would pay for everything.

"It's the least I can do."

Now, she was in the shower while I watched TV without really listening. They were talking about the July 9th gas attack on the Metrorail in Miami, as they had been for the past month since the attack had happened. According to what the authorities now knew, there had been three bags onboard the Orange Line going southbound in the morning rush hour. Three bags with a liquid gas in them that had killed seven passengers and left around fifty passengers still hospitalized. It was an act of terrorism, they said, but still, no one knew by whom and why. ISIS, most people guessed, but they had yet to claim it, as they usually did. According to experts, it had ISIS written all over it, but I wasn't so sure. ISIS had never used Sarin gas before.

"Sarin is a highly toxic and volatile form of nerve gas developed by Nazi scientists in the 1930s," the anchor on the TV explained. *"It's five hundred times more toxic than cyanide gas, which was used to execute people in gas chambers. It can be produced by a trained chemist with chemicals that are available publicly. The packages onboard the train leaked a thick liquid onto the floor, and people in the cars began to feel dizzy and lose their eyesight. Stinging fumes hit their eyes and struck them down in a matter of seconds. It left them choking and vomiting, while some were blinded and even paralyzed."*

"Don't you want to watch something a little more uplifting maybe?" Sydney asked as she came out of the bathroom.

"I like to keep myself updated," I said.

She shrugged and dried her hair with a towel. She was so beautiful it was almost unfair. I never thought an actress could be prettier in real life than on the screen, but she was.

"Filling yourself with all the terrible things going on in this world?" she said.

"It makes me forget," I said. "It makes my problems seem less. I look at this and think at least my daughter isn't one of the dead ones on that train. Not that I know of, that is."

Sydney sat down on her bed and began moisturizing her legs with some expensive looking creme. "You sure you shouldn't call home? Ask how the children are doing?"

I exhaled and bit my cheek. Sydney kept asking me this, and it was every bit as painful every time.

"I know they're fine."

"I know you do. Mom is taking good care of them."

"Their dad is with them too. He moved to Cocoa Beach, remember? He knows how to take care of them. He got himself a condo, and he promised me he'd take good care of them all while I was gone, no matter how long it took."

Just get our daughter back, were his words. I could still hear them in my head. I called him on the day I had decided to leave, and he said he had found a condo and that he would come down the next day. I never got to see him face to face, but we made an agreement on the phone that day. He would take care of the kids, make sure they had everything they needed, while I brought back our oldest. Chad trusted the police to be able to get her back just as little as I did. I knew I could do better, even if it might end up costing me my entire career and maybe even jail time. Before I left, I had sat down with my mother and explained everything to her as well before asking her if she could help with the kids while I was gone. She had always loved Chad, even after he cheated on me, so it was not a big deal for her. Together, they would hold down the fort, we agreed.

"I won't be able to contact you. I won't be able to see you or help you out with anything for a very long time," I had explained. "I won't tell you where I'm going, what I'm doing, or when I'll be back. Do you understand? The less you know, the better. They can't get out of you what I didn't put in there in the first place. If they take you in for interrogation, you won't be able to give up my whereabouts."

She had agreed, even though she had been slightly scared.

"The kids might miss you," Sydney said now, slapping more moisturizer on her well-shaped legs. "And you might miss them. What's one little phone call, huh?"

I swallowed and stared at the TV. We had this conversation over and over again.

"They know I'm all right. I told them this was how it was going to be. Before I left, I sat down with them and told them I was going to find their sister, but that it meant I was going to be gone for some time."

I closed my eyes and recalled Alex's and Christine's eyes as they stared up at me. Christine was crying but tried desperately to hide it. Alex had placed his little hand on my shoulder and looked me seriously in the eyes.

"Go, Mom. Go find Olivia. We'll be fine. Just bring our sister back."

Christine had sniffled and nodded. "Alex is right, Mom. We just want Olivia back."

"You can just call them from one of those burner phones you

carry around," Sydney said. "I know you're dying to hear their voices."

I was. She was right about that part. Every cell in my body was desperately screaming to see them again or at least hear their voices. I wanted to hug them and kiss them, but I wanted to hold their sister in my arms just as much, and right now she was the one who needed me the most, not them.

"It's too risky," I said. "By now, the police might have tapped all their phones. I can't risk them finding us and having all this been in vain. I almost killed a guy, Sydney. It's not small stuff."

"All right, all right. I hear you. I was there, remember?"

"I do," I said and turned off the TV in the middle of pictures from the gas attack. Right before the TV went out, I thought I saw something that made my heart stop.

What in the…?

Heart pounding in my chest I turned the TV back on, but as I did, they had moved on to another story and were interviewing some politician.

"No, no, no," I said and flipped to another channel, then continued till I was frantically scrolling through all the channels.

"NO!" I screamed and threw the remote toward the wall. It slammed against it, then fell to the carpet, the batteries falling out.

"What's going on?" Sydney asked and picked it up. "Why are you freaking out?"

I stared at her, panting and agitated.

"I…there was…on the TV, she was there!"

"Who was? You're making no sense, Eva Rae."

"OLIVIA!" I yelled, grasping my face. "She was right there. On that clip from the attack, the one they just showed. She was on the platform."

Chapter 11

"I'm taking you off the Baxter case."

Chief Annie looked at him from the other side of the desk. Matt wrinkled his forehead. The chief had closed the door behind him as he entered her office. This was serious.

"The bar stabbing case? Why? I have it almost wrapped up?" he said, confused.

What was this? Didn't she think he could handle it?

"Annie, I'm almost…"

She lifted her hand to stop him. "I need you elsewhere, Matt, that's why."

"Elsewhere? What's going on?"

She scratched her forehead, then exhaled. "I am lending you to Miami-Dade County. You're going to work on this case with a detective down there; his name is Charles Carter."

She pushed a file toward Matt, and he took it. He opened it and looked down at it then up at her.

"But this is…?"

She nodded. "I need you on it, Matt."

"But Annie, this is…?"

She leaned forward. "I need you to do this. I want you to keep an eye on the investigation. Report back to me."

"But don't they know that I'm personally involved in this?" he asked.

She shook her head. "No."

Matt nodded pensively, then looked at the file, skimming a couple of pages. It was odd to see the woman he loved described like this.

"She was last seen in Leisure City," Annie said. "A small town down south close to Miami. She struck a spa and a massage parlor down there. Miami-Dade has put out a warrant for her arrest, just as the Brevard County Sheriff has one out for what she did in Rockledge, and Broward County Sheriff's office has one out for what she did in Ft. Lauderdale. She's wanted for fraud, theft, assault and battery. You need to get her home before she digs herself in so deep there is no turning back."

Matt exhaled and felt his pulse quicken as he flipped through the case file.

"Listen, Matt. I need you down there to make sure she comes out of this alive. I care about her too much to simply let her dig her own grave down there in the search for her daughter."

Matt nodded. He grabbed the file, thinking this was going to be tough, but it was what was needed. He wanted Eva Rae home more than anyone.

"Any news on Piatkowski?" he asked, knowing that they were still trying to find Olivia that way.

"Our team is still trying to lure the Iron Fist out through the Dark Web, but so far, he hasn't taken the bait."

Matt cleared his throat, then stood to his feet.

"I'll go home and pack a bag, then leave right away."

Annie pulled into half a smile.

"Bring her home in one piece, will you?"

"I'll do my best. You know I will."

Chapter 12

I refused to go down to the restaurant and eat, so Sydney ordered us room service while I roamed the Internet on the laptop that Sydney had bought me in Palm Bay. I hadn't logged onto any social media on it, nor had I checked my email, knowing they might try and find me that way. But I used it for research, and now I was trying to find the clip I had seen on TV from the local TV station's webpage.

Later on, Sydney went to bed while I continued my search, not coming up with anything. I was beginning to think that maybe Sydney was right, and I was just seeing what I wanted to because I missed my daughter so much. Still, it nagged me. Something deep down inside of me told me it was her. What if she was on that platform when those trains were attacked? The thought worried me deeply. Was she exposed to the gas? Was she in the hospital?

I grabbed my phone and started calling the hospitals nearby that I knew some of the passengers had been sent to, but no one by her name had been treated there, they said.

Maybe she could have been admitted under another name?

I found more footage from the scene shown on the day of the attack and played it. A reporter was reporting live from the station, standing outside of the building, while ambulances were parked behind her.

I leaned back in my chair and listened to her words, my eyes fixated on what went on behind her when suddenly something caught my eye. A guy was standing behind her, looking confused while talking to a paramedic. I stared at him, then stopped the clip and looked at his face.

I know him.

There was no doubt. This was Ryan. Ryan Scott. Jack and Michelle's oldest son. They were a couple we had been friends with back in Washington, back when the kids were younger, and Chad and I were still an item. They had a younger son too, Blake, who was the same age as our Christine and went to the same school. We had hung out often when the kids were younger, until my job took over so much that I had no time for a social life anymore and neither of us really wanted to go to a dinner, pretending to be this perfect couple that we no longer were.

What was Ryan doing in Miami? Had he been on the train? Had he maybe seen my Olivia?

Chances were small, but not impossible.

I tapped my fingernails on the desk, wondering how I could contact his parents and ask for Ryan's info, then closed the lid on the computer, deciding to call them from a burner phone the next day. I stared into thin air, a million thoughts running through my mind, then rose to my feet and stared at Miami from my window. There was no way I could sleep knowing Olivia was out there in this big city somewhere.

I grabbed the car keys, wrote Sydney a note, then left the hotel room. I drove to downtown Miami, cruising through the streets, looking at the nightlife, staring at every girl or young woman I laid my eyes on, thinking it could be her; it could be my Olivia.

And then I spotted her. Standing on a corner by a streetlight, just as a car drove up to her and rolled down the window.

Chapter 13

"Oh, no, you don't!"

I parked the car on the side of the road, then grabbed my gun from my ankle-holster, and stormed out toward them.

"Freeze!"

The girl, who was wearing a short skirt and way too much make up for her age, pulled out from the window and looked directly at me. The sight made my heart drop.

It wasn't her.

It was a young girl about the same age who looked very much like her. She had a bad bruise on her cheek, and from one look into her eyes, I could tell she was drugged.

I lowered the gun, my heart pounding. The girl took one look at me, then took off running while the car drove off, tires skidding on the asphalt.

I stared in the direction the girl had disappeared, then put the gun away in its holster, knowing it would only be a matter of minutes before her pimp and his friends would come for me.

She's someone's daughter.

I backed up and went back to the Mustang convertible that Sydney had bought for us after we ditched the minivan in Leisure

City. I thought it was too flashy, but she had argued that this was what the tourists drove down here, and if we wanted to blend in, this was the way.

I had to admit; she had a point. With her big hats and scarves and the car, we did look like most of the tourists in this town. And I was beginning to think that the place we stayed was smart too. The people looking for me would never think to look for me at the big expensive hotels. They'd be searching the motels and creepy places where people thought it was easy to hide. And since we were using Sydney's credit cards, it left no trace back to me, since no one — except the people closest to me — knew that she was my sister.

I got back behind the wheel, then took off into the warm night, continuing through town, even driving through Overtown, the worst part of Miami. I made a lot of heads turn, but no one tried anything. I stared into the face of every girl I saw and couldn't help but see Olivia everywhere. So many young girls working the streets, it was unbearable.

What was she doing on that Metrorail platform? Why was she there? Who was she with?

I decided to drive to Government Center and stood for a long time outside of the train station, staring at the leftover crime scene tape, while wondering where Olivia was and if she was all right. Had she inhaled any of the gas? Was she out there somewhere sick and in need of help? Was anyone taking care of her?

"Please, God, help me find her. Help me figure out if it was really her that I saw. Was I just imagining it like I was with that other girl on the street? Or was it really her?"

A tear escaped the corner of my eye, and I let it roll down my cheek. I didn't even have my pictures of her since I had left my phone on the kitchen counter at my house when I left. I only had this paper school photo with me that I used to show people when asking about her, trying to dig my way through the underground world of trafficking in Florida. It was two years old, and she still had long hair back then.

In a weak moment, I dialed Matt's number on my burner phone.

"Hello?"

He sounded sleepy, and I guessed that I had woken him.

"Hello...? Is anyone there?"

I miss you, Matt. I miss your arms and your smile. I miss being with you.

I closed my eyes and held the phone tight to my ear, thinking about hugging him, smelling him, and feeling his strong arms around me.

"Eva Rae? Is that you?"

Pause. A deep sigh.

"Where are you, Eva Rae?"

I hung up, tears streaming down my cheeks, heart pounding in my chest. I was risking everything by doing what I was doing, but it was what I had to do. I had to do this for my daughter. I just prayed that Matt would understand that.

"I love you, Matt," I said to the dead phone and threw it in the trash.

I had never said the words to his face, and as I got back into the Mustang and it roared to life, I wondered if I was ever going to get the chance.

Chapter 14

"Ryan Scott?"

The man in the doorway looked at me skeptically through the crack. I had knocked on the door to his apartment after getting the address from his mother that same morning. Apparently, Ryan was in Miami because he was doing a summer internship at a local paper, she had told me. He had been on his way to work when the attack happened.

"Who are you?" he asked.

"You don't recognize me? I'm Eva Rae Thomas; well, I used to be Wilson back then in Washington. I know your parents, Jack and Michelle?"

He stared at me from behind the chain. "The FBI agent?"

I nodded. Sydney stood behind me, keeping her distance. "Yes, that's me."

"And who is she?"

"My sister. She's with me down here while we... Didn't your mom tell you I would stop by?"

"Maybe. What do you want?"

"I just want to talk to you for a second. Can we come in? Please? It's important."

Ryan stared at me, scrutinizing me, then finally opened the chain on the door and let us inside. The small one-bedroom condo was a mess — pizza boxes everywhere, trash bags that should have been taken out long ago, clothes scattered on the floor and the furniture.

"What's going on here, Ryan?" I asked as we came into the living room. "Have you been out of the condo at all since the attack?"

He ran a hand through his greasy hair. "I'm just having a little trouble getting outside. It's nothing."

"You're scared," I said. "It's only natural. But what about your summer internship?"

He shrugged. "I called it in right when it happened. I gave them the story, so they were the first to break it. But the next day, I couldn't get out of my condo, I was so scared it would happen again, so I called in sick. I haven't been there since. I can't seem to get past the door. I just need a little time; that's all. It'll get better."

I felt sad for him as I found a space on the couch that wasn't covered in old clothes or trash and sat down. This wasn't good.

"But that is actually why we're here," I said. "To talk to you about the attack."

Ryan's nostrils flared slightly, and he stared at me with wide open eyes. He rubbed his hair manically.

"The attack? Huh? W-what about it?"

He went to close the blinds on the window, then turned to look at me.

"You were on the train when the gas was released," I said. "What did you see?"

"I didn't see much," he said, still frantically rubbing his hair. "And if I did, I don't remember much of it."

"But what do you remember? Please?"

"I remember a liquid on the floor. It was coming out of a plastic bag. I remember seeing it, then somehow, I don't know why, maybe it was because I felt it stinging in my eyes, but I just knew I had to get out. So, I did, at Civic Center. I changed cars to the one behind it where there was no gas. I had no way of knowing that, though. It was dumb luck, I guess. They say it saved my life that I changed cars when I did."

"But you saw all the people who got sick, and some even died. That must have been terrifying. Did you see anything else?"

He thought it over for a while, then shook his head. "It was all so chaotic; I don't know."

I bit my cheek, then said. "Do you remember my daughter, Olivia?"

He gave me a look, rubbed his neck, then nodded. "The one with the red hair who played with my brother?"

I shook my head. "No, that's Christine. This is Olivia," I said and pulled out the old school photo. "She has short hair now."

He shook his head. "Maybe, I don't know."

"Look at it again, Ryan, please. I have reason to believe she might have been on the same train as you that day. I think I saw her on a surveillance clip on TV. She's been missing for three months, all summer, and I need to find her. Did you see her?"

He stared at the photo, then shook his head. "Maybe, I don't know. The police have been asking me about so many people, and I don't remember any faces. They say the gas might have affected my memory and maybe even made me paranoid."

I felt tears well up in my eyes but refused to let them overwhelm me. I had been so certain Ryan could help me.

"Look at the picture again, will you? Please?"

He did, then shook his head, fiddling nervously with his shirt. "I...I'm sorry."

I rose to my feet and looked at Sydney, who gave me back a glance of sympathy.

"I am sorry to have disturbed you," I said and went for the door.

"There is something," he suddenly said.

I turned around.

"What?"

"There is something that I keep seeing. I see it in my dreams and sometimes even when awake."

"What is it?" I asked, a little harsher than I wanted to. "Ryan? What is it? Tell me; it might be important."

He rubbed his eyes. Then he scribbled something on a note and handed it to me.

"I keep seeing this…this symbol. I think it was a tattoo or something on an ankle, I think. Maybe a wrist. I keep seeing it. I don't know. It might be nothing. It's just that, the past few days, I keep dreaming about it and seeing it everywhere. Again, it might be nothing."

I forced a smile, then took the note. "We'll keep it in mind. Thanks, Ryan."

Chapter 15

"Get up!"

A boot hit Olivia in the stomach, and she cried out in pain. Above her lingered a face. A man. She gasped and sat up, covering herself with the thin sheet she was sleeping with.

The man smiled creepily at her, then nodded toward the door.

"You're leaving. Now!"

All six girls stood to their feet and walked outside. It was the middle of the night, but still so hot she could barely breathe. Cicadas sang in the darkness while a dog barked somewhere nearby. She couldn't remember when they had last given her a shower, and she felt clammy and stinky all over. A girl walking next to her whimpered in fear. Olivia put her arm around her shoulder, but a guard saw it and slapped her over the head.

"Keep moving!"

They were taken to a truck and told to get in. A girl from another room fell to her knees and cried. Two guards rushed to her and started beating her up. Punches and kicks landed on her small body, and she couldn't get up. The other girls stared, unable to react out of fear of being next. Olivia saw it, then ran to the girl and grabbed her arm. She helped her get up from the ground. A guard pulled Olivia by the hair forcefully. Olivia screamed and was pushed away from the girl. Meanwhile, the girl had gotten to her feet and was now on her way into the back of the truck. Olivia stopped at the edge of the truck, then looked at the guard.

This is not the usual truck that takes us to the chicken factory. What's going on?

"Where are you taking us?"

The guard grinned, then pointed his rifle at her.

"Ask me again and feel the answer."

Olivia stared into the barrel of the rifle, her heart thumping in her chest.

"I didn't think so," the guard said, then nodded toward the back of the truck. "Now, get a move on. We don't have all day."

Olivia pulled herself up, and soon after the back was closed, and the truck took off. She felt how her hands were shaking and tried to hold them still but couldn't. Many of the other girls had told stories of being shipped from place to place and being raped over and over again. Was that what was going to happen now? Were they being shipped somewhere else? Would there be big sweaty men waiting for them, ready to rape them?

Please, God, no.

Olivia closed her eyes; then she felt something touch her hand. She opened them again and saw the girl from earlier. She could be no more than eleven or twelve years old. Definitely Hispanic. Her big brown eyes stared at Olivia, and she spoke to her in Spanish, but Olivia didn't understand. She just smiled comfortingly at her, then tried to control the deep panic roaming inside of her. That was when her eyes fell on something inside the truck with them, leaning up against the back wall, and her heart dropped.

Chapter 16

THEN

"It's like a secret sorority," Angela said excitedly as they walked up the stairs. She was gesticulating wildly as she spoke yet was almost whispering like it was some big secret. "We help each other out. You're gonna love it; just wait and see."

It had been a week since their last meeting at the restaurant where Angela had explained to Helen that she knew exactly what would help her get out of her depression and find purpose in her life again. She had told her she needed to meet with a group of friends that Angela knew, all consisting of famous actresses, billionaire heiresses like Helen, businesswomen, CEOs, and filmmakers. All had felt the same emptiness and lack of purpose in life, just like her.

As she entered the beautiful old house, a group of women turned their heads and looked at her. At first, Helen felt uneasy because of all the stares, and she wasn't sure she belonged there, but seconds later, they all greeted her warmly with handshakes, smiles, and some even with hugs. Someone handed her a cup of herbal tea, and they all sat on yoga mats in a circle, drinking tea, and soon after they were doing yoga, following Angela's instruction. Helen had always loved doing yoga, and it made them all relax in each other's company.

When they were done, she received another cup of herbal tea, and they sat on the floor, all sweaty and dressed in relaxed yoga outfits while laughing and telling harrowing stories about men and dating.

"Who needs men anyway?" a woman called Laura said. She was an heiress to a well-known cosmetic emporium.

That made them laugh, even Helen, who couldn't remember having laughed like that in months.

"So, how do you do it?" Helen asked. "How do you live without men?"

Laura smiled at her. "If you want to, we can teach you. It's called enlightenment."

"I want to learn," she said. "I don't want to be dependent on a man in my life. I want freedom and to be independent. Like you all are."

That made the others smile. They chuckled and nodded.

"Then, you've come to the right place," Laura said and rose to her feet. She went to her purse and pulled out a small book that she handed to Helen.

"Here. Read this. This is the first step. See if you like what this author writes. It's about finding your way to greater fulfillment. He's really good."

Helen looked at the book, then at the author's name. *Christopher Daniels.* From his picture, he stared back at her with deep blue eyes. She couldn't explain how, but he somehow made her feel better already. At least she felt like she was finally doing something to better her life, and the company of these women seemed like just what she needed right now.

"Thanks," she said and took the book.

Angela placed a hand on her shoulder. "That book saved my life," she said. "And now it will do the same for you."

Helen nodded, tearing up. "I can't thank you enough. All of you."

"It's gonna be quite the journey," Angela said, "but soon you'll be one of us, and then there'll be no more sad days. Ever."

Chapter 17

Detective Carter was a short, bald man who had sweaty patches underneath his armpits in his white shirt that was tucked inside of his black pants. Matt had only been with him for a few hours, but it was enough to know he was also a very stubborn man who didn't exactly want Matt there.

They were going through the case files together in Carter's office at Miami-Dade Police Department, and Matt was showing him what he had brought down with him, the case of the attack of the spa owner from Rockledge.

Carter had four other files to match it, all with the same MO. And he had the personnel file from the FBI.

"So far, she's wanted for fraud, theft, battery, and assault," he said. "But I assume you know that. It's the same charges you brought."

Matt looked at the small, sweaty man as he spoke. He sensed that he probably wasn't going to get very far by trying to defend Eva Rae. To this guy, a criminal was a criminal, no matter the motive.

Carter found a map and showed it to Matt. "These are the four places she has hit within our county. Now, the last place was in a strip-mall, the Harper Shop Malls, where we have this surveillance photo from a nearby ATM." He pulled out a photo and placed it in front of Matt.

"As you can see, Agent Thomas is clearly in the passenger seat of the mini-van. This fits well with our theory that she is not working alone. We just don't know who she's working with. We also assume that this person is the one paying for the party since Agent Thomas hasn't used her credit card in three months. There have been no transactions made or any withdrawals, but she must pay for lodging somewhere, right?"

Matt nodded. "Unless she stays with people she knows. She might have friends down here that we don't know about."

"True, but she needs to eat too, and she has made her way down south somehow, getting new cars on her way. Now, we know that the minivan they ditched after the last hit was registered to an address in Jupiter, and the owner says it was stolen, but as we looked into his finances, it turns out there was a deposit of twenty-thousand dollars in cash about a week before we found it. We suspect Miss Thomas and her accomplice bought it and told the owner to say it was stolen if we showed up, but we have no evidence to back that up."

Clever, Matt thought to himself, slightly impressed, but also concerned. Eva Rae knew all about how the police worked and could stay under the radar for a very long time, but what would happen once they finally caught up to her? Would she come out of it alive?

"We have eyes on her house and her kids in case she decides to come back to Cocoa Beach," Matt said. "She left her phone at the house, and as you said, her credit cards haven't been used. There's been no sight of her in Cocoa Beach or anywhere near it since she left."

"Dang it," Carter said. "I'd expect a woman like her to at least check in now and then on the kids."

"She probably knows it's too much of a risk. How did the owner of the car explain the money in his bank account?" Matt asked. "When you asked about it?"

Carter shook his head. "He gave us some story about selling a boat long ago and then not getting the money until now. He had no proof of ever owning a boat."

"So, where do you believe our suspect is now?" Matt asked. It felt weird talking about the woman he loved as a suspect, but he had to keep a professional distance. Carter couldn't know he was emotionally involved with her, or they would ask for someone else from his department to assist them. Matt wanted to be there; he needed to be on the front line of this investigation.

Or else he feared for the worst.

"We don't know," he said. "The car was found ditched here."

Carter pointed at the map south of Leisure City limits.

Matt looked up. "Could she have left town? Gone south?"

Carter smacked his lips, then nodded. "It's definitely a possibility. I say we push out her description and have it circulated in the police departments all over south Florida, even the airports and security and customs as well. In case she tries to get out of here. Meanwhile, I say we try and find out who is helping her. If we can locate that person, we might be able to find them by credit card transactions."

Matt nodded, biting his lip. He had a strong feeling he knew exactly who was with her, but he didn't dare tell Detective Carter. He wanted to find Eva Rae on his own and then maybe persuade her to come home with him. She would have to take responsibility for her actions, but both Matt and Eva Rae knew Greg, the DA in their home county, and maybe he would let her off easy if both Matt and Chief Annie testified on her behalf. No matter what, her chances were a lot better up north in her home county than down here. And right now, that was all that mattered… making sure her children still had a mother once this was all over.

Chapter 18

"Dang it. It's not there."

I leaned back in the chair. I was sitting in the hotel room and had been on my computer all day, while Sydney waited patiently on the bed, reading. She put the book down and gave me a look.

"What are you searching for?"

"The clip. I went through all the files on the attack to see if I could find the surveillance clip somewhere, but I can't find it. I can find tons of other ones, but not the one with my daughter on it. But then again, there are a lot of files, and it's going to take me days to go through it all."

"Is it safe to log into the FBI while on the run from the police?" she asked.

I sighed. It wasn't. If they knew I had been on, they could trace me, but I also knew the FBI wasn't looking for me. I had crossed no state lines. I hadn't given them a reason to take over the investigation. The local police were the ones who had it in for me.

"I don't know. But I had to check, you know? I called the TV station this morning, but they said they had shown so many clips, so if I couldn't tell them exactly which one I was looking for, they couldn't help me. I knew the FBI Joint Terrorism Task Force would be handling the gas attack since it's considered an act of terrorism. I figured they had more footage in their database. Maybe there'd be one with Olivia in it."

"So, what are they saying about it? Who's behind it?" Sydney asked and approached me.

"They don't know yet, but they think ISIS is all over it. They think there was a reason the gas was released at Civic Center while the train went on for two more stops and ended at Government Center. The latter services all the government buildings, the judges, state attorney's office, courthouses, etc. They think they were trying to target people working there. Surviving witnesses say there were bags onboard the train and it is believed that the terrorists were on board the train themselves and then poked a hole in the bags with the liquid nerve gas before getting off, leaving the gas behind to poison the remaining passengers, letting them die a slow and painful death. It makes me sick."

"But can't they just find them from CCTV cameras?" Sydney asked.

I shrugged. "How do you recognize who is a terrorist in a crowd? They've talked to many of the passengers, but there were several hundreds of them on board that train. Right now, they're going through the CCTV footage from the Civic Center station, where they assume the terrorists left the train, but finding each and every passenger will take months, maybe even years."

Sydney placed her hand on my shoulder. "Maybe it wasn't Olivia that you saw after all," she said and sat down in a chair next to me. She grabbed my hands in hers and held them tight. I still couldn't believe I had actually found my sister after thirty-six years. It felt so unreal. Yet I couldn't fully enjoy it. Not when my daughter was out there somewhere, lost, and I felt such anger toward my sister for bringing Piatkowski into our lives. I knew she felt it too. She saw it in my eyes, and she let go of my hands.

"It *was* her," I said, not entirely convinced. I had, after all, just thought I saw Olivia on the street the night before, feeling almost as convinced. Was I just fooling myself?

"Think about it," she said. "Your mind might be playing tricks on you, making you see what you want to see."

I turned away from her. "It was her. I know it was. No one has asked you to be here. If you don't like it, then you're free to leave. I sure don't need you here."

I stared at my screen, sensing Sydney's hurt from across the room. She sighed and rose to her feet, then went into the bathroom and shut the door. I closed my eyes for a second, wondering if I had taken it too far. The fact was, I needed her with me through this, but I couldn't get myself to say that.

Chapter 19

I couldn't stop thinking about that symbol that Ryan talked about. I felt like I had seen it before but couldn't put my finger on where. I stared at the note where Ryan had drawn the symbol, then tried to figure out what it could be. It looked strange, and I wasn't quite sure what was up and what was down. Could it be some sort of Chinese symbol? Or a Greek letter?

I searched for it on the computer. I didn't even hear the door to the bathroom as it opened, and Sydney came out. I was so immersed in my research that I didn't even notice she was packing her bag either. It wasn't until I had gone through all the Greek letters and had submerged myself into the Chinese alphabet that I realized I was all alone. The door slamming shut behind Sydney had caught my attention, but it was too late.

Darn it!

I stared at the closed door, then noticed that all of Sydney's things were gone. My heart dropped. What was I doing?

I thought about getting up and running after her, but for some reason, I didn't. I felt like I was paralyzed. Did she want me to come after her? Or was it too late already? Had I ruined it?

I can't deal with this right now.

I turned to look at my screen again, then continued to go through the Chinese letters, but my brain wouldn't focus. I kept thinking about my sister. As I reached the end of the first row of letters, I stood to my feet, then ran out into the hallway. I took the elevator down, my heart thumping in my chest, then ran into the lobby. But I was too late. As I came outside, I saw her ride away in a taxi, and seconds later, she was gone.

Shoot.

I stomped my foot and cursed, then realized there was a woman standing next to me, staring at me, eyes wide.

"I'm sorry," I said. "She left with my phone in her purse, and now I can't call her and tell her to bring it back."

"That's awful," the woman said.

"Sure is," I said, then hurried inside again and passed the bar that had a TV running. I had almost passed it when I stopped and walked back. On the screen above the bar, I saw my own face looking back at me. They had used an old photo from my days at the FBI. Underneath was written one word:

WANTED.

"Oh, Lord," I mumbled, then looked around to see if anyone had seen it. Luckily, the bar was almost empty. I bowed my head and rushed back into the elevator, then pressed the button to take me to the fifth floor. I hurried back into my hotel room and slid down on the carpet behind the door, keycard still in my hand, tears rolling down my cheeks. There was no way I could continue my search now. Not with my face plastered all over the screens in this town. I looked up toward the ceiling.

"What do you want me to do now, God? How am I supposed to find Olivia now?"

And that was when I remembered. In that very second, it popped into my head where I had seen the symbol before. I rose to my feet and hurried to the computer, then ran a search. A second later, the symbol came up on my screen, and my heart started to throb in my chest.

Chapter 20

It was the first time since his momma died that Jason wanted to go to church again. At only eleven years old, the boy had lost all his faith in God and His goodness. Jason's Aunt Judi, who never missed Sunday Mass, had asked him every week if he cared to go. And finally, this Sunday morning, he had said yes.

"I have a lot to talk to God about," he said determinedly.

Jason put on his Sunday clothes, took his aunt by the hand, and left the house where his father worked in his office, always on the phone, always busy, and never coming out for anything but to eat or rush off to work.

Judi was pleased that she was able to bring Jason to St. Mary's Cathedral on 2nd Avenue. It had been her home church since she moved to Miami five years ago, and to her, there was no better place on Earth to be — especially since her sister died. This was where she felt the closest to her, and she wanted the boy to experience that too. She wanted him to know that his mother was fine, that she was in a better place now. It was a promise she had made to Michaela as soon as she got sick — to keep taking the boy to church and make sure he was raised in the faith. Michaela knew her husband would never take care of that since he never went to mass and didn't believe in anything but making money and more of it.

"Do you really think Momma will hear me if I pray?" he asked as they parked the car and walked up to the cathedral.

Judi held the boy's hand tightly in hers. She was worried about him and what would become of him now that Michaela wasn't there anymore. Peter, his dad, had his own way of grieving, which mostly consisted of burying himself in work till he dropped. There was no room for the boy or his big grief and many questions. She had often thought about taking him in, asking Peter if the boy wouldn't be better off at her house. She had no kids of her own and could take good care of him.

"That's what I believe," Judi said. "I think she's with God now but that she's also keeping a close eye on you, making sure you behave."

She said the last part while tickling him gently in the side. The boy shrieked, then chuckled. His big eyes looked up at her.

"I miss her," he said as they sat down in the pew.

She kissed the top of his head. "I know, sweetie. I know. I do too — every day. I miss her calling me; I miss drinking coffee with her. What do you miss?"

She had read that it was important to talk to children about their deceased parents. Where most people just stopped talking about them since it hurt too much, children had a natural desire to speak about them and keep the memory of them alive.

"I miss hearing her laugh," he said after a second of thinking it over.

Judi smiled and nodded. "Yes, that's what I miss the most too."

Judi turned and looked behind her. The church was filling up slowly. A young girl sat down in front of them, and a couple came in after her and sat next to her.

What a nice family, Judi thought to herself sadly. She had never managed to have a family of her own, and her sister, who had, wouldn't be around to experience her child growing up. It was indeed a sad world they lived in.

As mass started and she stood to her feet, Judi felt her eyes stinging. She chalked it up to her being an emotional mess. It wasn't till her throat started to feel tight, and she could no longer breathe that she realized something was terribly wrong.

By then, it was too late.

Chapter 21

THEN

Angela was sitting on a mahogany stool in her kitchen. Her fifteen-thousand-square-foot, five-million-dollar home was tastefully decorated, overlooking the Intracoastal waters and the pool in the backyard. A series of photos of her with her teenage sons decorated the walls behind her. None of them was with her ex-husband, whom she had cut out of her life completely as soon as she ripped him of half of everything he owned after his affair with a woman from his gym.

A hairless cat sat in a bed, while the women in Angela's kitchen indulged themselves in the vegan and gluten-free dishes sitting on the granite counter island.

Helen knew most of the women by now, after many meetings like these. She had read the book by Christopher Daniels five times and taken several of his self-help classes in the hope that she might improve her life. It was expensive but so worth it. And so far, she was feeling more empowered with every step she took — just like the book had told her she would. She was getting stronger and slowly changing what she believed about herself. She wanted to get rid of all her fears and become as powerful and self-reliant as she was able to.

"I don't know how to explain it," Helen said.

They had been asked to share their fears and phobias as a part of their evolvement. Helen was telling them about her fear of dogs.

"It's like this choking sensation. I can't breathe every time I see a dog. Even if it's behind a fence, I just can't breathe. It's so devastating since I can't go to visit friends who might have a dog in the house. It doesn't matter what size it is or how sweet and friendly it is. I just can't be near a dog."

"It's an emotional trigger," Angela said. "Formed in your childhood. Can you remember ever being bitten by a dog? Or attacked by one?"

Helen shook her head. "No. That's the problem. I don't have any bad experiences with any dogs."

"We need to dig deeper," Angela said. "Explore the meaning of this trigger. It might be something more serious. Once you know what is really behind it, you can reduce the power it holds over you today."

"But how?" Helen asked.

"Hypnosis," Angela said. "Come."

She told Helen to lie down on a mat in the middle of the living room while the rest of the women joined in a circle around her. Angela asked her to close her eyes, and in a stream of intimate questions, spoken in nearly a whisper, she asked her about everything from her first meeting with a dog, to her parents' relationships. When they were done, she told Helen to open her eyes and sit up.

Helen felt dizzy and rubbed her forehead while Angela took her hand in hers.

"Your upbringing is what is causing this fear," she said. "The dog represents your own fear of success, your fear of independence. When you meet an obstacle or hardship in life, you run away; you hide from it, thinking you can't deal with it. Your parents have led you to believe that you can't do anything on your own — that you are incapable of taking care of yourself without a man. Meanwhile, your mother had a terrible life, and you believe she was forced into that life by your father. Your mother was unable to become an independent woman and chose to be a victim in her own life. Do you want that, Helen? Do you want to be a helpless woman? Or do you want to take control of your life? Do you want to be in the driver's seat of your own destiny?"

Helen stared at the woman in front of her, her childhood friend, and then at the women surrounding her. She had never thought about life in such a manner. The way they were teaching her was so different from anything she had ever encountered. Was it really true? Was she able to take control? All the things that had happened to her, the loss of ability to reproduce, the loss of her husband, the depression, was it all something she could get rid of? She had always gone running to her daddy when things went wrong in her life. What if she became the one person she relied on?

Helen closed her eyes and suddenly felt the tightness in her chest, which she usually felt all day, loosen. The anxiety that refused to let go of its tight grip daily was suddenly completely gone.

"How do you feel?" Angela asked.

Helen smiled. "I…I don't know what happened, what you just did to me, but I feel good. I feel better than I have in many years."

Angela smiled, and the surrounding women cheered.

"I think you're ready for the next step," she said, tears shaping in her eyes. "It's time you meet Christopher Daniels. But beware. It's a meeting that will change your life forever. We have all done it and it… well, you have to experience it to know just how life-altering it is. Are you ready for this?"

Helen didn't even have to think about it twice. Reading his book and taking some of his self-help classes, she knew that this man was capable of changing lives for the better. She had felt it over the past few months.

"Are you kidding me? It's my dream," she said, tearing up. "I would do anything to meet him. He's my hero."

Chapter 22

I woke up next to the computer, an almost empty bottle of wine next to me. My head was pounding, and my mouth felt dry.

Where am I?

I was still in the hotel room and had fallen asleep with my head on the desk. I had left the hotel the night before to go for a walk and clear my head; then on the way back, I had bought myself a bottle of red wine in a small food mart around the corner. I had wanted to drown my sadness and sedate the screaming voices in my head for at least a few hours, and I had succeeded. But now, they were back at full force, and I could add a thundering headache on top of it all. The anxiety was back, rushing through my veins, making me want to scream. The biggest question right now was how I was going to continue my search for Olivia without Sydney to pay for everything. I knew she had paid for the entire week for the room, so I was probably safe for a few days more, but then what? There really weren't many places I could go now with my picture everywhere. I had been on all the screens in the small homes, with my name associated with the words: *Dangerous fugitive.* I had read each and every article I could find written about me last night.

What am I going to do?

I got up, then felt dizzy and had to hold onto the back of my chair. I then staggered to the bathroom and splashed water on my face. I glanced at my face in the mirror, barely recognizing myself.

You can't do this alone.

I found my toothbrush, then rinsed the sour taste of red wine from my mouth and scrubbed the stains off my teeth. I spat, then looked at myself again, thinking it didn't matter what I did. If I didn't find my daughter, I was dead anyway.

You can't go back, Eva Rae.

I walked back into the room and sat down on my bed, a new burner phone in my hand. I tapped the first few digits of Matt's number, then paused and put the phone down.

No, I couldn't involve him. It was too much to ask. He had a son to care for, and he couldn't risk losing his entire career for me. I knew he would, and that was why I needed to keep him in the dark. I wouldn't be able to live with myself if he lost his job just because of me. I was a criminal, a fugitive on the run, and if he withheld information about my whereabouts or about me contacting him, then he would be in serious trouble. I couldn't do that to him. I refused to.

I put the phone down with a sigh, then thought about my children, praying they were all right. Between my mother and Chad, I was certain they were doing fine; both Alex and Christine were probably in heaven for being with their dad again. I didn't have to worry about them. I knew that much.

I found a painkiller in my bag and swallowed it with water, then laid down with my head on my pillow, waiting for it to kill that throbbing headache, when there was a knock on my door.

Chapter 23

"Sydney?"

I stared at my sister, standing in the hallway. She was holding her suitcase in one hand and her purse in the other. She rushed past me inside, and I closed the door behind her.

"What are you doing here?" I asked suspiciously.

"I came back," she said. "I spent the night in another hotel close by, but then I saw your picture everywhere and realized I couldn't just leave you. You need me."

I crossed my arms in front of my chest.

"What I don't need is your pity; thank you very much. I can take care of myself."

She groaned. "Why do you have to be so stubborn?"

"*I'm* stubborn?" I asked.

She shook her head. "You know what? Never mind. I shouldn't have come back. You obviously don't want me here."

Sydney grabbed the handle of her suitcase and was about to leave again when I stopped her.

"Yes, I do."

She gave me a look.

"I need you terribly," I said. "I can't do this on my own."

Sydney exhaled. She let go of the handle on her suitcase. "You have got to stop pushing me away. You do this to everyone you love. Matt, your mother, me. You have to stop it, Eva Rae. I'm here to help. Yet you treat me like dirt."

"I know," I said. "I'm sorry. I'm just under a lot of pressure right now. It's just… a lot."

She nodded. "I know. I feel awful too for bringing that man into your life. There isn't a day when I don't beat myself up over it, when I don't think back at all the alarm bells that should have gone off, at how blind I was for not seeing him for what he really was. And I am sorry, Eva Rae. I really am. But at some point, you have to forgive me."

I nodded, feeling my eyes fill. "I will. I promise. I know it isn't your fault; I just… well, blaming someone makes it easier to handle somehow. At least I thought it did, but it doesn't anymore. It makes me miserable. Fact is, I can't do this without you, Syd."

She sniffled, then pulled me into a deep hug. "I hate that name."

"I'm sorry. Kelly, then."

She let go of me then looked into my eyes. "No, that seems odd coming from you. I think I like it better when you call me Sydney."

"Really?"

"Yeah, it's kind of growing on me. It feels familiar somehow, homey, almost."

I wiped a tear away with my sleeve. Sydney walked to the second bed and placed her suitcase on top of it.

"So… where are we? Any leads? That's how they say it in the crime shows, right?"

I nodded and approached the laptop, then sat down on the bed with it in my lap.

"I found the symbol, the one that Ryan Scott talked about. I know what it is."

Chapter 24

The owner of the food mart looked at him suspiciously from behind the counter when Matt showed him his badge.

"I'm looking for a woman, early forties, red hair, blue eyes, about five-five, a little on the chubby side, but in a cute way," he said and showed him a photo of Eva Rae. Her eyes stared back at him from the counter, and his heart felt warm. All he wanted was to be with her again.

It was Chief Annie who had called this same morning and told him that Eva Rae had used her credit card the night before. They had someone from IT monitoring her activities, and last night, there had been action for the first time.

"I know she was in here last night," Matt said. "She used her credit card at this terminal at nine forty-two."

The cashier nodded. He was a small Indian man with a speech defect, so it was hard to understand what he said.

"Yes, yes. She was here. Bought a bottle of red wine and some gum."

"Was she alone?" Matt asked. "Or did someone come in with her?"

"She was alone. Just her."

"No one waiting for her at the door or outside, maybe?" he asked.

He shook his head. "I don't think so."

"Did she come by car or walk here?"

"Walk. No car."

"Okay," Matt said and wrote it down on his pad. If she walked there, it could mean that she was staying somewhere close by.

"Did you see which way she went when she left? Did she turn right or left once outside of the door?" he asked.

"I did not see," the man said, shaking his head while smiling in a friendly manner.

Matt lifted his glance and spotted a small camera in the corner under the ceiling.

"Could I take a look at that? From last night?"

"Yes, yes," the man said and made way for Matt to come in behind the counter. He showed him into the back office, where a computer was placed on the desk. He tapped on it, clicked with the mouse, and the surveillance footage appeared.

"Here you go."

"Thanks."

Matt sat down and pushed back the timeline to the night before. He stopped and started the video from when someone entered right before nine forty, wearing a hoodie covering their head. Pretty sure it was her, he then watched Eva Rae as she came in through the door and took a quick glance around before walking to the wine section and picking out a bottle. As she did, she turned to face the camera before walking to the counter where she picked out a pack of gum. Knowing her, he knew it was probably because she didn't want to look like an alcoholic.

Happy to see her again, Matt chuckled to himself and stopped the video right when she looked up at the camera from underneath her cap. He could almost see how she froze in place when realizing that she had been spotted.

"What are you up to now, Eva Rae?" he mumbled in the dark room. "When will this ever end? How is it going to end? You're gonna get caught, and then what? Will you come willingly, or will they have to take you down? What's your plan?"

Matt grabbed his phone, then took a video with his phone of the footage, running it all again, making sure he got everything down to the door closing behind her after she had paid.

Why did you use your credit card, Eva Rae? You know better than that. Was it just a moment of weakness?

"Did you get what you needed?" the man asked, and Matt nodded, then rolled the chair back in place.

"I did. Thank you very much."

Matt left the store and walked into the parking lot, feeling worried. He was closer to her than ever in this search, yet he felt like she was slipping between his hands.

Matt hadn't told Carter what he was doing this morning and, luckily, Carter hadn't asked. He was too busy living through his fifteen seconds of fame, doing interviews with all the local TV stations, telling them about the dangerous fugitive that was on the loose in Miami, to even notice. Matt wasn't going to tell him now either. He couldn't risk Carter finding Eva Rae before he did.

Matt drove to the Miami-Dade Police Department. But as he reached the station, he was met by the sight of maybe fifty uniformed officers running out of the building, storming toward their cruisers, and driving off in a rush, sirens blaring.

A sergeant passed him, and Matt stopped him.

"What's going on?"

He shook his head. "You're not gonna believe it," he said, eyes flickering back and forth, terrified.

"Try me."

The sergeant panted agitatedly. Matt guessed it wasn't from running, but from the fear rushing through him.

"There's been another attack."

Matt wrinkled his forehead, fear and worry spreading like wildfire inside him.

"What do you mean by attack?"

He shrugged. "Terrorists probably, what do I know?"

Matt's eyes grew wide. "Terrorists?"

"Listen, all I know is that we have about two hundred people at St. Mary's Cathedral who have been exposed to some type of gas. Just like it happened on the Metrorail last month."

"You're kidding me?"

"I wish I were, buddy. I wish I were."

Chapter 25

We left the hotel and drove to downtown Miami. Sydney had bought us each a coffee, and I was slurping mine while looking at the town outside my window. It was Sunday morning, and the streets were nearly empty. High-rises and palm trees surrounded us, and the scorching sun was burning through the windshield. We had put the roof on the convertible to keep the heat out, and I cranked up the AC and made sure the air blew in my face. It was already unbearably hot. Big fluffy clouds were building over land, and in a couple of hours, they would turn black as the day's first thunderstorm approached.

The cars on the four-lane road drove slowly and, as we passed one of them, I realized they were tourists busy taking pictures with their phones through the windows.

We stopped at a red light. A man walking on the side of the road was pushing a rusty shopping cart in front of him. Another was begging for money with a sign around his neck pleading to us passersby:

I AM HUNGRY

We passed a Marriott and took a left when I spotted a police car in the side-view mirror. It was coming up behind us.

"Shoot," Sydney said when she saw it in the rearview mirror. Her hands with the many rings on her fingers began to shake on the wheel. "What do I do? Eva Rae? What do I do?"

I looked at her briefly, then at the police cruiser coming up behind us. It turned on the siren.

"Oh, dear God, he knows it is us; he's coming for us, Eva Rae," Sydney gasped. "We're going to jail."

My pulse was beginning to quicken as I watched the cruiser come closer behind us, siren wailing. The sound made my heart pound. Was this it? Was it over?

There was no way I was giving up now.

I felt my gun in my holster, clutching my hand on the grip. My palms felt sweaty. I really didn't want to have to hurt a colleague, but if he stopped us and came to the door, then there was no telling what might happen. One thing was certain; I wasn't going down today.

"He's right behind us now, Eva Rae; what do I do? What do I do?" Sydney said.

"You slow down, then drive the car to the side of the road and stop. Nice and easy," I said. "And you remain calm."

Sydney whimpered something, then did as I told her. She eased off on the accelerator, then turned the Mustang toward the side and slowed even further till it came to a stop.

The police cruiser behind us came closer still, and we watched it, hearts beating fast, holding our breaths, till it continued past us, sirens blasting loudly as it disappeared down the road.

I exhaled with profound relief. Sydney moaned and leaned on the wheel.

"Oh, my God, that was close," she said.

I chuckled and leaned my head back in the seat, my heart finally beginning to calm down. It was like every cell in my body was pumping.

Sydney held her chest and laughed. "God, I was scared."

As we sat there, catching our breath, another police cruiser rushed past us on the road, and then another one and one more. I stared at them as they made their way through traffic, then looked at Sydney.

"What's going on?" she asked.

"I don't know, but it's something big. I've seen more than fifteen police cars drive by in the past minute or two, and now I can hear firetrucks too."

Chapter 26

W e continued, going slowly, trying hard not to attract unnecessary attention. As we came further down the road, we saw where all the police cars were going. They had parked in front of a big yellow church building. There were fire trucks and ambulances too, and the area in front of it had been blocked off.

"What the heck is going on here?" Sydney asked. "It looks serious."

There were hundreds of people outside of the church, most of them on the ground. Some were wrenching in pain like they were having seizures, others throwing up. Most of them didn't move at all.

Because they're dead.

I bit my lip, feeling anxious. I had seen pictures of situations just like this, many of them — when I went through the FBI files of the nerve gas attack on the Metrorail last month.

This had to be another one.

The thought was horrifying. One terrorist attack was a terrible thing, but two within this short period of time? It was going to unleash a panic unlike anything we had seen.

But that was, of course, usually the terrorists' purpose. To make people afraid of living their lives the way they used to.

Choppers were above us now, hovering over the area. Police choppers and news choppers were circling our heads.

"We should get going," I said. "Before someone sees us here."

"Isn't that…?"

Sydney pointed, and I turned my head to look. Right there, talking to someone in a hazmat suit, was Matt, the man I loved.

What is he doing here?

"What the heck?" I said.

"That's your boyfriend; isn't it?" Sydney asked. "That detective?"

I nodded, blushing slightly. I missed him so terribly. I hated myself for leaving him the way I had, for running off. I just hoped he knew that I only did what I had to do. We had known each other all our lives, and I just hoped he knew me well enough to forgive me.

"What's he doing here?" Sydney asked. "Did you know he was down here?"

I shook my head. "I haven't spoken to him since before I left Cocoa Beach."

I stared at my beloved boyfriend, my heart thumping in my chest, then looked at Sydney.

"We should go before he sees us, or before anyone else does, for that matter. We're kind of suspicious the way we've parked across the street from them."

"Right," Sydney said and put the car back into drive. We drove slowly past the scene, and I caught one last glimpse of Matt. As I did, he turned his head and looked directly at me, and I ducked down.

"Go faster," I said. "He's looking at us."

Sydney pressed her foot down, and the car jolted forward in between the tall buildings. Sydney floored it, and soon we were back to blending in among the tourists.

Chapter 27

I t was like a warzone. Matt would know since he had actually been to one. As a young recruit, he was sent to Afghanistan, and what he had seen there, he tried to keep in the box of things he didn't like to think about. But seeing all those people on the ground, some fighting for their last breath, others having drawn theirs long ago, brought back some very unpleasant memories and popped that box right back open.

Two firefighters dressed in Level A Protective Personal Equipment, Hazmat suits, and SCBA, self-contained breathing apparatus, carried a woman out of the church and put her at his feet. Matt knelt down and looked at her face. She was alive but fighting to breathe.

"We've got a live one over here," he yelled as loud as he could. "Any available paramedics?"

A paramedic came running to him and took over. Matt backed away, sweat running down his spine and behind the gasmask.

"It's a God darn mess," one of the forensics coming up to him said, while Matt fought to calm himself down. The woman was fighting for her life on a stretcher, while the paramedics put her on respiratory support, giving her atropine in an autoinjector.

Matt was wearing a hazmat suit to protect him against the gas, and he had been inside, helping to carry out the churchgoers, trying to get them to a safe place away from the gas.

"I have never seen anything like it," the forensic said.

"Was it Sarin gas like the first attack?" Matt asked.

He nodded. "In the liquid form again. It's easier to transport, and fortunately, a lot less deadly, but still enough to kill all these people. Luckily, they have it all contained inside the church. I can't believe it. What kind of a sick mind tries to kill peaceful people going to church on a Sunday morning?"

Matt watched as more people were rushed away in ambulances, while the paramedics were fighting desperately to save them in time.

"It's like a darn insecticide," he said. "It's colorless and odorless. You won't know you've been exposed to it until it's too late and you feel your throat and eyes burn. Once you've been exposed, you have only a few minutes before it kills you. It's nasty."

Matt felt a shortness of breath himself behind the mask when thinking about it. He nodded heavily.

"When the first responders got here, they thought it was just a couple of churchgoers that had fallen ill," he said. "They sent an ambulance to deal with it, but when the paramedics arrived, suddenly there were twenty people who had fallen ill, and that was when they knew. The first responders were exposed too, though, and have been taken in for treatment."

Matt sighed and walked away from the area when he was told that everyone had been taken out of the church. A group of people who hadn't been exposed and showed no symptoms were gathered on the other side of the church. They were crying and holding each other. Matt took off his mask and helmet, then continued to where they were standing. Carter was taking their statements along with the other detectives. Each and every one of them had to be interviewed. It was vital to do it now when the memory of what had happened was still fresh to them. Maybe one of them had seen the person carrying the gas inside? Maybe they could get a description of the terrorists this time?

They had called in everyone from the surrounding departments, and the place was crawling with uniforms and suits.

"Anyone said anything useful so far?" he asked Carter as he approached him.

Carter took in a deep breath. "A guy saw a plastic bag on the floor and saw liquid inside of it," he said. "He didn't think about it but walked right past it and went to the right front side of the church to sit with his fiancée and her family. When he saw it, the bag wasn't leaking, so we assume there was no hole in it at that point."

"So, you're thinking that someone placed the bags there, then pierced them with something and left."

Carter nodded. "That was how they did it on the train, right? But so far, none of the witnesses remember seeing anyone leave the church."

"The FBI Joint Terrorism Task Force is here and will be taking over now."

Matt nodded toward the big black SUVs as they arrived.

"That's our cue, I guess," Carter said. "They'll be taking over then. Always know how to swoop right in after all the dirty work is done, am I right?"

Matt didn't answer. He was happy to leave it in their hands and get back to searching for Eva Rae. As he turned around, he recognized one of the FBI agents. It was an old colleague of his, Patrick Albertson. Patrick saw Matt too and hurried toward him.

"Matt, my man, what are you doing all the way down here?" he asked, and they shook hands. "Aren't you still up on the Space Coast?"

"I am, but I was working on another case down here when this happened."

Patrick nodded. "Eva Rae Thomas, huh? Yeah, I heard what happened. I can't believe she would go rogue like this."

"You knew her?" Carter asked.

"Not well, but back when she was still an agent, I knew her a little bit. She was so good at her job, though. Never would take her for someone who would go nuts."

She didn't go nuts, you idiot. She's just desperate.

"Well, there's two sides to all stories," Matt said, calming himself down. "Now, if you'll excuse me."

Matt turned around to walk away, but as he did, he spotted a car parked across the road from the church, on the other side of the police barrier, where many spectators were standing, along with the reporters and their cameras. It was a yellow Mustang convertible. He didn't know why, but somehow, he felt like the people in the car were watching him, and he felt strangely drawn to the car.

Who was in there and were they really watching him or was his mind just playing games with him?

Just as Matt stopped to get a better look, the car suddenly took off in a hurry, driving fast back down the street it had come from, and soon disappearing between the high rises.

Could it be... was that... was it you, Eva Rae?

Chapter 28

THEN

"I'm sweating like a pig. Can you tell I'm nervous?"

Helen looked at Angela, who smiled comfortingly. She reached over and stroked her cheek gently.

They were sitting in the waiting area in front of Christopher Daniels' office in his multimillion-dollar estate. It was beautifully decorated with gorgeous art and lots of plants and had a soothing aura to it. The surroundings made Helen feel less nervous, but she still had this sensation deep in her stomach that wouldn't go away. She was about to meet the man whose books she had read cover to cover, whose classes she had taken. To her, he was the smartest and most enlightened person in the world. He had changed her life.

"No. You look great, sweetie. Just relax. Christopher is really nice. There's nothing to be nervous about."

"Exactly what is supposed to happen during this meeting?" Helen asked, trying to keep her hands calm.

"This is how you become a full-blown member of NYX and join the inner circle. It'll blow your mind. You'll see. Just go along with it. All of it."

Just go along with it? What an odd thing to say.

It didn't make Helen feel less nervous, and as the door opened, she hid her shaking hands behind her back, then rose to her feet.

"Go ahead," Angela said and almost pushed her forward. "You can go in."

"You're not coming with me?" Helen asked.

Angela shook her head. "No. This is your time to shine. Go."

Helen took in a deep breath, then walked to the door and went inside. A man stood by the window, looking out. He was dressed in white from top to bottom; his long brown hair was hanging down below his shoulders. He had an air of peacefulness around him, and he smiled gently at her as he turned his head. She recognized him from all the books and papers in class.

It was really him. Being the heiress of a billionaire and growing up in her father's self-built entertainment empire, Helen had met all kinds of important people in this world, even presidents. But none of them had made her feel the way she felt in this instant. It wasn't love, not the way she had loved Brian; it was something else, something bigger.

Infatuation.

From the moment he put his eyes on her, it was like she was put under his spell.

"Close the door behind you," he said, and she did, heart pounding in her chest.

"Come into the light," he then said. "So I can get a good look at you and *really* see you."

She did as she was told, and he came closer, studying her, but it didn't make her feel uncomfortable. On the contrary, she found that she enjoyed it; she liked the way he looked at her with his deep blue eyes.

"There you go. Now, I see you," he said. "Now, I really see you. I see so much beauty in you, and it's time you stop hiding it."

Helen blushed. "Really?"

He came up close behind her, and she felt her stomach flutter. She felt his warm breath on her skin and closed her eyes for a second. When he put his hand on her shoulder, it felt like an explosion inside of her.

Chapter 29

"Lori Moore?"

The woman in the white shirt with the yellow scarf tied around her neck stopped in her tracks. We had driven to Bal Harbor in Miami Beach, a small wealthy community at the north end of town. There were tons of exclusive shopping malls and high-end restaurants. The cars were Ferraris, Maseratis, and Teslas. This was the type of environment that Sydney felt at home in and was accustomed to. Not me.

The woman in the high heels came walking into the lobby of the Ocean View Hotel, a luxury hotel that she owned.

"Who's asking?" she said while signing something a young woman was holding out for her. The woman then rushed off with the signed paperwork. Lori Moore gave me a suspicious look. I was wearing a baseball cap and had dyed my hair black on Sydney's recommendation. Apparently, my red hair was way too obvious now that I was a wanted person. It was the type of dye that would wash out after a couple of days.

"I want to talk to you about NYX," I said, leaning forward and speaking in almost a whisper.

Our eyes met, and hers grew serious. Lori looked around her, then signaled for us to follow her. We took the elevator to the twelfth floor, and she showed us into her office. It had an incredible view of the ocean on one side and Intracoastal on the other, and then Miami downtown towering in the distance. It was quite breathtaking.

Lori closed the door behind us.

"Please, sit down."

We did, and she sat on the other side of her desk and leaned back with a deep sigh.

"Why are you here?"

"We are investigating NYX," I said. "I know you used to be a member and that you have spoken out against them on your blog. I believe this is their symbol, am I right?"

I showed her the note that Ryan had drawn for me. Lori looked at it, then nodded.

"What do you want to know?"

"Everything. What is NYX? How does it work? What do they do?"

Lori leaned in over her desk, folded her hands, then exhaled. "NYX is a self-help organization. Or that's their cover. It's built around the founder, Christopher Daniels. It's supposed to be a way for you to get a better life. Daniels has written several books, and you can take his self-help classes or workshops with the aim to take power back over your own life."

"But the classes are expensive, right?" I asked. "It's not for just everyone."

"Very. A five-day workshop would cost you between seven and ten thousand dollars. And it does work. It has helped a lot of people. Many who graduated from his classes have managed to stop smoking, to overcome their fear of flying or public speaking, and so on. It empowered them to do things they didn't know they could."

"As far as I have read," I said, "it has attracted a lot of famous and successful people. Billionaire heiresses and businesspeople, even actors and the daughter of Venezuela's former president. But there is more to it than just self-help, am I right?"

"Yes. I was introduced to it through a friend when I went

through losing my dad in a car crash. I was going through a rough time dealing with the grief. The courses were mostly self-improvement workshops, based on therapeutic techniques, including hypnosis and Neuro-linguistic Programming, which is basically a behavior modification regimen. But the deeper I got, the more I realized something was off. There was a group within the group, like a sorority that my friend became a member of, but soon things started to change with her. She withdrew from me, became more secretive, and she lost weight, a lot of it. I realized it was all part of the behavior modification technique. She told me she had to lose her identity to gain a new one, that she was starving herself as a part of the therapy because it helped her connect with her inner self, her true self. I think she was just easier to control that way, and that Christopher Daniels just wanted to make sure she didn't resist him. I sensed that something was very wrong and left. I tried to warn my friend and asked her to come with me, but she wouldn't. She seemed scared. It's hard to explain, but I felt like I lost her completely, like they were controlling her. They said it was all about women's empowerment, but what I saw was the exact opposite."

"Wow," Sydney said. "I think I heard about this before. One of my friends talked about joining something like it and explained how taking those classes changed her life. Come to think of it, I haven't seen her in a long time."

"You're Kelly Stone, aren't you?" Lori suddenly asked, smiling. "I thought I recognized you downstairs. I love your work."

Sydney nodded. I didn't mind that Lori recognized her since I had a feeling that made her feel more comfortable with us. She didn't seem to recognize me, which was fortunate. I guessed a woman like her was too busy to keep up with the news of wanted criminals, which worked to my advantage.

"You be careful you don't end up in their claws," Lori said addressed to Sydney. "They'd love to have someone like you in their inner circle. You're just their type. Rich, successful, and famous."

Sydney chuckled. "I'll remember that."

I stared at the woman while thinking about this cult and the leader. I had no idea where I was going with this, but my instinct told me it was important. Ryan had seen the NYX sign at the attack somehow, and my daughter was on the surveillance camera footage. How, or if these things were connected, I had no chance of knowing. But it was all I had, and I was clinging onto it for dear life.

"Have you ever heard of the Iron Fist?" I asked.

Lori shook her head.

It was a long shot; I knew it was. But I had to try.

"Tell me about the founder, Christopher Daniels," I said. "I read that he is quite mysterious and rarely seen in public."

"That is true. I never met him myself, as I said, only the inner circle people get to do that."

"Do you have any idea how to get in contact with him?" I asked.

"Are you sure you want that?" she asked while grabbing a sticky note and writing on it. She ripped it off, then slid it across the table. "This is the NYX estate. He lives there, as far as I know. I know this because I was supposed to meet with him a couple of weeks ago in order to join this so-called inner circle, but I never showed up. I don't want to end up like my friend."

I grabbed the note and looked at it. "Did they get angry with you for not showing up or for speaking up afterward?"

She shrugged. "Their lawyers tried to shut down my blog, but I have lawyers too. They can try all they want. They can't touch me."

Chapter 30

They brought in new girls. Olivia was sitting on her mattress, crying when the door opened, and they came in. A young girl, no more than thirteen or so, landed next to her. Her face was swollen from being beaten. She looked up at Olivia like she expected her to explain to her what would happen now, but how could she? How could Olivia tell her what was about to happen to her?

"What's your name?" the girl asked.

"Olivia," she answered without looking at her. She didn't want to care for her; she didn't want to become friends with her. If there was one thing she couldn't do in this place, it was to care for any of the other girls. So many had come and gone, and that taught Olivia an important lesson. If she was going to survive this, she had to keep to herself and never care about anyone else. It was easy with the girls who came from China or Ukraine as some of them did because she didn't understand their language, at least not most of them. It was easy to keep them at a distance, but this girl was American like Olivia. That made it harder to cut her off.

"I'm Tiffany," she said with a sniffle. "I'm from Chowchilla, California. Do you know where we are?"

Olivia shook her head, trying to not look at the girl. Why was she so talkative? Normally, when new girls arrived, they wouldn't say a word for the first day or so.

"I don't know," Olivia whispered.

"I have been so many places," she continued, crying lightly. "It was my mother's boyfriend who took me. He beat me up at the house where we lived, and when my mother didn't do anything, I ran away. But I had nowhere to go, and he picked me up on the side of the road. Not knowing what else to do, I got in the car, and then he took me to his friend's house. That friend raped me. He kept going for hours and hours till I couldn't scream anymore. Then another of his friends came to his trailer, and they put me in a van and drove off. Since then, I have been so many places; I have no idea where I am or who I'm with."

Olivia exhaled. She had heard similar stories repeatedly over the past few months while being held there. It was so much tragedy; she couldn't bear it. It also frightened her to the core, especially when she heard of the amount of time some of these kids had been kept as slaves.

Was she ever getting out? Would she ever go home?

Olivia looked up toward the ceiling, stifling her tears. She'd had a lot of time to think about how to get out, and so far, come up with only one way. But it was too dangerous, and she wasn't sure she dared to follow through with it.

"Do they rape you here?" Tiffany asked.

Olivia shook her head. "No."

"Really?" Tiffany said, her eyes gleaming with hope.

"Yes, really. But they make you work for them."

"What type of work?"

"Cleaning chickens, mostly. In a factory. But there's other stuff too."

"Like what?" she asked.

Olivia put her head down on the mattress. She didn't want to kill this girl's hope by telling her the truth.

"Just stuff. You'll see. Now, go to sleep. They usually come at night, so you won't get any sleep if you don't sleep during the day."

Chapter 31

I glanced at the note from Lori Moore with the address on it. We were back at the hotel, and I had looked it up online and found the mega-mansion located a little south of town with views over Biscayne Bay. It wasn't far from the hotel where we were staying. It was an area that, according to the Internet, Jennifer Lopez also owned a house in and so did one of the Bee Gees, along with some of the wealthiest politicians and TV anchors in the country. I stared at the Google view from the top of the mansion. With its red-tiled roof, pool, and tennis court, it looked like all the other mansions in the area. It was a twenty-seven-thousand-square-foot house with both pool house and guest quarters, according to Zillow.

Sydney brought me coffee from downstairs and placed it in front of me. I sent her a grateful smile and sipped it, leaning back in my chair in the hotel room.

"Anything?" she asked and blew cautiously on her coffee before sipping it.

I exhaled. "I've gone through everything I could. I couldn't even find a driver's license for him in the DMV register. I tried to get information on his financial situation, but according to the IRS, he hasn't made any money in the past ten years. Yet he lives in a mansion in one of the most exclusive neighborhoods in the world. But the house isn't in his name. It's registered to a woman, whose name I also found on the board of NYX."

"Wow."

"He had another company earlier on, under the name Daniels, but that was shut down fifteen years ago because it was accused of being a pyramid scheme. He has a file with the FBI from back then, and it states that he doesn't even have a bank account in his name. He's keeping his name out of everything, so they can't get him for anything. Yet the company owns a jet."

Sydney lifted her eyebrows. "Are you logging into the FBI database? Are you sure that's a good idea?"

"Probably not. I'm using my former partner's login, though, and I don't think he'll notice. But listen to this. I looked through old articles written about the group, and in 2011, a woman disappeared after an NYX session in California. Her car was found abandoned in a parking lot, and on her phone, they found a video she had recorded of herself saying that she was brainwashed, that she didn't realize it, but she was already dead. Then she told whoever found the video to please contact her parents and tell them how sorry she was. Her body was never found."

Sydney almost choked on her coffee. She stared at me, eyes wide. "Did she kill herself; do you think?"

I shrugged. "Who knows? But something is off. Something is very much off here. I can smell it."

Sydney placed a hand on my shoulder. I looked up at her.

"I smell it too, Eva Rae, but what about Olivia? I thought we came down here to try and find her? All we know is that you think you saw her on the platform after the gas attack."

I stared at my sister, feeling a pinch of guilt in my stomach. I knew she was right. I was getting off track here. I feared that too. The fact was, I had no idea if it really was Olivia I saw on that clip, and I had let myself be blinded by the investigation into this strange cult instead.

It was time for me to get back on track — back to what I had come there for in the first place.

To track down the Iron Fist.

Chapter 32

S ydney watched TV, flipping through the many news stations and their breaking news about the possible terrorist attack on a local Catholic church in Miami. Meanwhile, I sat by the laptop and, through a downloaded Tor-browser, I accessed the Dark Web, using a VPN for protection.

Now, the Dark Web is pretty easy to get access to, and thereby to all the illegal stuff going on there, but the hard part is finding the right sites. You have to know where you're going once you enter the browser. And I did. Back when I started my search for Olivia, I had found a list of pages where human trafficking was taking place. I knew that the FBI had a team of operators operating on the Dark Web to catch people engaged in criminal activity, and I gained access to their files. After finding a lot on murderers for hire, child pornography, illicit sale of body parts, and weapons for sale, I had found the pages that were known to the FBI to facilitate human trafficking, the buying and selling of people as slaves. Going to those sites got ugly really fast, and it made me sick to my stomach, plus I risked getting all kinds of malware on my computer. But it was on one of those sites that Piatkowski had sold my daughter, so I kept going back to see if the Iron Fist showed his ugly face.

So far, I had no such luck.

Until today.

I had recently entered a hacker forum and found someone willing to track down the Iron Fist for me, for an indecent number of bitcoins, naturally. Now, as I entered the chatroom, he wrote to me that he had found him. He then shared a link with me that would lead me to a chatroom he was in. I stared at the screen, my palms growing sweaty. I knew that if this link led me to child pornography, I was in trouble. I would be doing something illegal. I took in a deep breath, then decided to trust this hacker, and I clicked the link.

I held my breath as the page appeared, and a chat opened. Then I saw his name in the forum. There he was. Right in front of me. The Iron Fist. He was writing in the chat, asking for help. He needed four girls, fast.

I almost threw up.

Why is he asking for more girls? What is he doing with them? Does that mean he doesn't have Olivia anymore? What did he do to her? Did he sell her to someone else? Did he kill her?

Someone answered. He had a shipment coming in, tonight. PortMiami. Midnight.

I stared at the chat as they agreed on a price, then went silent. I snapped a picture of the entire conversation on my phone. There was no way of tracking people who entered the Dark Web, but this was the best I could do. I stared at it, my hands shaking, my breath caught in my throat. I looked at my watch. There were still four hours until midnight.

I lifted my glance and studied Sydney for a second. She was engrossed in the news broadcast from the church. I wondered what to do about her. I couldn't really bring her. I didn't want her to get too deeply involved in what I was doing. It was too much of a risk for her. She had a career to think about.

I had to do it alone.

Chapter 33

THEN

"Aren't you going to ask me any questions?"

Helen looked at Christopher, her legs feeling wobbly. He was standing in front of her now, looking into her eyes, moving a lock of hair. It felt like his eyes saw straight through her.

"About myself?"

Christopher chuckled. "I already know everything."

"How so?"

"Just by looking at you, I can tell that you are strong, a lot stronger than you think. You have a defiant air about you. You're a rebel. I know that you showed up to your first workshop in a ripped T-shirt, refusing to look like the others, refusing to show off your wealth and take part in in the upper-class materialistic way of life. I know that you are protesting against the bourgeois environment in which you grew up. I know that you are angry at the world and that you think more highly of animals than humans and that you would rather be with horses than humans. I also know that you have a terrible relationship with your father, who thinks he can buy anything or anyone. I also know that, through my workshops, you have looked deep into your psyche and been able to get rid of fears that have tormented you for years. I know that you can't have chil-

dren and that you suffered from depression before you came to us
for help. I know you married a man who left you when he realized
you couldn't have children."

Helen stared at him, out of breath.

"Wow."

He took her face between his hands. "You are no surprise to me,
Helen. I know you better than you know yourself. And now it is time
for you to submit to me fully."

Helen swallowed. "W-what does that…"

He hushed her, and she stopped talking. He touched her hair
gently, then ran a hand down her chest, lingering a few seconds by
her breast before continuing down her arm, where he stopped by
her wrist. He held it tight in his hand when the doors opened, and
two women wearing white dresses entered.

"Who are they?" Helen asked. "What are they doing here?"

He hushed her again, then looked into her eyes. "Do you
trust me?"

She swallowed hard, then nodded. "Y-yes."

"Good," he said.

He nodded, and the women approached. One of them held a
cauterizing device. Christopher took it in his hand, then looked at
Helen. It was sizzling in his hand — one of the women filmed with
her phone.

"It is time for you to let go of your past, Helen. You're a part of
us now. Your old family is holding you back from becoming all you
can be. We're your family, and with this mark, I brand you, so you'll
know where you belong always. You belong to me. Say these words
after me: I give you, Christopher Daniels, full and complete control
over my life."

Helen gasped lightly, but one look from his blue eyes made her
feel at peace with this. It was the right thing to do. It was the next
step, and she wanted it badly.

"I g-give you, Christopher Daniels, full and complete control of
my life."

He then placed the cauterizing pen on her arm and pressed it down on her skin. Helen screamed in pain. Christopher smiled and lifted it again, and a mark was left on the skin, burning like crazy.

Helen looked down at it, then up at the two women, who clapped and cheered.

"Congratulations," one of them said. "You're one tough woman."

"And now you're one of us," the other said. As she spoke, she lifted her arm proudly to show Helen her own branding mark.

Christopher grabbed her by her chin, then turned her head to face him. He then leaned forward and placed a deep kiss on her lips.

"You belong to me now. Come," he said and pulled her by the hand. "Don't resist me. It's your upbringing that makes you think you need to resist me, but you need to liberate yourself from it. Only then can you reach healing."

The two women left, and Christopher slowly undressed Helen. He placed her on a yoga mat in the middle of the room, lit all the candles surrounding her, then climbed on top of her.

Chapter 34

Lori Moore stared at her wrist and turned it in the sparse light. Then she felt it. The smooth skin felt nice under her fingertips, she thought with a deep sigh. She was thrilled she had pulled out in time, before she too was branded like her best friend was, like all who became part of the inner circle were — branded for life.

Always reminded of what they had agreed.

Lori sipped her glass of Chardonnay while looking at the lights in Biscayne Bay. Out there, the cargo ships waited to be docked in the port, while cruise ships left for or came back from the Bahamas or the Virgin Islands.

She had left the office early, right after the visit from Kelly Stone and her strange companion. Their visit had stirred something up in her that she didn't care for, and she treated herself to the rest of the day off, something she never did. But today, she needed it.

Lori sipped her wine and felt the warm breeze on her face. The light in the pool lit up the entire back yard while the dark windows from her mansion looking back at her reminded her how alone she was.

Living in an eighteen-thousand-square-foot home could be quite lonely when it was just one person.

Lori had never wanted children and a family. It had been pretty clear to her when she became an adult. She wanted a career. She wanted to make something of herself. Growing up poor, she had never thought she would actually live on the ocean one day, in one of the most exclusive neighborhoods in the state. She never thought she would live in a house like this or that people would talk to her with awe and respect the way they did every day. But that was her life now, and boy, was she proud of it. If only her mom wasn't always high on drugs, she would invite her to see it, to see for herself what her daughter had accomplished, even though she always told her she would never amount to anything in life, that she was so ugly she should *consider herself lucky if she made it as a whore*.

Those had been her words when Lori was a teenager, and they had lingered with her ever since, making her determined to prove her wrong.

And this was where it had brought her — a huge mansion, Chardonnay in hand, and more than a three hundred employees beneath her.

But was it enough? Did it satisfy her?

When Lori had entered NYX, she had thought that the classes would help her deal with this sense of emptiness that was growing inside of her. She had believed this was what she needed to fill that void that she had thought would go away when she reached her goals in life.

And for a little while, the teachings of Christopher Daniels had done just that. But then he had asked to have sex with her when she saw him in his office. Lori had refused. She hadn't told this part to Kelly Stone and her friend since it was too private to share. But the fact was, Lori had run out of his house, and even though several men had tried to stop her, she had managed to make it out, running away and never returning.

Now that she had left NYX, she had also lost everyone she knew. She had become a social outcast since most women in her social circles were members, and a lot of them inner circle members. All her network collapsed at once, and now she was more alone than ever, especially after she started writing her blog about what had happened, excluding the sex part since it was too embarrassing, at least for now.

But the fact was, she couldn't have sex with this man. Not because she refused to; no, she could probably have closed her eyes and gone through with it just because of the benefits and status it would give her later on… becoming part of the inner circle. But the thing was that Lori had once been Lorenz. She looked like a woman, yes, and she felt like one. But there was still one thing left that technically made her a man. She hadn't been able to go through with the full transition and become a full-blown woman, removing the one last part that made her a man at birth.

That was why she could never go all the way with Christopher Daniels or any other man for that matter. Not even if she wanted to.

And she hated him for putting her in that position. She hated that he was the reason she had lost her entire social network, her only friends, because of it. Now she was all alone again, as she had been for most of her life.

Lori sighed and rose to her feet. She swung the glass and almost empty bottle in her hands, then staggered barefoot toward the sliding doors, barely keeping her balance.

As she entered the house and closed the sliding doors behind her, she turned around and stared straight into a set of eyes.

"What the heck are *you* doing here?" she asked, forcing herself to focus and stand still, but couldn't help swaying from side to side.

"What do you want?"

Chapter 35

Sydney was asleep when I left. I wrote her a note, then snuck out, shoes and purse in my hand, feeling like I was cheating on her or doing something criminal. I just didn't want her to know where I was going. She would only try and convince me not to go, to call the police instead, or she would end up coming with me.

I couldn't risk that happening. I needed to do this alone, without the police, without Sydney. Why? Because it was the only way I could get to the Iron Fist. Chances were slim that he would actually be there himself, but someone else might, someone that might lead me to him. This meeting was my only lead to him and Olivia.

I couldn't risk losing that. I had to find him. I had to track him down so I could get my daughter back home.

I rushed out through a back entrance, trying not to be seen by the front desk of the hotel. We had made sure it was Sydney who spoke to them every time we came back or left — to make sure they didn't recognize me. I was disguised pretty well with dyed dark hair and fake colored contacts and glasses, but still. We couldn't risk anyone calling the cops.

So, I snuck out the back entrance and found the Mustang in the parking lot behind the hotel. I drove it out into the street and hit the accelerator, finding the roads leading to the port.

Port Miami was located on Dodge Island; a slim island squeezed in between Miami Beach and Miami downtown on the mainland. It was both a cargo port and a cruise ship port.

The meet was at the cargo port, between the container ships. I found it easily and parked the car. I then ran toward the container terminal, which was a huge glass building. I rushed past it, running down the port, passing a big whale of a cargo ship that was lying there, empty, having just been unloaded, while hundreds of containers were on the dock next to it.

"SS Attra, that's her," I mumbled and looked at the name on my phone from the chat.

Holding the grip of my gun with one hand, I looked around until I spotted a guy standing by the corner of a container, obviously being the lookout. He was the type to be heavily armed, so I hid between a row of containers, pressing my back up against them.

I could hear voices, people talking. I snuck around the other way and came out on the other side of the containers, then ran across an open space until I could hide behind another container. As I peeked around a corner, I spotted them. A group of people was gathered there. They were chitchatting with one another, one even laughing like it was a typical greeting between old friends.

For a second, I thought I might have been wrong, but as I snuck closer, I spotted the girls. They were sitting in the opening of a container, an entire row of them. They were huddled together, trying to hide from the men surrounding them. They weren't even crying. It was obvious they didn't dare to, or they were too drugged even to try.

Seven young girls, some of them a lot younger than Olivia, about to be sold like slaves into prostitution or hard physical labor.

It was gruesome.

Somewhere, seven mothers are missing their children. Seven mothers are crying themselves to sleep at night.

"Not on my watch," I mumbled, just as a car drove up and someone stepped out.

Chapter 36

It was hard to see from where I was standing, so I snuck closer. As I did, someone spotted me, and soon all hell broke loose.

The armed guards yelled and ran toward me. I lifted my gun, but as they turned the corner, they started to shoot, not asking questions. I fired back, then ran around the corner at the other end. I heard screaming coming from the open area. Shots were fired after me, and I turned around the corner, then fired, hitting first the guy to the right, then the one to the left. Both went down. I then ran forward as fast as I could, stormed into the area where I had seen the girls, just in time to watch them trying to get them into the truck that had arrived just a few seconds ago.

"STOP!" I yelled.

More shots were fired while people scattered. I fired back, hitting another guy, just as he tried to shoot me. They gave up on getting the girls in the truck and shut the door, then took off instead. I stopped and fired a round at the truck. The bullets ricocheted off of it, but it kept moving.

"Oh, no, you don't!" I said, then looked in between the containers. I took off running, knowing if I went fast, I would be able to cut them off on their way since they'd have to take a detour around the containers.

I panted agitatedly as I reached the end of the row of containers, then turned left, and now stood right in front of the truck.

"STOP!" I yelled and pointed my gun at them.

The truck accelerated violently and, as it did, I fired two shots straight through the windshield, hitting the driver. The truck turned sideways, then ran straight into a crane pole.

I stared at the crashed truck, my gun still pointed at it, shaking between my hands, but nothing happened. A few seconds later, the door to the passenger seat opened, and someone jumped out on the other side of the truck. The person took off running. I fired a shot and yelled for him to stop, but he didn't. He was way faster than me and soon gone.

I stared after him, then cursed while wondering if he had been the Iron Fist.

I returned to the truck and opened the driver's door. The driver was hunched over the wheel. I had shot him in the shoulder. His forehead was bleeding from the impact when hitting the crane.

I grabbed his head and pulled him back to see his face. Then I let his limp body plunge back down while cursing again. As I let go of him, I spotted something else. A guy was in the back. He had hurt his head when the car slammed into the pole, and he was dead. But he didn't look like any of the others. This guy was well dressed in a nice suit, a very expensive one. His shoes were of the same caliber. This was no ordinary man.

The Iron Fist?

Unlikely. He wouldn't come to something like this on his own. Someone working for him? More probable.

I stepped inside the truck, then pulled him back to see his face properly. As I did, I saw his wrist as it poked out from beneath the shirt.

A wrist with something branded into the skin. A symbol I knew a little too well.

"NYX," I said, gasping lightly. I fumbled with my phone, then took a picture of it before letting him go. I searched through my phone, then sent all the pictures to a secret email address I had recently created, one that no one knew of except myself.

I got out of the truck with the phone clutched to my ear. I walked back toward the open area and saw the girls. They were huddled up inside of the container again, having gone back to what I assumed had been their home for quite some time, while they were transported across the ocean.

Then, I called the cops.

"I'd like to report a shooting. At the port. You'll find several dead men and some young girls that were supposed to be sold as slaves inside of a container."

I gave them the exact address, then threw the phone in the trash before disappearing, hurrying to my car. I took off into the night while hearing the sound of sirens blaring behind me.

Chapter 37

Esther Hermane pressed in the code to the door. Her fingers were shaking, and she had to take in a deep breath in order to calm herself. She tapped in the wrong code, then shook her head.

"Where is your head today, Esther?"

She tried again, and the gate opened. She walked inside, holding her purse close to her body. Inside of it was her phone, and she had to make sure that she could hear it if it rang. She would have to keep it close all day while cooking and cleaning.

Coming from Haiti ten years ago, getting used to things here in America, and especially Miami had taken her a long time. But life was better here. It had been better for her son James to grow up here than back home. After ten years, Esther had thought they were safe here now. She had worked hard over the years to provide a good life for him, but the night before, he had been taken in by border agents.

He had been visiting his aunt in Naples as he had done so many times before, going by bus, as usual, when agents had entered the bus right as they reached Miami.

They had asked for his ID, then asked if he was illegal, and he had said yes. He was eighteen years old and had never been able to tell a lie. They had told him they'd take him with them, and then he'd be deported within the next two weeks. He had gotten the right to call his mother, and he had done so, then told her the entire story. Esther had contacted an old friend, who had gotten them an immigration lawyer who worked with cases like these, and today, James was supposed to appear in court.

It was still early in the morning, and the court appointment wasn't till eleven, so she had time, but Esther was already anxious. She had been up all night worrying, wondering if James was all right in that place they had taken him to and whether they had treated him properly.

Was he being fed?

Just thinking about it made her stomach churn, and Esther tried to shake it. She walked up to the front door and pressed in the next code, thinking about the day she had in front of her. Usually, she cooked breakfast for Mrs. Moore before Mrs. Moore left for work, and Esther had the house for herself the rest of the day, cleaning and making sure everything was perfect for when Mrs. Moore came home, which was usually pretty late. Esther would make a meal for her and place it in the fridge, covered in wrapping, so all Mrs. Moore needed was to put it in the microwave whenever she made it back.

It was a good job, Esther had always thought. She liked Mrs. Moore, even though she found her to be a strange creature. Not really man or woman, in her opinion. The fact that someone could simply decide they were of another gender amazed her, but then again, so many things had surprised her in America. It wasn't the place she had expected it to be or dreamed of when she was younger. And living in constant fear of being found by the border agents wasn't living at all. Esther couldn't stand it, couldn't stand being constantly worried about her son and their future. She didn't understand why this was happening now, after all these years. She had been a hard worker; she had taken the jobs no one else wanted. She had stayed out of trouble, and so had her son. And James was doing great in school. All they were guilty of was trying to earn their way to better, safer lives. She wasn't harming anyone. Neither was James.

Esther shook her head and pushed the big door open and entered the house. The first thing she saw was the broken bottle of white wine that had scattered across the tiles and the wine had run across the floor and seeped into part of the expensive Persian carpet. Esther's heart sank when realizing that Mrs. Moore had been drunk again and cleaning up after her would probably take most of the day.

"Stupid American woman-man, wasting away in this big mansion big enough for my entire village to live in," she hissed, then went with determined steps for the closet with the cleaning supplies. As she put her hand on the handle, she spotted the blood on the white tiles.

Now, while growing up in Haiti, Esther had seen some gruesome things. She had seen people lying murdered in the streets and even witnessed her own father being shot. But what she saw in the kitchen on this day was nothing in comparison.

It made her long to go back for the first time in ten years.

Chapter 38

It was late in the morning, and Matt had just gotten his second coffee when Carter approached him.

Matt had hoped that the day would be quiet for once. Just him responding to possible sightings of Eva Rae. Ever since detective Carter had been on TV, the calls had been coming in non-stop. But so far, none had proved to be true.

Matt was still focused on the area around the food mart, and he had planned to visit a few of the hotels surrounding it later in the day when Carter was too busy to ask questions. He had been focusing merely on small motels and crappy places, but then realized that if Eva Rae was with her sister, then maybe they were, in fact, hiding in plain sight, frequenting the more exclusive hotels, since Kelly Stone — or Sydney — would be paying. Matt had thought about getting a trace on her bank account, but he would have to do it behind Carter's back, and that made it harder. It was also more difficult because she was a celebrity. There would be questions asked, and he wasn't sure a judge would allow it when Matt couldn't prove that she was actually with Eva Rae. She could be traveling or staying here for work. A call to her agent hadn't cleared things up since he had no idea whether Kelly was in Miami or not. He also said that Kelly Stone often took off without saying where she went, not even to him. She did this when she wanted to go on a vacation, or just have time off for herself. Then she would go off the grid until she was ready to resurface again and let the world know she was back. It was all to avoid paparazzi on her vacations. The fewer people who knew where she went, the better the chances were for her actually to get some vacation time.

Matt couldn't blame her. He had always thought it had to be awful to live a life as a celebrity and never be able to go anywhere without having the paparazzi chasing you or people gathering to get your autograph or a silly selfie with you.

It had to be exhausting.

Matt had been minding his own business, going through all the latest so-called sightings, and called back on several of them, when Carter had approached him and told him to grab his badge.

"Something happened."

And now they were standing in front of an expensive white mansion in one of the most exclusive neighborhoods south of Miami... Coconut Grove. Patrol cars blocked the street, and the blue lights lit up the palm trees in the driveway. Carter pointed at the house next door, then mentioned casually that Bruce Willis lived there, according to his sources. Matt nodded, even though he had the feeling that Carter was just showing off. So what if he lived there? Celebrities didn't impress Matt much.

"Why are we here?" Matt asked. "What happened?"

Carter signaled for Matt to follow him, and he did. The house was crawling with crime scene techs, and Matt was soon suited up and had put on gloves. A tech showed them inside, and they followed.

The victim was in the kitchen, naked, tied to a chair. The body was drenched in blood. There were already flies in the eyes and the wound on the slit throat.

Matt clasped his mouth, and for a few seconds, he couldn't hear anything but the rushing of his own pulse in his ears.

Chapter 39

"Who is she?"

Matt wanted to turn around and look away but managed to keep his cool. Carter stepped closer, grinning as he looked up at Matt.

"I think she was more of a he," he said and pointed down to the crotch. A penis had been split in half down the middle, and Matt almost threw up again, thinking about just how painful it had to have been. A knife had been secured as evidence. There was a trail of blood across the white tiles, where the body had been dragged. Matt wondered if she had been still alive, if the killer had dragged it out, just for the pleasure of it.

"*She,*" Carter said, "is the owner of Hotel Ocean View in Miami Beach."

Matt looked away. "Could it be a hate crime?"

Carter shook his head. "You'd think, right? But no. I have another theory. The detectives on the case called once they spoke to her secretary. Mrs. Moore here had a visitor yesterday at her office that might be of interest to us. They pulled the surveillance from the lobby as she entered."

Their eyes met, and Matt's heart sank.

"Eva Rae Thomas?"

Carter clicked his tongue. "Bingo."

"Wait," Matt said. "You don't honestly think that…?"

Carter bit his lip. "Oh, yes, I do. She was the last person to see Mrs. Moore alive. After her visit, Mrs. Moore told her secretary over the intercom that she was going home, then left taking the back door."

Matt could hardly breathe. This wasn't good. This was going from bad to worse.

"Why? Why would Eva Rae Thomas murder this woman?"

Carter lifted his eyebrows. "That's what we need to find out. But so far, she is wanted in connection with the murder. This gives us a lot more elbow room to work. I have asked for roadblocks to be set up around town. Cars will be searched, and that means she won't be able to go anywhere without being discovered. The Miami-Dade chief is giving us extra manpower. He wants her caught yesterday."

"Okay," Matt said and nodded anxiously. It was getting harder for him to hide his worry. Eva Rae was in serious trouble, and he found it difficult to see a way out of this. "I guess we have work to do then."

"It gets better," Carter said, grinning again.

"Really?" Matt asked nervously.

Carter nodded. "There was another woman with her on the surveillance footage. You'll never guess who she is."

Matt swallowed hard. "W-who?"

"Kelly Stone," he said, sounding proud, like he was the one who had made the discovery, when in fact, it was another detective who had contacted him and told him this.

"Yes, the actress. The very one and only and get this. They're sisters."

Matt lifted his eyebrows and tried to act surprised. He was never much of an actor or a liar, and he knew it would come off as awkward. He wanted to yell at this guy and tell him that he had known Eva Rae since he was three years old, and there was no way she would ever hurt another human being like this.

Not Eva Rae.

But, of course, he couldn't say that. He needed to stay close to the investigation, and they wouldn't let him if they knew the truth. So, he continued to play dumb.

"Really?"

Detective Carter nodded pensively. "Makes sense, right? Why we couldn't locate them. She's been living the life in first-class, letting her sister pay for everything. Meanwhile, we've been looking in all the wrong places. But that's over now. We're breathing right down her neck, and it's only a matter of time before she walks into our net. And when she does, I am taking her down. She won't know what hit her. There's only one thing worse than a criminal, and that's a criminal cop. I can't stand that. It's a dishonor to the badge. But I know how to get her now. I know exactly how to sniff her out."

Chapter 40

"Did you go out last night?"

Sydney and I had just gotten into the Mustang when she asked me the question. I paused before inserting the key in the ignition.

"What do you mean?"

"I woke up around midnight, and you weren't there."

I shrugged. "I went for a walk," I lied. I didn't want her to know what I had been up to.

"I see," Sydney said and looked out the window.

I turned the engine on, and the Mustang roared to life. I sensed that she didn't believe me, but I couldn't deal with that now. I had seen the cult's symbol branded into the skin of that man in the truck the night before and I hadn't been able to think about anything else since.

I hit the accelerator, and we left the hotel's parking lot, then drove into the street. I wondered about the night before and if the police had found the girls and taken care of them. All morning, I had been flipping through newscasts but hadn't heard anything. I worried about those girls.

"So, where are we going?" she asked and looked up at the sky above us and all the tall palm trees that were rushing by.

"NYX headquarters," I said and pressed the accelerator to make the car jolt forward.

Sydney sat up straight. "Excuse me?"

"I got the address from Lori Moore, remember? Well, I thought we'd pay them a little visit, or at least you would. I'm kind of exposed."

"You want me to walk into NYX's headquarters and do what exactly?" Sydney asked, surprised, and maybe slightly appalled by the idea.

"I want you to pretend like you want to take a course. I want you to ask questions and seem interested. I want you to go as you, as Kelly Stone, the famous actress, and let them know you're interested. I want you to ask to see the founder, Christopher Daniels."

Sydney stared at me, mouth gaping. "Me? Why?"

"You heard what Lori Moore said. They'd love to get their hands on someone like you. You're just the type they want. And you're an actress; you can easily pretend like you're very naïve and gullible."

Sydney nodded. "O-okay, I guess I can do that. But what do I do when I get in? What if I get to see him? What do I do then?"

"I don't know," I said and turned right on red.

Sydney gave me a look. "You don't know?"

I exhaled. "I just know that somehow this Iron Fist is connected to the cult. I know they're also somehow connected to the trafficking of young girls. I just don't know how."

Sydney crossed her arms in front of her chest. "And just exactly how do you know this? Yesterday, you didn't seem so certain. Did you discover this when out *walking* last night?"

"You might say so," I said and drove up another street and into a far more expensive part of the neighborhood. I drove up to the house I had seen on Google maps, then parked the car down the street from the entrance so as not to seem suspicious or get caught on a potential surveillance camera.

"Listen, Sydney. Just trust me on this. This cult, and probably its leader, is hiding something, and that something might have to do with my daughter. You've asked me a ton of times how you can help make things better; well, this is it. If you do this for me, it might help me get Olivia back. So, please."

Sydney looked at me, her eyes growing softer.

"Okay. I'll do anything for you; you know that."

I eased up and fell back in my seat. "Thank you, Syd. It means the world to me."

Chapter 41

THEN

The sex was intense. Christopher was insatiable, and it felt like he could continue forever. Helen was exhausted by the time he finally got off her, and she felt so embarrassed.

She had wanted this to happen, a big part of her had, and she had let it, but at the same time, she felt like she had no choice. Christopher held that type of deep power over her so that she was incapable of saying no to him.

He rose to his feet, ran a hand through his hair, then looked down at Helen's naked body while getting dressed. The yoga mat underneath her felt sticky. His eyes glaring at her made her feel uneasy.

He smiled like he enjoyed looking at her, and that made her blush. She felt like asking what would come next, what was expected of her, but she didn't dare.

The thing was, she enjoyed him and the way he looked at her. Somehow, she had known that she would from the first time when reading his book and looking at his picture. She had known that she wanted to sleep with him. He had that raw sexual energy in his eyes. But he still scared her slightly as well.

Helen reached for her dress on the floor and was about to put it on when he stopped her.

"Wait."

She paused and looked up at him. He pulled out his phone and took her picture. Helen froze, wondering what he was doing. He took another picture, then crept really close to her, spread her legs, and took a series of pictures of her vagina.

"What are you doing?" Helen shrieked. She reached her hand down to cover herself up, but he laughed and removed it.

"Don't be shy. I'm just taking a few pictures of you."

"W-why?" she asked and grabbed her dress, then held it up to cover her body.

He grinned and showed her a picture on his display of her vagina up close, then swiped so she'd see herself lying naked on the floor. Helen winced at the sight.

"Why?" she asked again. "Why would you take those pictures?"

He leaned over her, pushing her back, then kissed her intensely. As his lips parted hers, he looked into her eyes.

"I call it collateral. Now that I have these, you won't tell anyone what goes on here. I own you, and if you tell anyone about us or about what this group is, or if you refuse to do as we tell you to, then these pictures will be sent to everyone you know, starting with your parents."

Helen stared at him, eyes growing wide. She pulled away, appalled. It took a few seconds before she was able to speak again.

"W-what do you want from me?" she asked while pulling the dress back over her head, her heart pounding in her chest. Never had she been treated in such a manner with so little respect. "Is it my money you're after?"

He smiled and tilted his head as she rose to her feet. He grabbed her by the shoulders, then kissed her again.

"What is this?" she asked.

"This is me taking control of you. You're my slave now, and you do everything I tell you to, do you hear me? Everything."

Chapter 42

The new girl, Tiffany, stayed close to Olivia at all times. It was getting slightly annoying to Olivia, and she often tried to lose the girl, to push her away, but Tiffany refused to let go of her side. Often, she clung onto her arm so tight, Olivia couldn't use it.

It got them in trouble at the factory that night, and after that, Olivia ignored Tiffany when they got back to the house. She went to bed, hoping that by giving her the cold shoulder, she might give up and finally leave her alone. Olivia didn't have the energy to take care of anyone else.

"I'm sorry," Tiffany whispered later as they were trying to sleep.

Olivia lay with her back turned to her, eyes open, but pretending to be asleep.

"I'm just so scared," Tiffany continued, her voice quivering. "And you remind me of my sister. I miss my sister so much."

Olivia exhaled. She really didn't want to know more about Tiffany or her family. She didn't want to know any details about this girl because that would mean that she'd have to care about her, and she didn't want to. She couldn't allow herself to do that.

Yet she still sat up and looked at the girl, then smiled. "I have a sister too. And I miss her… a lot, even though she can be very annoying at times. What's your sister's name?"

Tiffany wiped her nose on her arm. The stench from the factory and the dead chicken lingered in Olivia's hair constantly, and she felt so sticky.

"Her name is Ariana. She's two years older than me," Tiffany said. "She used to help me with my homework. She's really good at math."

Olivia felt a knot in her throat. She had forced herself to not think about her family for so long, simply because it hurt too much to do so. She tried hard not to picture her mom because, if she did, she would see how sad and desperate she was, not knowing where Olivia was.

There was nothing worse to Olivia than to see her mother cry. She didn't want to think about it.

"I used to help my sister with math too," Olivia said, then chuckled lightly at the memory of her and Christine struggling over math problems. "She was terrible at it."

Olivia bit her cheek, realizing that she had spoken about her sister in the past tense like she didn't expect ever to see her again. Did that mean that she had given up hope?

Maybe.

She had seen several of the girls die while she had been kept there. Only the toughest made it through to the next day. And so far, Olivia had been among the tough ones. But for how long?

"Do you think we'll ever see them again?" Tiffany asked, her big hope-filled eyes lingering on Olivia's face.

Olivia pictured her sister's face, then her brother's, and finally, her mother's. Then a tear escaped her eyes and rolled down her cheek.

"I'm sure we will," she said. "I'm sure we will."

But they both knew it was a lie.

Chapter 43

M att was staring at the whiteboard in front of him, his hands shaking lightly. On the board, looking back at him, was the surveillance photo of Eva Rae and her sister, taken in the lobby of the Ocean View Hotel. They had both dyed their hair, and Eva Rae was also wearing a cap and glasses, but he could still see it was her. He'd recognize that sweet face anywhere.

Matt closed his eyes for a brief moment and pinched the bridge of his nose, leaning forward.

What am I going to do? How am I supposed to get her out of this mess?

As he opened his eyes, Carter stood in front of him, a file in his hand, and a smirk on his face. He placed the file in front of Matt.

"Our little friend was busy last night."

"What do you mean?" Matt asked, feeling tense. Could it possibly be more bad news? He wasn't sure he could take any more.

Carter nodded at the file, and Matt opened it, then flipped through the top pages before looking back up at his partner.

"There was a shootout at the harbor last night. Three men were found dead. Others were badly injured. No one is talking, though. Seemed to be gang-related at first. But get this, they found seven young girls in a container. All fresh in from Guatemala."

"Trafficking victims?" Matt asked.

Carter nodded, grabbed a chair, and sat down. "Looks like an Eva Rae Thomas project, doesn't it?"

"But... what time did this happen?" Matt asked. "If we assume she was at Lori Moore's house, she couldn't have been at the harbor too. She can't possibly have been at both places?"

Carter leaned back. "I had a feeling you might say that, but unfortunately, one doesn't exclude the other. The medical examiner says Mrs. Moore was murdered between two and four a.m. The shootout took place right after midnight. It's a twenty-minute drive. She could easily have performed both. No matter what, we're looking at at least three homicides at the harbor, and then a possible homicide in Coconut Grove. We're waiting for ballistics on the shooting victims. But I'd say we have ourselves a serial killer now. This is the big stuff, Matt. This is what can make or break a career."

"Except we have no evidence placing her at any of those scenes," Matt said, his voice shivering in desperation.

"Ha. That's where you're wrong," Carter said. "Turn to the next page."

Matt did, his hand shaking so badly it was hard to hide. A surveillance photo of someone getting out of a yellow Mustang appeared. It was obviously a woman, a woman wearing a cap.

"Taken at the port at exactly five minutes to midnight," Carter said. "Notice, she's wearing the exact same clothes as she was on the surveillance from the hotel earlier in the day, the last time anyone saw Lori Moore alive."

Matt's heart sank. There was no way around this. It was her. It was Eva Rae in that photo, placing her right at the scene of a triple homicide.

What the heck are you thinking, Eva Rae!

Matt stared at the photo. Tears were welling up in his eyes, but he managed to stifle them.

"Say... are you... you're not personally involved with this woman, are you?" Carter asked, scrutinizing Matt.

Matt sniffled and shook his head. "No. Of course not."

"It's just... you seemed a little emotional there."

He closed the file. "Well, I'm not. It's just allergies."

"Allergies, huh? Yeah, they can get pretty bad down here at this time of year." Carter looked at him, and Matt felt uncomfortable, sensing that Carter didn't buy it.

Luckily, his phone rang, and he picked it up, leaving Matt to wipe his eyes on his sleeve. Carter walked away for a few seconds, talking on the phone, while Matt cleared his head, convincing himself to remain professional. If Eva Rae had killed these men, then she had done so for a reason.

Eva Rae was many things, among them a strong and protective mother. But a murderer, she was not. And Matt was going to make sure the world knew it.

Somehow.

Carter returned, looking annoyingly cheerful.

"Kelly Stone has been seen at a hotel downtown," he said and grabbed his car keys and placed his badge on his belt. He lifted his eyebrows.

"We've got them. Let's go."

Chapter 44

"These guys are good."

Sydney got back in the passenger seat. I could tell she was shaken up. She was pale, and her voice trembled when she spoke. She had just come out of the NYX headquarters after spending about an hour inside. Meanwhile, I had been sitting in the car, listening to the radio announcer talking about the shootout at the harbor the night before and that the police wouldn't comment on whether they believed it was gang-related. There was no mention of the girls.

I shut the radio off as soon as Sydney approached the car and got back in. She wiped her sweaty palms on her skirt.

"What do you mean?" I asked.

"You were right. They were all over me as soon as they realized who I was. It was crazy. But they were so nice at the same time. Very friendly and not in my face at all. I felt very comfortable. I hadn't expected to. I spoke to one of the women there, and she told me so many good things about how this could be a journey for me, how I could develop into a much stronger individual, and she even guessed that I had a fear of flying, which I've never told anyone. Because in my line of work, you have to fly places all the time, but the truth is, I loathe it, and now I know why. Because I was taken from my family and put on a plane back then when my dad took me. I was forced on a plane and taken thousands of miles away to a life where I would miss my mother and sister every day until my dad convinced me they were the ones who didn't want me, and I stopped longing to get back. But the fear of flying still lingers inside me. Can you believe it? I was in there for what? An hour? And they already made me realize this? I can't imagine how much more they could do for me if I took one of their workshops."

"Wow," I said.

"Are you sure they're not legit?" she asked. "I mean the people I met sure seemed professional. They knew what they were doing."

"That's probably how they get you hooked," I said. "Did you get to meet Christopher Daniels?" I asked.

She looked at me, then nodded. "I was shown into his office, and they served me herbal tea. Then he came in. He was such a handsome man, so charismatic; you won't believe it. He shook my hand, and we spoke for about ten minutes, mostly him asking me questions about my life and what I expected to get out of his classes, what I wanted to change in my life. I told him I would think about it, then get back to them, then shook his hand again and left. But he was so nice, Eva Rae. I didn't expect him to be. I felt so welcome and even at home there. I have never felt anything like it."

"Did you see anything that could help us? Any young girls in the house or pictures, or did he mention anything?" I asked. "Maybe they're working for them?"

She shook her head. "Not at all. The woman who served me herbal tea was about my age and didn't seem to be in any distress at all. I tried to look into her eyes, and she seemed almost blissfully happy. I have to say, Eva Rae, I'm not sure this has anything to do with your daughter and what happened to her. Why do you even think that it has? Because that Ryan guy saw their symbol during the attack? It's a little far-fetched; don't you think? I mean he might have seen it on a bag or something and then just kept remembering it. It doesn't seem to have any connection to Olivia, whom we don't even know for sure was on that clip on TV. There's a lot of loose ends here, Eva Rae."

I started the car up, disappointed, and took off. I don't know what I had expected she'd find in there, but at least something. Instead, I now doubted everything. Could Sydney be right? Was I just going crazy and clinging onto something I had imagined in my mind?

That guy in the back seat of the truck had the symbol branded into his skin.

No, something was definitely off here, and it had to do with this cult. I might have been a hothead, blinded by my desire to get my daughter back, but I just knew it had to, no matter what Sydney said. No matter how nice and wonderful these people were.

Life had taught me that the line between good and bad people was thinner than you'd think.

Chapter 45

I drove up in front of the hotel, then hit the brakes, hard. Sydney was thrown forward and landed with her hands on the dashboard.

"Hey!" she yelled. "What's going on?"

I stared at the entrance to the hotel for a few seconds, my heart pounding in my chest. I watched as Matt came out of the sliding doors with a shorter, slightly overweight bald guy. The entry was packed with police cruisers.

Sydney saw it too, then looked at me.

"What do we do?"

"We need to get out of here," I said as I turned the wheel and slid the car back onto the road, making sure not to go fast and cause suspicion. I drove nice and casually past the hotel and continued down the street, then took a right turn and parked in front of Flanigan's Seafood Bar and Grill.

"Let's go get some coffee," I said, then felt my stomach growl. "And maybe some lunch."

We walked inside and sat down in a booth. We ordered coffee and mahi-mahi burgers. I was starving, yet my stomach was almost too upset to be able to eat. The burger was good, though, and it made its way down. Getting food helped me to think more clearly.

"What do we do now?" Sydney asked. "That place was crawling with cops. They were there for us; weren't they?"

I exhaled. "Yes. There's no doubt in my mind. They found us, so we're not going back there; that's for sure. They'll ask the front desk to alert them as soon as we try."

Sydney breathed heavily. She ate a bite of her fish burger, then chewed and swallowed.

"Maybe we should just turn ourselves in," she said. "Before things get out of hand."

I looked up, and our eyes met. I felt a pinch of guilt. I could hardly tell her that things had already gotten way out of hand. I regretted having brought her with me in the first place. Why had I dragged her into this? She risked losing everything.

I stared at my burner phone on the table, then grabbed it and rose to my feet.

"I need to make a call," I said, then left, dialing a number. I walked outside to the parking lot while waiting for him to pick up.

Come on; come on.

Finally, he did.

"Matt Miller."

"Why are you here?" I asked. "Why are you following me?"

It took a few seconds before he said anything, and I assumed he needed to get somewhere where no one could listen in on our conversation. His response came in a gasp.

"Eva Rae? Where are you?"

"Wouldn't you like to know?" I said. "What are you doing down here, Matt?"

"I'm trying to help you," he said agitatedly. "What on Earth do you think you're doing?"

"I'm looking for my daughter. You know this, Matt."

"Last night was a disaster, Eva Rae," he said with a moan. "You've gone too far."

"They were traffickers. Seven girls' lives were about to be destroyed. I saved them."

He sighed. It didn't sound good. I closed my eyes and missed feeling his breath on my skin, and his lips pressed gently against mine. I thought about the last time we had been together and desperately wanted to feel that again.

But it was impossible.

"Eva Rae, please turn yourself in," he said heavily. "This has gone as far as it can."

"I haven't found Olivia yet, so, no."

"Eva Rae, dammit. You're wanted for murder!"

"It was self-defense. They tried to kill me. I liberated those girls."

"No, no, not that. Well that too, but you're also wanted in connection with the murder of Lori Moore. You were there at the hotel before she went home. Next thing, she's found murdered in her house. You were the last one to see her alive."

My heart dropped. "Lori Moore is dead?"

"Yes. They think you killed her or at least that you had something to do with it. Please, come in and tell your side of the story. I know you didn't kill her, but I can't convince everyone else if you keep running. Running makes you look guilty. You, of all people, should know this, Eva Rae."

My heart was hammering in my chest now. I kept staring out over the street and the palm trees on the side of it. A woman walked by with her small dog, not noticing me at all.

Lori Moore was dead? Right after we had been there to see her?

"They think I did it? But… but they're wrong."

"And that is what you need to come in and tell them. Please, Eva Rae. Stop running. We'll find Olivia together. The right way. Through thorough police work. I know it takes a lot longer than what you care for because you'll need the warrants and surveillance for months before we can strike those joints, but we will. Eventually, we'll find her."

"I don't think so," I said. "Eventually isn't good enough. Months is too long. I want her home now. And I am going to continue chasing them until I find her. There's nothing you can do to stop me."

"I love you," he said, right as I hung up.

I stared at the phone in my hand, a tear escaping my eye. Then I whispered: "*I love you, too.*"

I threw the phone on the ground, then stepped on it, shattering it, and threw the remains in a trash bin with a loud cry.

I then gathered myself and walked back inside the restaurant, my heart feeling completely shattered. I looked at Sydney, who was about to pay with her credit card.

I stopped her.

"Use cash instead. They might be tracking your cards."

She swallowed nervously, then nodded. She found a handful of cash, then left it at the table.

"We need to get out of here," I said. "Things have gone from bad to worse. I'll explain later."

Chapter 46

"I love you."

He said the words again, but the line had gone dead. Matt stared at the display, then wondered if she had heard him. He still had never heard her say the words back to him, and it tormented him.

Did she love him?

"Miller!"

Carter waved him back toward the entrance of the hotel, and he rushed to him, his heart feeling heavy in his chest.

Would he ever get to kiss her again? Would he ever smell her skin again or just look into those blue eyes of hers?

"Where were you?" Carter asked. "We need to get back. They're not here. We searched their room and the entire hotel, but they're not here. Dammit. I was so certain we'd get them this time. Who were you talking to?"

"Just my mom. She's taking care of my son back home and needed to know where his cleats were for lacrosse. He has a game tonight."

Dang, I am a good liar.

Carter gave him a look of disinterest, then felt his bald head. "All right. The front desk will alert us once they get back."

"Did you find anything in their room?"

Matt had been up there with them going through the few belongings they had left there. Seeing Eva Rae's clothes again had made him almost lose his cool.

Carter shook his head. "They didn't bring much. We took the laptop on the desk in there. Hopefully, it'll contain something we can use in our case against those two."

"What about the fingerprints on the murder weapon? The knife in Mrs. Moore's house?" he asked, hoping to find anything that might clear Eva Rae as a suspect in that case.

"What fingerprints?" Carter said. "The killer wore gloves, I'm afraid. They left nothing. Still waiting to hear if she left any DNA on the body, though. The ME moved our case up because of its urgency, but they're still very busy with the many deaths from the Sarin gas attacks."

"Naturally," Matt said and walked with Carter back to the cruiser and got in.

Carter turned on the engine, and they took off toward downtown. Soon, they were stuck in heavy traffic. Matt stared at the tall buildings, then at the people walking the streets, and at the many cars. Where was Eva Rae now? Would she try to get out of town? Would she go to a motel somewhere? Would she be safe? While talking to her, he had wanted to reach into the phone and rip her through it to keep her safe. Being out there was dangerous for her now. The cops were terrified of her and would shoot if she gave them any reason.

"I can't believe they were right there all this time," Carter said. "Living in one of the most exclusive hotels in Miami, and we had no idea. Makes you feel kind of stupid, right? But we'll get them. Don't you worry. I have one more card up my sleeve."

Chapter 47

THEN

"I haven't seen you in forever. How are you?"

Helen stared at the woman sitting in front of her in the tearoom at the NYX headquarters. Helen lived there now while going through her healing process. The woman who had come to visit was her sister, Aubrey, and she wore a worried look and a slightly tilted head.

"You've lost weight," she said. "You look thin, Helen."

"Well, I've never felt better," she said. "I'm finally in control of my own life."

Aubrey looked like she didn't believe her. "Really? You don't exactly look fine to me. You've gotten so skinny. It doesn't look very healthy."

Helen cleared her throat. Losing weight was part of her self-development, part of the process she was going through. To deny herself food was a way of regaining control.

"Christopher says that…"

"Christopher? As in Christopher Daniels?" her sister said. "You're on a first-name basis with him?"

Helen nodded and sipped her tea.

"Mom and Dad are worried too," she added. "They haven't seen you in almost a year."

"I've been busy. We're busy here."

"We? It's *we* now?"

Helen nodded. "I'm part of something bigger than myself, so, yes."

"Dad says you've completely given up the horses. You never go to the farm anymore and have stopped riding? That's not like you, Helen. Those horses were your entire life, remember?"

"Christopher says it's part of evolving into an enlightened version of myself. It means giving up what has held me back all these years. Everything from my old me no longer applies. I've cleansed myself of everything from my past and can't go back anymore."

Aubrey sighed and leaned back in the white couch. "You should hear yourself; I can't believe you, Helen. Don't tell me you've given them money too?"

Helen chuckled. "It's always about the money with you people. I'm finally free of all that. Christopher says that money is just energy that needs to flow through us. Giving away your money is never a loss. You'll get empowerment back."

Aubrey gestured, annoyed, and groaned. "Can't you hear it? Listen to your own words, Helen. They've completely brainwashed you. Are you also having sex with this Christopher character, huh?"

"Wow. I didn't believe it when Christopher told me, but now I see it clearly that he was right. You're jealous of me. You're jealous of all that I have become, that I have managed to finally free myself from the world we grew up in, from our parents' claws. Don't you see that they're holding you down with all their money? Your ego is so big, you can't see it. But they're controlling you, telling you what to do, and I don't have to be a part of that. Finally, I have found a group that likes me for who I am, where there is nothing but love and peace, and where there is room for me and just me. All my life, I've had this void inside of me, this empty space, and finally, it's been filled in. Finally, I feel whole. And Mom and Dad can no longer touch me. They hold no power over me."

Aubrey rose to her feet, annoyed. "And what happens when you run out of money, huh? When you can no longer pay for the party? What will they ask you to do then? Where will you go when they throw you out? You can't come home. Dad's been very clear about that."

Helen shook her head with a gentle smile.

"You don't understand, sister. I *am* home. This is my home."

Chapter 48

My eyes were focused on the road, my hands sweaty and shaking slightly as we drove away from the restaurant, the Ritz-Carlton, and the exclusive neighborhood of Coconut Grove. I approached the end of 27th Avenue when the traffic slowed down.

Sydney gave me a look. "What's going on? Why are we stopping?"

I shrugged. "Traffic, I hope."

I looked ahead of us. The rows of cars were slowly crawling forward toward blue flashing lights.

"Could it be an accident?" Sydney asked.

I spotted the patrol cars, then officers in the road peeking inside of cars.

"It's a roadblock," I said. "They put up a darn roadblock."

"For us?" Sydney shrieked.

"Yes, for us," I said, then looked in the rearview mirror. There was still no one close behind us, so I put the car in reverse and backed up, swirled the car around, then drove the wrong way back down the road until I found a small street and turned, while the oncoming cars honked loudly at me.

We drove through the back streets in a smaller neighborhood, then reached a Home Depot before heading out on Dixie Highway, leading out of town. I pressed the accelerator down, and we roared southbound until the traffic suddenly slowed down once again and we came to a full stop.

"What the heck?" I said.

"Another roadblock?" Sydney asked and looked at me perplexed.

A chopper circled above us and made me nervous. The traffic crawled forward, and I found a small exit, leading us back again.

"Shoot," I said and slammed my hand on the wheel.

I took another turn down toward the Chinese Village but ran into yet another roadblock and had to turn around again and drive back.

"They've blocked all the exits," I said. "We can't get out of here."

I hit the accelerator again, and we rushed back toward Coconut Grove. I found a park and stopped the car, trying to clear my head for a few seconds, and looking at the map.

"We've tried all the exits," I said. "There's no way out. We have to stay here, somehow."

"But, Eva Rae, I don't understand," Sydney said. "Why are they chasing us like this? Is there something I need to know?"

I exhaled and leaned back in the seat. "They think I killed Lori Moore," I said. "I called Matt earlier, and he told me. I didn't want to worry you. That's why I didn't tell you."

Sydney stared at me, barely blinking. "Lori Moore? She's… she's dead? But we saw her yesterday?"

"And that's why they think I killed her. We were the last people to see her alive. She was found murdered in her house this morning."

The panic was visible in Sydney's eyes.

"Murdered? But… but… can't you just tell them you didn't do it?"

"It's not that simple. I'm already wanted for a lot of other stuff. And I don't exactly have an alibi for when she was killed."

"You don't? Oh, wait... it happened last night? You snuck out last night... but... why, Eva Rae? What were you doing?"

I started the car back up with a roar. "I went for a walk, remember?"

I didn't want to tell her what I had done. I was still processing it myself. Three people had been killed, bad people, yes, but still. They weren't supposed to have died. It was an accident. I didn't want Sydney to know; I didn't want to give her more to worry about.

"We need to find somewhere to hide," Sydney said and gave me a look.

"I don't think any hotels will take us," I said. "Even if we found a small motel, they'd recognize our faces."

"Maybe we don't have to," she said. "I have an idea. But you're not gonna like it."

Chapter 49

"You've got to be kidding me."

Sydney had taken over the wheel and driven us back to Coconut Grove and into the south end of the neighborhood, far from the Ritz-Carlton. She parked in front of a big mansion and looked at me.

"Think about it. They'll never look for us here. We'll be right under their noses."

"But... Sydney. This is NYX headquarters?"

She nodded eagerly. "I know. It's perfect."

Sydney got out of the car, and I reluctantly followed her. She grabbed my hand in hers and led me to the entrance, where we rang the doorbell. A tall, gorgeous woman wearing white linen pants and shirt opened.

"Kelly Stone!"

"We need your help," she said. "Can I talk to Christopher again?"

The woman nodded. "Of course. Of course. Come on in."

We walked inside the big hall and were told to sit down on a set of couches. A huge flower arrangement on the table in front of us smelled heavenly. All the walls and furniture were white, and everything was very bright.

Even the man coming toward us was dressed in a white suit, his salt and pepper hair slicked back, his piercing blue eyes lingering on my sister.

"Kelly Stone, twice in one day. How did I get to be so lucky?" he said and gave her a warm hug.

"This is my sister," she said and pointed at me. "Eva Rae, this is Christopher Daniels."

The gorgeous man pulled me into a hug as well. His embrace felt warm and genuine. I had to admit, I enjoyed it, and it brought me great calmness.

He looked into my eyes, still while holding me.

"Wow, you're tense."

He turned to face my sister, finally letting go of me.

"My assistant told me you needed our help?"

Sydney nodded. "Yes. We need shelter for the night. The entire town is looking for us."

Christopher Daniels stared at her, scrutinizing her. "I have a feeling I shouldn't ask why. We don't watch the news here and, to be honest, it doesn't matter why you're running. We all run from stuff in our lives. We are here to help."

"We can pay you," Sydney said.

Christopher put his hand up. "We don't need your money. It'll be our pleasure to host you and your sister for as long as you need. I'll put you up in one of the guest cottages in the back. No one will think about looking for you there."

Sydney exhaled, relieved. I was still tense, maybe even more now as I saw the way he looked at my sister.

"Thank you so much. You have no idea how big of a help this is."

Christopher Daniels placed his palms against one another, then bowed.

"It is my pleasure to help. At NYX, we believe in kindness toward everyone."

He turned to face the woman who had opened the door for us.

"Angela here will make sure you have everything you need; won't you, Angela?"

The woman nodded, smiling. As she moved her arm and her sleeve was pulled up, I noticed she too was branded with the symbol, just like the guy I had seen in the car at the port. Seeing it made my blood freeze.

"Of course," she said. "If you'll follow me, I'll get you installed."

Chapter 50

Matt sat at his desk, sipping coffee, while people rushed around him, talking on phones and tapping on computers. He stared into the empty screen, not knowing what to do. He could still hear Eva Rae's wonderful voice and missed her so terribly. It was like his entire being was screaming for her to come back. The whole town was looking for her now. He was terrified that she would put up a fight and they'd end up killing her.

Carter had ordered roadblocks all over town, especially tight around Coconut Grove, so they wouldn't be able to leave the neighborhood without being caught.

So far, Matt hadn't heard anything, so that was still good news. But Matt felt nervous beyond anything else. If they did catch her, then there was no telling what might happen. Would she resist arrest? Would she try to run? Would they shoot at her if she did?

He couldn't see any good ending to this, and it tormented him.

Chief Annie had called earlier in the morning and told him she too was worried. What she was hearing from down there made her nervous.

"You and I both know she didn't do it," she said. "She couldn't kill that woman — not that way. In self-defense maybe or trying to do something good, yes, but not a brutal slaughter like this. You have to stop them, Matt."

"How?" he had asked her. "I tried to get her to turn herself in, but she refused to. Not until she finds her daughter."

"So, she must have some intel that puts Olivia in Miami," she said. "Maybe she knows that the Iron Fist is there."

"That's what I've been thinking too. But I've asked around and even searched their files down here. They have nothing on this Iron Fist."

"It's probably just a name he uses online," she said with a deep exhale. "They might know him by another name."

"I've asked to look into their human trafficking files, and hopefully that'll pay off."

"And that guy, Carter? Does he suspect that you know Eva Rae?"

"I'm afraid so. He asked about it earlier, but I think I managed to talk myself out of it."

"He can't know, Matt," she said. "You've got to play along, so we know what's going on. We want Eva Rae home alive."

He sighed. "I'm beginning to think it might be hard. This guy wants her taken down. It's become like an obsession to him."

"That's not good, Matt."

"He still doesn't have anything that places Eva Rae at Lori Moore's house at the time of the murder."

"That's good," she said. "I'll try and pull all the strings I can from up here, but there's a lot of heat on her right now, so I fear it might be tough."

They had hung up, and Matt had felt like screaming but kept his cool. Now, he spotted Carter coming down the hallway, a file under his arm, whistling happily.

I don't like that look on his face.

"Guess what?" he said as he approached Matt's desk.

Matt forced a smile. It became awkward, but Carter didn't seem to notice.

He reached inside of his file, then placed a photo in front of

Matt. On it was a necklace with a golden heart at the end of it. Seeing it made Matt feel sick to his stomach.

Matt had given Eva Rae this necklace for Christmas.

"Recognize this?" Carter asked, then showed him a photo of Eva Rae where you could see her wearing the necklace.

"That's right," he added. "It's hers, and guess where it was found? You guessed right. In Lori Moore's house, in the kitchen where her body was found. This places Eva Rae Thomas at the scene of the crime. This is exactly the evidence we've been waiting for."

Chapter 51

The guest house they gave us was really nice — decorated in white furniture and with flower arrangements on the tables, two bedrooms with queen-sized beds, and a small kitchen. It was all we needed.

I took a shower, then threw myself on the bed and fell asleep right away. I slept heavily until Sydney woke me up and told me it was time to go to dinner. I still felt groggy and exhausted when I followed Sydney into the big dining room.

Many eyes were on us as we found two seats and sat down. The food was nice and reminded me of my mom's. Being vegan and plant-based, it was something she might cook. I ate while thinking about her and the kids, wondering if they were all right. I didn't allow myself to think much about them since it hurt too much if I did, and I had to focus on the task of finding Olivia.

I had been so close to the Iron Fist the night before at the port. And now, I didn't even have a computer to gain access to the Dark Web. It annoyed me greatly that I had finally found him in there, found a chatroom where he was arranging the meets, and now, I couldn't even get back to it.

I had been so close, and yet I blew it.

Not everyone in the dining room had been branded on the arm; I realized when looking around. It seemed to be only a few, and those few seemed to be in charge of the rest. Most were women, but there were also a few men. The founder, Christopher Daniels, sat at the end of the table, smiling and chatting to the people sitting next to him. Sydney fell into talking with several other women sitting next to her, and she seemed like she was enjoying herself. Meanwhile, no one spoke to me. I guess I didn't exactly give out the vibe of wanting to chat.

Gosh, I miss my family. Has Alex lost that loose tooth he was so proud of? Will my mom remember to give him money from the tooth fairy? Is Christine remembering to practice her double bass?

Talking to Matt earlier had almost made me lose it. I wanted him to reach in through the phone and hold me tight. I needed to feel his touch, his warm kisses on my skin. I craved to be close to him again. But instead of telling him how badly I missed him, how deeply I loved him, I had been distant and cold toward him.

Because I had to be.

I just hoped he understood that.

When dinner was over, we helped clean up along with everyone else in the big kitchen. I filled the dishwasher and, once I was done, I walked outside on the porch overlooking the big pool area. Two women were in the pool, swimming.

I realized there were four guest cottages like ours on the property, and one of them was located by the edge of the property, its windows covered with plywood. Somehow, that cottage gave me the creeps, and I couldn't stop looking at it.

"You enjoying the view?"

It was Christopher Daniels. He came out on the porch, an orange in his hand that he began peeling. He smiled at me when I turned around.

"Just enjoying that I still have my freedom," I said, feeling heavy. I knew this was a good hideout, but it wasn't going to last. At some point, I had to face what I had done. I just hoped I found Olivia before it happened.

I added, "For now."

"I sense you are weighed down greatly by your past," he said, his eyes scrutinizing me.

Really? How insightful.

"You know there are ways to let go of all this, right?" he asked. "We have workshops that can help you."

I forced a smile. "I'm good for now. But thanks."

"Suit yourself," he said, then finished peeling the orange and opened it. He handed me a piece. I took it to be polite. He slurped his as he ate it, and the sound made me cringe.

"You know it's not your fault that your sister was kidnapped when you were younger," he said.

I almost choked on my piece of orange. I coughed to breathe. He didn't seem to notice.

"You've carried that weight since you were a child," he continued. "But that's not all of what is weighing you down. And this is becoming a problem between you and your sister. Because, deep down, you also blame your sister for what happened. Because she strayed. That day at the supermarket. She walked away from you; she left you to look at Barbie dolls. The man, your father, grabbed you first but then took her instead. You're secretly angry at your sister for letting it happen when she knew she was supposed to keep an eye on you. And now that she's back in your life, you're angry with her because she got the easy part. She got to grow up with your dad while you were stuck with a mother who was emotionally unavailable. She got to become a beautiful, beloved actress, while you became an FBI agent in the attempt to redeem yourself for not being able to save her. She grew up guilt-free while you carried all this weight around. But you need to forgive her in order to be able to move on. Or else it might end up destroying your entire relationship. You need to let go of this. It's important for both of you."

I stared at the man next to me, eyes wide open, my nostrils flaring. At first, I didn't know what to say.

"Did my sister tell you all this?" I ended up asking.

He shrugged. "Does it matter?"

I was about to say something, but as I turned to look at him again, he had left. I stood alone on the porch, warm wind blowing in my hair, feeling myself blush in anger.

Who did this guy think he was?

Chapter 52

Matt couldn't sleep. How was he supposed to fall asleep with all that was going on?

He was lying in his hotel room, staring into the ceiling, wondering about Eva Rae and how to help her get through this. He also wondered about the necklace and how on Earth it could have been found in Lori Moore's house if Eva Rae hadn't been there on the night of the murder.

Part of him was beginning to worry that maybe she had been there. Maybe Eva Rae had killed that woman?

What if she did?

No, you fool. It's Eva Rae we're talking about. You've known her since you both were three years old.

Matt closed his eyes while rubbing his forehead. He had a headache coming along, and it had been lurking behind his eyes all evening.

His thoughts returned to Eva Rae. He had gone through the case from the port this very afternoon and looked through all the pictures. Three men were killed. Seven young girls rescued. Matt didn't know what to think. Those guys were obviously criminals of the worst kind, buying and selling young girls. But the thing was, if Eva Rae had killed them, then maybe she had killed Lori Moore too. If she was involved somehow in the trafficking? Could she have been some sort of ringleader?

Two of the men were killed in a car crash. The driver had been shot through the windshield, but that wasn't what killed him. The impact was. One was shot in what looked like self-defense. They didn't have their throats slit in their kitchen. Nor had they been mutilated. No, that kill was of another caliber. That was the work of a vicious murderer.

Matt exhaled and lifted his head from the pillow. His watch said two a.m. He looked at his phone to make sure she hadn't called again. But the last incoming call was from his mother when she called for him to say goodnight to Elijah. As usual, the boy had been completely silent on the other end while Matt spoke. It hadn't exactly helped their relationship that he was gone for so long. Matt had thought about taking the boy to counseling to make things better between them. His mother and Eva Rae had both told him to give the boy time, but Elijah blamed Matt for the death of his mother, and it didn't seem to get any better, no matter how much Matt tried.

"Maybe you're trying too hard," Eva Rae had said back then when Matt had taken the boy in. "Maybe he needs a little space."

It had been eight months now, and Matt saw no improvement at all.

Maybe I'm just not good enough to be a dad.

He sighed and put the phone down. He couldn't stop thinking about Eva Rae and how distant she had been earlier in the day when they had talked on the phone. Matt knew she was under a lot of pressure, more than what most people would be able to sustain, but still.

Didn't she miss him at all?

He wondered where she was hiding. There were roadblocks all over town, and they would continue all night and into the next day. How had she managed to avoid them so far? She couldn't go back to the hotel. She couldn't go to any hotel in the area without them calling Carter. Her face was everywhere, on all the screens in the small homes. How was she still keeping herself under the radar?

Carter had said he had one more card to play, one he believed would smoke them out. He wouldn't share it with Matt in detail, but Matt got the feeling that it was bad news for Eva Rae.

Chapter 53

S ydney took a late-night yoga and meditation class, while I stayed in the guesthouse raging over Christopher Daniels and the way he believed he knew me. The fact was, he didn't know me at all.

I kept glaring down to the end of the property toward the cottage that was all boarded up. It had me curious. What was in there and why did it have to be boarded up? There hadn't been a hurricane going through since Irma two years ago. Had they simply just never removed them? Because they didn't use it?

Or was there something in there that they didn't want to see the light of day?

Sydney came back after it had gone dark, looking all blissful and relaxed. She took a shower, then threw herself on the bed next to me with a deep sigh.

"My God, I needed that. You should have come, Eva Rae; it was so good, and so empowering," she said.

I looked at her, thinking about what Christopher Daniels had told me earlier, then forced a smile, trying to push down the feeling of jealousy I felt toward her and always had felt since she came back into my life. I wasn't going to let this control me or let Sydney sense it. I could deal with my guilt and blame on my own. I didn't need their workshops to help me. Christopher Daniels might think he knew me, but he didn't know me at all.

"I just feel so refreshed," Sydney said and dried her hair gently with the towel. "Like I'm brand-new. I really like it here. It's been a while since I felt so good about myself."

"That's great," I said, not meaning it.

"You know what Christopher told me?" she asked.

"No, what?" I said, wanting to roll my eyes, but refraining from doing it. I didn't want her to know how I felt about him and all his so-called insight.

"He said something that really resonated with me deep down. And I am a little embarrassed to admit this, but he told me it would be good for me to tell you. He told me that I was secretly blaming you for being the one who wasn't kidnapped back then at the Wal-Mart. I mean, our dad did grab you first, and then he took me instead. According to Christopher, that has been bothering me all my life, and secretly, I've been blaming you for it. And I'm jealous of you for having grown up with our mother. I grew up lacking one my entire life, thinking she didn't want me. It's tough once you get to that age where you really need her, especially as a teenager, you know? I mean, who was I supposed to talk to about getting my period, huh? Dad? He blushed when I even asked him to buy the pads I needed."

I stared at her. "You think Mom talked to me about periods?"

"Didn't she?"

"Mom barely talked to me at all. I would scream for her attention but never receive it. She could freeze me out for days at a time. She couldn't even look at me because it reminded her of what had happened. After you were gone, it was like I didn't exist to her anymore."

Sydney looked at me with compassion in her eyes. "Oh, dear God, Eva Rae. I didn't know."

I shrugged. "How could you? You weren't there."

I rose to my feet, feeling all kinds of emotions stir up inside of me. I hated to admit it, but Christopher Daniels was right. I was upset about Sydney getting to grow up with our dad and leaving me alone with our distant and cold mother.

Dang it, he was annoying.

Chapter 54

I sat outside of our cottage for a long time, maybe a few hours; I didn't know. All I knew was that I felt angry and sad at the same time and that I was sick of feeling this way. Yet I didn't know how to get rid of it, how to solve it. Maybe I should take one of his workshops?

As I sat there, looking up at the stars and the night settled everywhere, I suddenly saw activity down by the boarded-up house. Two people with flashlights approached it, speaking in low voices.

I looked at my watch and realized it was two a.m. Why were they up and walking around down there?

I rose to my feet, then hurried across the lawn, past the two other cottages, then stopped when I got closer. I watched them from afar as they unlocked the door and opened it. When they had entered, and the door was closed behind them, I ran up to the cottage and stood by the window, leaning my ear against it.

I heard whimpering coming from behind it. Someone was crying. Crying and pleading with them.

"Please, let me out, please."

My eyes grew wide. Someone was being kept in there? Against her will?

"You can't get out," a voice said. "You must finish what you came here for first."

"It's part of the cleansing process," another voice said.

"Please," the woman said.

"Remember what Christopher said," the first voice said. "It's for your own good."

"I know," the woman said. "I know."

"Don't you want to reach enlightenment? Don't you want to get rid of your old persona and become like new?"

"I do. I really do."

"Then you must let go of your old ways. Your excessive pride is holding you back. This is the only way to become free from it."

"I know. I know."

I can't believe these people. They're keeping her in there? Locked up? And then they tell her it's for her own good?

I gasped lightly as someone placed his hands on my shoulders. I stood up straight while he held me tightly between his hands.

"Oh, my, still so tense," he said.

Christopher Daniels!

I froze in place while he leaned over my back. I could feel his body really close to mine as he whispered in my ear and breathed down my neck.

"You really need to learn how to relax. I can teach you."

"Just like you're teaching that woman in there?" I said.

He laughed, then closed his arms around my neck, a little too tight for my liking.

"She's in there voluntarily," he said. "No one forced her."

"How long has she been there?" I asked. "Voluntarily?"

"Does it matter?" he whispered. I felt his lips close to my ear, and it made me very uncomfortable.

"I heard her pleading to be let out, yet they didn't do it. Why is that?"

"Because she doesn't know what is best for her. It's part of the process, to strip her of her pride. But no one said it was going to be easy. It's our job to make sure she doesn't give up in the middle of the process."

Dear God, what is this place? We need to get out of here before it is too late.

His arms were still wrapped around me, and he was holding me tight. I wanted to get out of his grip, but he wasn't letting me go. Instead, he chuckled as I struggled to get loose.

"Your life is just one long struggle, isn't it?" he asked. "It doesn't have to be. It could be so much easier."

"Let me guess, if I give in to you and your ways?" I said. "What else do you keep locked up in this place? Do you have any young girls here too? Kidnapped young girls?"

Finally, he let go of me. I panted and turned around to look at him, breathing agitatedly.

He stared at me. The way he looked at me made me feel uncomfortable, and I backed up. Our eyes locked for just a second, and I took off running back to our cottage.

Chapter 55

"I think Christopher Daniels is the Iron Fist."

I had barely slept all night. Once my heart had calmed down enough for me to find a little rest, the many thoughts in my mind wouldn't let me sleep.

"Excuse me?" Sydney said.

She was sitting up in bed when I entered her room and sat down next to her. She looked gorgeous, even when having just woken up. It annoyed me.

"Why would you say something like that?" Sydney continued. "He's been nothing but nice to us."

"He's keeping a girl locked up in the cottage down by the end of the property. I heard her plead for them to let her out, and they wouldn't. Then he came and put his arms around my neck, tightly, like he wanted to hold me down."

"That's a technique he uses," she said. "To make you connect with the Earth again. He did it to me yesterday too."

"The guy is a sleaze bag," I said. "Why are you defending him?"

"Why do you keep accusing him? Need I remind you we're staying here for free while the entire police force is looking for us because of you."

I stared at my sister, biting my lip.

"I still think he's the Iron Fist."

"You're insane," she said, then grabbed her burner phone. I had asked her to get rid of her old phone now that they knew she was with me. It was too easy to track.

"Now, if you'll excuse me," she said. "I have to check my emails. I assume this thing can access the Internet?"

"It can. I only bought those that can, assuming we'd need it. The data is prepaid for by cash. But do you have to check your email now?" I asked. "It's risky."

"Yes, I need to do this every now and then. Since I have been on the run with you, I have been completely off the grid, and I need to check in to make sure there isn't some big offer for the role of a lifetime that I'm missing out on."

"Be careful," I said. "They might send you a link for you to click, but it could give up our whereabouts."

She gave me a look that reminded me of Olivia. It almost made me cry. I hadn't realized until now how much those two actually looked like one another.

"There's an email from my agent," she said and pressed on the display of the LG burner phone. I had bought a ton of them at Wal-Mart before we left, so we could get rid of them as soon as we were done using them. I had purchased the most expensive ones since they would be able to do more, like use navigation and access the Internet, but they were still only thirty bucks per phone.

"Oh, dear God," Sydney said.

I looked at her, and her face turned pale.

"What's wrong?" I asked.

She lifted her eyes, and they met mine.

"They're threatening me to turn you in."

"They're what?" I asked.

Her eyes teared up. "The police have contacted my agent and told him that if I don't turn you in, they'll go to all the newspapers and magazines and tell them I am a suspect in a murder case. So far, they have kept it from the public that they are looking for me too, but now they're willing to leak it if I don't turn you in. It'll ruin my career. Oh, Eva Rae, I don't know what to do."

Chapter 56

"What is happening? Where are we going?"

It was in the early morning hours, and Olivia and Tiffany were sitting on the floor of the blue van. The armed guards had woken them up around sunrise and told them to get in.

Sitting next to her, Tiffany whispered the words to Olivia. Olivia didn't look at her. She fiddled with the hem of her jeans that had become ripped from the many hours working at the factory. The jeans were so dirty you could barely see the blue color anymore. Olivia's black Converse were worn out, and her pinky toe was poking out the side.

"Olivia?" Tiffany said. "Where are we going?"

Olivia shrugged, then looked away.

"Please, Olivia?" she said. "What's happening?"

Olivia took in a deep breath, then finally looked at the girl. She reminded her so much of her younger sister; she almost teared up just looking at her.

"Remember that I said that sometimes we do other stuff besides work at the factory? Well, this is it. This is the other stuff."

"But what is it, Olivia? What are we going to do?" Tiffany asked, her lips shaking.

Olivia shrugged. She had grown to care for the girl. Even though she had promised herself she wouldn't, it had happened anyway. And now she was worried about her. It was the last thing she needed right now, to have to worry about someone else besides herself. But spending days with this little girl, having no one else to talk to, she had done what she decided never to do. She had gotten to know her. And now she feared something might happen to her. She wanted to protect her.

"Just follow my lead when we get there," she said. "And don't ask questions."

"But...?"

Olivia sent her a look, and she stopped. Olivia felt her hands begin to shake as she worried about what was ahead.

They soon ran into a roadblock, and they could hear the driver talking to an officer outside, while the guards signaled for the girls to be very quiet. The talk lasted a few minutes, and Olivia had to bite her lip hard to not scream for help. But when looking at the guards' guns, she knew there was no way she dared to do it. They would only kill her.

Someone walked up behind the van, and they heard voices. Hope filled Olivia and made her stare at the door, praying they'd open it and find them all.

We're in here; Please, help us!

But the door never opened, and soon the voices faded out, and the van started back up again. Olivia felt her heart hammering in her chest as she stared at the guards with their guns. Sweat was springing from her forehead as she slowly realized they had passed the roadblock. A tear escaped her eye as her hope dwindled.

When the van came to a halt again, she gasped and looked up toward the door that was opened, and a face appeared. Their leader smiled widely at them.

"It's time, girls."

They rose to their feet and walked in a line out of the van, Olivia making sure that Tiffany was right behind her. Once outside, they were told to stand in a line up against a wall. The area around them was void of people. The guards had new clothes for them to wear along with plastic bags and sharpened pencils.

"Now, some of you have done this before and know what to do," one of them said, staring each and every one of them into the eyes to make sure they understood. "The new ones follow what the rest do. As soon as you're inside, you place the bags, hiding them under a chair or a bench, and then you poke the bag right before you leave and rush back outside, where we will be picking you up at the back entrance."

The bags were handed to them, and Olivia took hers along with the pencil. Tiffany stared at the bag between her hands with the liquid inside of it. Olivia could tell she wanted to ask questions but held it back like Olivia had told her to. The guards and the leader didn't like them asking questions. Olivia had seen them beat a girl until she could barely walk because of that. If you wanted to survive, you just did what they told you. Those were the simple rules to follow.

The leader came up in front of them, then walked down the line and pointed at one girl, then at another.

"This one. And that one. And…?"

The leader stopped in front of Tiffany, then placed a hand on top of her head.

"This one."

Olivia's heart stopped when she saw it.

"No!" she yelled and stepped forward, nostrils flaring. There was no way she could let this happen.

The leader stopped. A furious set of eyes landed on Olivia.

"Do you want to take her place?"

Olivia swallowed, then looked down at Tiffany, who was crying now. Olivia nodded.

"I'll take her place."

"All right," the leader said. "As you wish."

As they had changed and began walking in a straight line, Tiffany tugged at Olivia's shirt.

"What was that? What did you do?"

Olivia exhaled. She felt her hands begin to shake.

"Every time we do this, they choose three girls who will be the ones who go in first. They usually don't make it out alive. Our leader wanted you to be one of them, but I took your place."

Chapter 57

They were told to merge into the crowd and look like any of the other children there. They had given them uniforms to wear and had even given them backpacks on their backs to make it look like they were just kids going to school. The grown-ups pretended to be teachers and wore skirts and carried briefcases.

Olivia walked with the two other girls toward the crowd entering the school, then blended in with them, and she lost sight of the two others. They were instructed to be the ones to go upstairs and place the bags there. By the time they made it downstairs, the girls down there would already have poked holes in their bags, and it would be too late for them to make it out. Olivia knew the drill. She had done it twice before.

But the other two times, she had been among those to survive. This time was different. She had chosen to sacrifice herself.

Olivia's hands were shaking as she followed the other children inside. She had no idea what had become of Tiffany since she had stayed behind and would enter with the four others, the ones that were going to survive. One of the adults looked at her, and she could tell she was scared too. But there was no way around it. The first time, on the train, one of the girls had tried to run before they got on the train. Two guards grabbed her and took her away. They never saw her again.

What they did was terrible; Olivia was well aware that it was. She knew the bags held a gas in them and that it killed people once it was released. She looked at all the kids hurrying to class, grins on their faces. She saw the girls chatting by the lockers, happily, only worried about the next test or maybe a boy, not knowing what was about to happen. She felt such terrible pain in the pit of her stomach.

How was she supposed to do this to them? They were nothing but kids like herself.

"If you run and we find you — and we *will* find you — you will be killed. If you talk to anyone, you will be killed. If you refuse to do as instructed, you will be killed. Is that understood?"

Those were the words before they sent them off, just as they had been the two other times. Olivia had listened to them, shaking, and she hadn't dared not to do as she was told. She had wanted to survive.

She still wanted to survive. But the guards waited by the entrance and exits of the school. They would catch her and kill her if she tried to escape.

The first time they had sent them into the trains, Olivia hadn't known what was in the bags. She had been instructed to go one stop and then place the bag under her seat, poke a hole in it, then get out of the car and into another one, the only one that wasn't attacked. Then as they rode one more stop, she was told to get out and walk away like nothing happened. *Don't look back*, they had told them. *Just keep walking till you reach the stairs*. But Olivia had stopped and turned to look. That was when she had seen them. Hundreds of people that had fallen out of the car that she had been in first, and crawled across the platform, gasping for air, some screaming in pain, others squirming until they took their final breath. Three of them had been girls she knew from the house. They had been in the first car at the end of the train and didn't make it out in time. Olivia had stopped for just a second and stared at them, then realized that she had done this, that what had been in those bags had caused this.

Her stopping had cost her a beating when they got back to the truck because she almost exposed herself, they said. Olivia hadn't cared. She thought she deserved a beating for what she had done.

Now, she was up the stairs and looking down the hallway at all the smiling faces. Olivia realized it was August, and school was back in session. She had been gone all summer, and school had started back up without her. The thought made her tear up.

I am never going back to school. I am never going to be with my friends. I am never going to see my parents or my siblings again. I will die here, squirming on the floor like a worm until I can't breathe anymore — like they did on that train and like they did in that church.

"No, I will not. I will make it out, somehow," she told herself, shaking her head.

She then walked inside a classroom and placed the bag underneath a chair. She was instructed to wait until right before class started. A couple of kids looked at her strangely, probably wondering if she was a new student. She looked down, then placed her foot against the bag to make sure it was still in place. She felt the pencil in her hand. It was amazing how heavy such a little pencil could feel when it held the power of life and death.

Chapter 58

What does it matter if I'm dead anyway?

Olivia stared at the pencil in her hand and felt the pointy end of it with her finger. Still more kids were coming into the class and putting their backpacks down. Two boys were goofing around and fighting for fun. Three girls were watching, giggling at their stupidity, hoping one of them would look their way.

Olivia looked at the clock on the wall. There were still ten minutes until class started. She spotted a girl sitting a couple of desks down, on her phone.

Heart hammering in her chest, Olivia made a decision, one she feared she would end up regretting.

"Can I borrow your phone for a second?"

The girl looked up at her. She was wearing black lipstick, and her eyes blazed in anger.

"No. Why would I loan my phone to someone I don't even know?"

Olivia leaned over her desk, then said with a low voice. "Because if you don't, we're all going to die."

Now she had her attention. The girl looked up at her, eyes wide, mouth gaping.

"What did you just say? Is this some kind of joke?"

"Listen to me," Olivia said. "I'm trying to save your life here, but I need you not to panic, okay?"

The girl scrutinized her for a long time. Olivia was certain she could hear the clock on the wall ticking loudly in her head. She had no time to spare. She didn't know what the response time was around here. Would they be able to make it in time?

"Just let me borrow the phone, please," Olivia said with the calmest voice possible. Sweat was springing from her forehead, and her palms felt clammy.

"Please."

The girl swallowed, and Olivia could tell she knew this was serious. She looked down at the phone for a second before finally handing it over to Olivia.

Relieved, Olivia grabbed it, then dialed.

"9-1-1. What's your emergency?"

"There's going to be a gas attack on a school," Olivia said, keeping her voice low, hoping that the other students wouldn't hear her and panic. If they started to run, the girls in the other classrooms would poke their bags prematurely as they had been instructed to. People would die.

"What school are we talking about?" the dispatcher said. Olivia could hear her tapping on a keyboard. Olivia found it difficult to calm her pounding heart.

"I…I don't know…" Olivia said, then looked at the girl with the black lipstick. She seemed to understand and pointed at the emblem on her shirt.

"Our Savior's Catholic school," Olivia said, her voice trembling. "It's the same as what happened on the trains and at the church. The gas is in bags. But you must hurry. It's gonna happen in six, no wait, only five minutes. Please, hurry."

Chapter 59

"What's going on?"

Matt saw the officers begin to run. Carter looked up from his desk too. A sergeant came to them.

"Sarin gas attack on a school. Someone called it in. Apparently, the attackers are still inside, and it hasn't happened yet."

Matt rose to his feet, then looked at Carter.

"I'll drive," Matt said and grabbed his gun. They stormed to the cruiser and took off, sirens blasting, following the nine other patrol cars that were leaving at the same time.

"We need the entire perimeter sealed off," Matt said. "If the attackers are still inside, then they'll come out at some point, trying to get away, and there will be someone waiting for them. We need to get them."

Over the radio, they learned that firefighters and paramedics were almost there, but they were told to stay back in case the terrorists were armed. If they were to stop this, then they had to play their cards right. They also learned that JTTF were on their way, but coming up behind them, so Miami-Dade police were to intervene if possible once they got there.

"Leaving the tough work to us normal cops," Carter grumbled under his breath. "As usual."

"We're talking ten terrorists, armed with Sarin gas, inside the school," the radio informed. "One of them called dispatch. She's on the top floor. She's just a young girl. She informed dispatch that there were seven young girls who were forced to do this. And three adults."

"They're using young girls?" Matt asked, startled.

It suddenly made sense. He had been going through the files from the two previous attacks and seen that there had been at least three young girls in each place that were unaccounted for. They had been in the age range from ten to seventeen. And so far, no one had looked for them, and they hadn't been able to ID them yet. Some were Hispanic looking while others were assumed to come from Eastern Europe. Only one girl had been ID'ed as being American, and her parents had been notified. They had told the police that she had run away from home two years earlier. How she ended up in a Catholic Church on a Sunday morning in Miami had been a puzzle until now.

"They're using trafficked girls," Matt mumbled.

"What's that?"

"To do their dirty work," he said.

"The terrorists?"

Matt nodded as Carter drove up in front of the school and parked behind the many other patrol cars. They each grabbed a vest and put it on. They were going to be there with the first responders, and Matt felt anxious. It was almost eight o'clock. They had thirty seconds to get in there, identify the terrorists, and stop them before they pierced those bags like they had at the Metrorail and the church.

The responders leading the charge suited up in hazmat suits and put on gas masks. Matt waited outside, gun clutched between his hands, while the men in suits stormed inside and the screaming began.

Chapter 60

As the first scream resounded, all in the classroom turned to look at Olivia. She had explained the situation to them and told them to remain calm, that the police were on their way.

"Why can't we just run?" a girl said, her entire torso shaking in desperation.

"Yeah, I want to get out of here," a boy standing next to her said, his eyes flickering in fear.

"Don't," Olivia said. "The police have just entered the building; that's why they were screaming downstairs. But as they did, the bags were most likely poked, and the gas has started to seep out. If you run out in the hallway or down the stairs, you'll run right into it, and then you'll be exposed."

The kids stared at her, eyes brimming with terror. More screams were coming from downstairs, and it made another wave of fear go through the classroom.

"They'll come for us," Olivia said. "But until they do, we keep the door closed and stay in here."

More screams made a boy rise from his seat. "I can't stand this. I can't stay in here!"

Before Olivia could stop him, he ran for the door, opened it, and stormed out into the hallway. Olivia slammed the door shut behind him, crying helplessly.

Barely had she backed away from the door before it opened, and a man made his way inside. Seeing his face made Olivia's blood freeze. He was one of them; he was one of the men that had brought her there.

He took one glance at Olivia, then at the bag on the floor beneath the chair.

"We've been compromised. You know what to do next," he said. "Poke the bag."

Olivia stared sat him, her hands beginning to shake. In his hand, he was holding a gun, and as the other kids in the class saw that, they screamed and backed up.

Olivia stared at him defiantly, blocking his way to the bag.

"It must be done," he said and lifted the gun to her forehead, then clicked the hammer back. "You know this."

She closed her eyes and shook her head. If he shot her, then so be it. She wasn't going to risk all these children's lives.

"DO IT!"

She opened her eyes and stared into his, determined. Then she opened her mouth and said:

"No."

The man trembled in anger and pressed the barrel of the gun against Olivia's skin. She prepared herself, readied herself to pay the ultimate price.

She didn't see the chair as it flew through the air until it was too late. It slammed into the man's back and knocked him to the floor. Olivia glanced toward where it had come from and spotted the girl with the black lipstick holding it, panting agitatedly.

Next thing she knew, she was on top of him, her hands gripping over his and over the gun. Olivia didn't know where she got her strength, but it just happened. The man let go with one hand, and Olivia pulled the gun out of his grip, but as she almost had it, he gave it a push, so it flew across the room. He then punched Olivia in the stomach and blew out all the air from her lungs. Olivia panted, and the man managed to squirm away. It was too late when Olivia realized that he had a pencil in his hand, and she couldn't stop him before he poked a hole in the bag, and the green liquid slowly seeped out onto the classroom floor.

Chapter 61

Olivia lunged at the man, but it was too late. A shot blasted through the air and whizzed above her head. The bullet hit the man in the forehead, and he fell to the floor, instantly dead. Behind her stood the girl with the black lipstick, gun between her hands, shaking. She let it go, and it dropped to the floor.

Screams of panic soon filled the classroom, and Olivia stared at the leaking gas, panting and agitated.

"Get away from it," she yelled at the top of her lungs. "Go to the windows and open them!"

Someone lifted a chair and threw it through the window. The window was pushed out of its frame, and soon the boy crawled out. He stood on a ledge, screaming his heart out.

"Help! Help us!"

A girl crawled out after him but slipped. Her hands gripped for the ledge, and she was now hanging there, screaming. There were two windows in the classroom. Olivia ran to the other, the one that faced the other side of the building and spotted the firefighters below. She pulled the blinds off, then pushed the window open. She yelled at them to come to the other side of the building. They did and entered the school courtyard below. The firefighters spotted the kids on the ledge and soon backed a ladder-truck up in the court-yard. The girl dangling outside the window let go of the ledge with a scream and jumped into the arms of a firefighter on the ladder below who took her to safety. Seeing this, the two others soon followed.

"Hurry," Olivia said and looked back at the gas at the other end of the room. Luckily, the hole in the bag wasn't very big, and it was coming out very slowly. She couldn't even feel it in her eyes yet, and she knew of several other girls who had survived that. As soon as it pinched the eyes, that was when you should run; she had learned from them.

Run, if you can.

Olivia turned to the others, then pointed at the window. "Get out there, and they'll take you down. It's the only way to survive this. If you stay here, you'll die. We can't wait for the police and para-medics to come up here. We need to go now."

One after another, Olivia helped them crawl outside, and they were soon crawling down the ladder. When it was the girl with the black lipstick's turn, she stopped.

"You go first," she said.

"No, no, it's all my fault; I'll go last."

The girl looked into her eyes. "No. You go first."

"I don't want to," Olivia said.

"Listen," the girl said. "Once we get down there, they'll start looking for you. You saved us. I don't want the police to get their hands on you; you hear me? There are only three of us left, and we all agree you should go now, so you'll have time to get away. Please, just go."

Olivia sighed deeply. "Thank you."

"I'm Emma, by the way," the girl said and hugged her.

"I'm Olivia."

Olivia gave Emma one last glance of gratefulness, then slid her body out of the window and stood on the ledge, looking down. The area was now crawling with cops, and her legs were shaking badly.

Right before she let the firefighter help her onto the ladder, she spotted a set of eyes belonging to someone standing behind the crowd and looking into them made her scream.

Chapter 62

I stared at my burner phone when the breaking news sign filled the screen. I had been sitting in our guest cottage on the bed with Sydney ever since she told me that the police were pressuring her to turn me in. Neither of us had a solution to the problem, though, and now we were sitting in silence when the phone vibrated.

BREAKING NEWS: SCHOOL ATTACKED WITH SARIN GAS IN DOWNTOWN MIAMI.

"What the heck?" I asked and looked up at Sydney. "Another one?"

I turned my phone to show her. She had turned hers off completely in anger because of the email. She had told me she wasn't going to do it, that her sister came before her career at any time, but I sensed it was tough for her to make that choice, and I wasn't sure I wanted to put her in that position. I didn't want her to have to make the choice.

You'll never work in the business again, had been her agent's words.

I pressed the link, and it led me to a TV station's live feed from the scene. A chopper flew above the school and filmed as the chaos unfolded beneath. I watched as students came out of the school screaming, some falling to the ground, and the paramedics were rushing to them. My heart cried when I saw the panic and chaos as the chopper continued to the other side of the school building, where kids were standing on the ledge, reminding me of the horrific scenes from nine-eleven.

Luckily, the kids were being rescued by the firefighters. But as the chopper paused above them, lingering as close as it could get, I saw something that just about made my heart stop.

I saw her. I saw Olivia.

I was so surprised; I burst out in almost a shriek.

"Olivia?"

My voice cracked, and Sydney looked at me. "It's her," I said. "It's her; look. She's on the ledge."

Sydney looked over my shoulder and saw her too, just as she was helped down by a firefighter.

"She's going to make it," I almost cried while Olivia crawled down the long ladder. "It's my Olivia, Syd; it's her. We've found her!"

"I can't believe it," Sydney said, tearing up as well. "It really is her."

"But…how? What is she doing at a Catholic high school?" Sydney asked.

"I…I don't know," I said, almost laughing when I saw Olivia put her feet on the ground. She was soon greeted by a flock of students, and I lost track of her as she blended in.

"Where is she? She disappeared," I said.

Then the chopper suddenly took off. It moved away, then took a turn and returned to the main entrance.

I shook the phone in my hand in frustration.

"No! Stay there. Stay on these students. I need to see where she's going!" I yelled at the phone in my hand, but it didn't help. The cameras were now on the front side of the building where more students were carried out. They were lying on the grassy area outside of the school, making it look like a warzone. I gasped and clasped my mouth.

"Do you think she was exposed to the gas?" I asked. "She was in there, just like those other kids."

Sydney grabbed my hand and made me look her in the eyes.

"Eva Rae, no. We saw her. It was her. She was fine. She got down. Eva Rae, listen to me. This is good news. She's alive, and she's here. She's in this town. We found her, okay? We found her."

Chapter 63

Matt ran around the building. The first responders were still working on the inside, trying to get all the victims out, and everything was total chaos. His job was to make sure none of the terrorists escaped and to help the victims as they came out.

Never had he seen anything like it. So many kids came tumbling out of the building, coughing and screaming in panic. The terrorists had let the gas out just as the first responders entered the school building, and after that, it was all turmoil.

Later, he had heard about the kids on the ledge of the second floor and run to help.

Now he was staring up at one of the kids standing on the ledge, and his heart dropped. He couldn't believe who he was looking at.

Olivia.

He walked closer, heart throbbing in his chest. Could it be? Could it really be her? Or was it just someone who looked like her? Was his mind playing a trick on him?

No, it's her. It is definitely her.

Matt hurried closer. Olivia didn't see him. She seemed to be staring at someone else, and Matt discovered it too late. Someone was standing behind the crowd, poking his head out, and as she got onto the ladder, her eyes locked with his. Olivia then screamed before climbing down.

Matt rushed to her, running, but as soon as she had her feet on the ground, she ran fast. She ran toward a flock of kids who were all wearing the exact same uniform as her. They surrounded her, and she blended in so quickly, he lost track of her. He couldn't see her anywhere.

"Olivia?" he yelled. He reached the crowd and stood in the middle of it, surrounded by kids the same age as Olivia. They were all were wearing the same uniforms. Matt was turning around, frantically looking into each and every face, repeating her name, when he finally realized that she wasn't there.

Olivia was gone.

Heart hammering in his chest, he looked toward the man that she had been looking at when she climbed down and realized he too was gone. He was nowhere to be seen.

NO!

He left the flock of kids and ran toward where the man had been standing, then jumped behind the row of bushes and spotted a street behind it — one that was beyond the police barrier. At the end of the street, he saw a blue van disappear.

"Stop that van!" he said and began to run after it, sprinting down the street. The van turned right and, with the tires screeching, it swung into traffic. Seconds later, it had completely vanished out of Matt's sight.

Matt ran to the end of the road, screamed his anger out, then slammed his fist into a light pole next to him in frustration.

"Dammit!!"

Chapter 64

I waited until Sydney had her meditation class, then grabbed my purse and put my burner phone in it. I wrote her a note on a small notepad in the room that was supposed to be used for us to write down our thoughts during our *cleansing process* or something. I wasn't listening when the branded woman told us about it when we first got there.

I left the note on Sydney's pillow, then grabbed my purse and left the cottage. Most of the entire group was at the meditation class, so this was a perfect time to get out of there without anyone asking questions.

I knew that Sydney would be upset with me for leaving her like this, without a word, but I also knew that if I told her about it, she would ask to come along. And I wouldn't be able to say no.

It was time for us to split up. I didn't want her to go down with me. She still had a career, and I wanted it to remain that way. I didn't want her to give up everything for my sake. I wouldn't be able to live with myself if she did.

I walked across the lawn to the main house and in through the dining hall, finding it empty as I expected. I peeked inside the kitchen and grabbed a banana and a pack of bread to keep me alive for a little while since I was going out into the world without any money, and I couldn't risk using my credit card again. I had made that mistake once, and I had a feeling that's what led Matt right to me.

I turned around, ready to walk out through the main hall when a voice stopped me.

"Eva Rae Thomas. Running away, are we?"

It was Christopher Daniels. He was standing right in front of me, flanked by two of his goons. There weren't many men here at his cult headquarters, but the few that were here were big and looked like they could take me down without using much effort.

"As a matter of fact, yes," I said. "I'm leaving today because I've gotten news about my daughter and her whereabouts. I need to find her. I thank you for your hospitality; it's much appreciated. As you'll see, my sister will be staying a little while longer."

I tried to walk past him, but he blocked my way.

"How's that song go again?"

"What song?"

"*You can check out anytime you like, but you can never leave.*"

I lifted my glance and looked into his eyes. "What the heck are you talking about?"

"You can't run away now. Not when you have begun the process of becoming a better human being. You are so close, Eva Rae. The world out there will tear you apart, literally. They'll arrest you, and then what? In here, you can reach enlightenment. You don't have to care about what goes on out there. You don't need the world. We'll take good care of you."

"Excuse me? Are you telling me I can't leave this place?"

"I do believe it's a bad idea."

"You can't keep me here against my will," I said. "Is it because I saw that woman in the cottage? And now you're afraid I might tell the police about her? You know what? I don't have to tell anyone. I don't even plan on talking to them, so there you go. You can let me leave."

I was lying so terribly, it had to show; I just knew it did. Of course, I was going to tell the police everything. Are you kidding me? I was the police, or at least I used to be. I tried to reach inside my purse for my gun but didn't manage to grab it.

"I don't think so," Christopher said, then signaled for his goons to approach me. They ripped my purse with my gun away from me, then grabbed me by the arms and lifted me into the air. They then carried me away, kicking and screaming.

Chapter 65

It was getting late, but none of them were even thinking about going home. The Miami-Dade Police Department was overwhelmed, and Matt and Carter had been asked to help with the interrogations. They walked into the interrogation room and sat down. The woman in front of them stared at them, her eyes big and scared.

"Helen Wellington," Carter said and looked into her file. He looked up at her, expecting her to confirm. She did with a silent nod.

"They made me do it," she said, her voice trembling. "Said they'd kill me and my entire family if I didn't."

"Let's start at the beginning, Helen," Matt said. "You were stopped outside of Our Savior's Catholic School during the attack today. You were coming out of the building when we stopped you. Several witnesses claim to have seen you place one of the bags of Sarin nerve gas in a classroom, poke a hole in it, then leave and close the door behind you."

Her nostrils were flaring, her body shaking. "I had to do it. They forced me. They forced all of us, even the young girls."

"Who?" Matt asked and leaned forward. "Who forced you to do this?"

She turned her head and stared into his eyes. He saw deep fear in them, and it made him feel uneasy.

"They did. NYX."

"And what is NYX?" he asked.

"It's a cult," Carter said. "That's what they call it around here. A cult for rich people. Their founder is known to run these workshops for self-awareness that he charges the rich women tens of thousands of dollars for."

"So, you're telling me that this group, NYX, told you to walk into the school and place the bags of nerve gas for them?"

Helen nodded with a light whimper. "I never wanted to hurt anyone. I'm not evil. You must believe me."

Matt looked at her file. Helen Wellington was the heiress of a billion-dollar entertainment empire that her father had built. He wondered how a woman like her had ended up in a situation like this.

"You don't know how they are," she continued. "They'll convince you that you're worthless without them. That you need to cleanse yourself of your old self, that you need to become a new person, and that you have to do stuff for the group to get rid of your old pride. They starved me for months and even locked me up in a small cottage for two entire months. I didn't get to see any sunlight or eat anything but dry bread and drink the little water they brought to me."

"They held you locked up against your will?" Matt asked.

She sighed. "That's the thing. I never told them no. I went along with it. So, in that way, it wasn't exactly against my will. I thought I wanted it because they told me I did, that I needed it to become a better person, to reach enlightenment. But that's how they work. They push you and push you until they can get you to do anything for them."

"Like placing Sarin gas in a terrorist attack," Carter said with an exhale. "Doing the dirty work."

Helen stared at him, then lowered her eyes and slumped her

head down. "You don't know how awful I feel. I don't understand how it got this far."

"The starvation and being locked up made it easier for them to brainwash you," Carter said. "Stories like these have been heard before concerning NYX — accusations of brainwashing of their members."

"But you said that there were also young girls," Matt said, thinking about Olivia on the ledge.

Had she been one of them?

"Where did they come from? Were they members of the cult and brainwashed as well?"

"No, that was even worse," Helen said. "Those are trafficked girls that they buy online to perform these attacks. They use them because they are expendable. No one will miss them if they die. You'll find them among the victims in both the train attack and the church."

Chapter 66

I t was beginning to rain, and the sky cracked above her head.
Olivia looked up and realized a thunderstorm was approaching,
and she had to rush and find shelter.

Since she ran away from the school, she had been wandering the
streets of Miami, not daring to stop for even a few minutes in case
the armed guards in the blue van came looking for her.

She still couldn't believe she had managed to escape their claws.

It had gotten dark out, and Olivia was beginning to feel unsafe.
Tourists had disappeared from the streets, and now groups of shady
looking men had taken over. Their eyes lingered on her everywhere
she went, and she rushed past them. Now she was running because
of the typical Florida rain that came with the thunderstorm, and
she spotted a bridge where a group of homeless people had found
shelter.

Hoping there could be room for her, she ran toward them,
trying to cover her face from the rain.

As she came in under the bridge, all eyes were on her and her
school uniform that she realized made her look very out of place.
She sat down on a piece of the pavement underneath the bridge,
pulling her legs up underneath her, trying to become as unnotice-

able as possible. A young girl who couldn't have been more than five or six came up to her and stared at her. Her face was dirty, and her eyes were lacking that healthy spark a young child her age would have.

"It's the Blue Lady," she said like Olivia knew who she was talking about. "She's watering her plants."

"Who's she?" Olivia asked. "This Blue Lady?"

"You don't know about her? My mom says the Blue Lady brings us love and protects us from the Bloody Mary, who will take your soul. She once cured my headache. I saw her standing outside the window, her skin pale, her eyes blue, and she looked in through the window at the shelter where we were staying. When she left, the window broke."

Olivia looked behind the girl when she heard two adults arguing. She realized it had to be the girl's parents. They seemed drunk. The woman was trying to stop him from eating their last can of sardines. She yelled at him, and he yelled back. Another man sitting on top of his black garbage bag let out a high-pitched laugh when the man slapped the woman. The girl didn't even turn to look at her parents. Instead, her eyes were fixated on Olivia.

"That's Crazy Jack," she said. "Don't go near him either."

Olivia tried to smile. "I won't. Thanks for the tip."

The girl turned around and left Olivia. Her parents were still fighting and yelling at one another, while Crazy Jack's high-pitched laughter bounced off the walls of the bridge. Olivia exhaled while wondering if she would be able to sleep there at all at night or if it would be safer for her to stay awake. She didn't have anything they could steal, but she was afraid of being raped or beaten. But not as much as she feared being found by the men in the blue van. If only she knew if they were still looking for her or not. She had a feeling they wouldn't give up so quickly and realized she had to keep moving. As soon as the thunderstorm passed, she would have to leave.

Chapter 67

I was on the bare ground, lying on concrete, trying to stay cool inside the small cottage they had put me in. The woman from earlier was no longer there, and I assumed they had finally let her out. At least I hoped that was what had happened and that it wasn't because she had died.

At first, I had tried hammering on the doors and boarded up windows, but when nothing happened, I had given up and laid myself down on the concrete floor to try and get a little cooler. No air was moving inside the cottage, and it was so hot I could barely stand it.

As the night approached, I dozed off, dreaming of Olivia and seeing her standing on that ledge of the school building over and over again. Every time she reached the ground below, I woke up with a shriek, sweat dripping from my forehead.

She's so close and yet I can't get to her. I can't stand it!

I lay on the floor, rage roaring inside of me, fueling me despite the heat and lack of food and water. I was going to get out of this place, no matter what. If only I could somehow alert Sydney to what was going on. But I had left that stupid note, telling her I had taken off on my own to find Olivia. So, of course, that was where

she thought I was, while she was having the time of her life medi-
tating with that embezzler, Christopher Daniels. I had seen through
him from the beginning but was starting to get the feeling that I
hadn't seen half of what he was actually capable of. Both him and
this place gave me the creeps.

I thought about the branding I had seen on the dead guy's arm
in the car at the port. I still couldn't escape the thought that Christopher Daniels could be the Iron Fist. After all, the *Iron Fist* was a TV
show about a rich guy growing up in a monastery among warrior
monks that taught him how to fight and meditate before returning
for what was rightfully his. Maybe he identified with him somehow.

I opened my eyes with a sudden gasp in the darkness.

"She was at both attacks," I mumbled, then sat up. "Olivia was
at both the attack at the train and the school. I saw her at both.
Maybe she was at the church too?"

A gazillion thoughts rushed through my mind in this instant as a
picture began to take shape. It wasn't one that I liked very much,
but it made sense.

They were using her and the other trafficked girls to perform the
attacks. That's why they kept buying more girls online. That was
why there was a member of NYX at the harbor. He was the Iron
Fist's representative. He was supposed to bring the girls back here so
they could use them. It was a smart trick since no one would come
asking for the girls anyway, and their dead bodies couldn't be traced
back to the cult. It was actually very clever. But did that mean that
NYX was behind the attacks?

Probably.

"Oh, my God," I mumbled while the pieces fell into place. They
had used my daughter to carry out terrorist attacks all over town.

The realization caused an even deeper rage to well up inside of
me, and I rose to my feet and started pacing back and forth, determined to get them for this.

These people were going down.

Chapter 68

C arter had left for the night to get in *a few hours of sleep before the chaos started all over again in the morning*, as he put it. Matt didn't feel ready to leave just yet. Helen Wellington's dad had posted the bond of one million dollars earlier that night, and she had been picked up in a limousine. They had told her she could expect to be brought in for more questioning in the future, and she had said that she'd be willing to help in any way she could and that she just wanted NYX punished for what they had done. She wanted the truth out about who they really were.

Now, Matt sat at his computer and began researching this alleged cult, NYX. He had found a lot of articles about its founder and many positive accounts from people who believed their lives to be much better after having attended his workshops.

Then he found a blog, and that was when the blood froze in his veins. It was an old blog, about a year old, but it was the person who was behind it that made him curious. It was written by the now-deceased Lori Moore, the woman who Carter believed Eva Rae had murdered in her kitchen. And it wasn't exactly saying nice things about the cult. In long descriptions, Lori Moore wrote about how this leader had made approaches to her and how she had seen a good friend lose weight to an almost dangerous level and seem deprived of any self-will after having become a member of the inner circle of the cult. She also talked about how they were branded and had sex with the leader and told that they now belonged to him. According to Lori Moore, he had a harem of women that obeyed his every wink and never left his side. Meanwhile, he had kept a woman imprisoned for almost six months in a cottage because she had sex with another man when she was only allowed to have sex with the founder, telling her *it was all for her own sake, for the better of her future, so she could reach enlightenment.*

Matt couldn't help but find all these descriptions very familiar. He remembered something about a Japanese cult leader and then Googled it. He found many articles about this doomsday cult and its leader that had been executed just the year before. The cult carried out a deadly Sarin gas attack on the Tokyo subway, along with several smaller gas attacks back in the mid-nineties. The attack on the subway was known as Japan's worst terror incident. Thirteen people were killed, and thousands injured.

Reading through all the articles, Matt suddenly saw many parallels to the NYX cult and its leader, Christopher Daniels. They too promised their followers a more meaningful life and gained tens of thousands of followers in its peak. Their leader was even invited to speak at universities.

Matt quickly figured it couldn't be a coincidence that Lori Moore was killed after criticizing them in her blog. She was a defector. She was dangerous to them. She might have known details about the attacks or their plans, and that was why they got rid of her.

But what was their aim? A new world order?

The Japanese cult leader, Shoko Asahara never explained any motive for the attacks, and the media was left to guess why a man like him would do something like this. Maybe there was no reason at all, some wrote, while others speculated that the followers of the cult believed that the end of the world was coming, that another world war was about to begin, and only the cult's members would survive.

Was this the same madness?

Matt wondered about it while turning off his computer and getting ready to leave the station. As he walked out of the building, he felt a small beat of hope. If only he could prove that NYX was behind the murder of Lori Moore, then there was still hope for Eva Rae.

Chapter 69

I had dozed off when I woke up to the sound of someone outside the door, trying to get in. I opened my eyes with a deep gasp, then rose to my feet.

More scrambling behind the door followed.

I prepared myself for it being Christopher Daniels or one of his goons coming to finish me off. They had no use for me, and no one knew I had ever been here except for Sydney who thought I had left. No one would come looking for me here, and they could just tell Sydney that I had disappeared while trying to find my daughter.

It was the easiest thing in the world, and they would get away with it in a heartbeat.

I scanned the cottage for any type of weapon I could use to defend myself, but I knew there was nothing in here. I had searched every corner for anything to help me break out.

All I had were my fists and my will to live.

The door squeaked open, and I lifted both my fists in the air, ready to go down fighting when a face peeked inside and signaled for me to be quiet. I almost cried.

"Sydney?"

She shushed me, and I let my fists come down as she sneaked

inside. "I stole the key from Christopher's office earlier. I pretended to want to get closer to him and asked to have a personal meeting with him. He said he wants me to join the inner circle and that I will need to come in and have another meeting with him. He then kissed me, and I let him because I wanted him to believe I was all in, that I want to go to the next level, but the fact was, I knew something was off the moment I saw your note. There was no way you'd ever leave me like that. Not after all we had been through. It had to be fake. I remembered that you told me about the woman they kept in the cottage by the end of the property line and thought I'd check it out. While Christopher kissed me, I spotted the keys he had in a cabinet behind his desk. I also saw your purse in there and knew I was right about you still being here. As soon as everyone went to sleep, I snuck back there and found both the keys and your purse."

I stared at my sister, mouth gaping. I had to admit I didn't think she'd ever pull off anything like that.

She smiled. "I am so glad I did this."

"I...I'm so sorry you had to kiss that charlatan," I said.

Sydney chuckled. "That's nothing. I am an actress, remember? I kiss nasty guys all the time and pretend to be in love with them. It's what I do."

"I...I don't know how to thank you," I said.

She looked me in the eyes. "You get out of here, and you find Olivia. That is the best reward I can get."

"But what about you?" I asked. "I can't leave you here. What will they do to you when they find out I'm gone?"

"You have to. It needs to look like I had nothing to do with it. Besides, my face is too well known out there, and I will get us arrested if I try to run with you. You're better off without me. For now, at least."

"But...?"

Sydney shook her head. "She's out there somewhere, Eva Rae. Don't think of me. I'll be fine. This is what we came down here for. Go get your daughter and bring her home."

Chapter 70

She had fallen asleep. She never meant to; she really tried to stay awake, but no matter how much she fought her eyelids, they still ended up closing, and soon she was asleep under the bridge while the rain poured down.

Olivia dreamt about her family. She was with them on the beach, and her dad was there too. She was young, only seven or eight, and Alex hadn't been born yet. They were building a sand-castle together, and her mom was laughing.

Olivia opened her eyes with a deep gasp. She could still hear her mother's happy laughter, but there was also something else. The sound of a car — then the tires screeching as it stopped.

Olivia spotted the blue van as it opened its doors, and two men jumped out. One of them pointed at her and then they began to run.

Olivia rose to her feet, her heart hammering in her chest. She stared at the men running toward her, then took off running. She climbed up the slanted side.

On the plateau above, she found around twenty tents. Someone she had been sitting with below had warned her that those were the sex offenders who had no other place to go after being released from jail. He also told her to stay far away from them.

One of them was awake and looked at her. He had blankets and lots of plastic bags, even a rug, and a TV. He gave her an indifferent look as she stormed past him. Hearing the men gaining on her, she ran to the end and climbed the grass area and came to a road above. She jumped over the railing, then ran down the road, her perpetrators coming up right behind her. Olivia sobbed, pushing herself forward, tears forcing their way through her chest and into her throat. Cars passed her on the road, but most didn't see her because of the darkness. One saw her too late and honked loudly. Olivia screamed as she saw the men gaining on her and could hear their footsteps on the asphalt behind her.

Olivia panted agitatedly and turned left down a smaller street. Soon, she was surrounded by brick buildings and not a streetlight was in sight. Olivia didn't know if that was bad, or maybe it would work to her advantage. Maybe the perpetrators gave up when they couldn't see her anymore.

Unfortunately, she had no such luck. As she turned to look, she spotted them coming up right behind her, and she knew they would soon catch up to her. Quickly, she glanced around her and saw nothing but old flat-roofed buildings. A sign above her said *Welcome to Historic Overtown*.

Olivia had learned about this neighborhood and knew it wasn't somewhere you'd want to be walking through alone at night. She looked behind herself, then realized the men were gaining in on her. She continued ahead, then as she ran past an open door leading into a courtyard, a set of arms reached out, grabbed her, and pulled her inside. Olivia started to scream, but as she looked into the face of the one who had grabbed her and saw the black lipstick, she immediately stopped.

"Emma?"

Emma shushed her when the men stopped right outside of her door. Emma then used her fingers to whistle and running out came five big black guys with clubs in their hands. One of them swung his club at one of the men and hit him straight on the shoulder. The man screamed and backed up, and soon both of them were gone, running down the street.

Chapter 71

Emma signaled for Olivia to follow her inside, where she sat down on a chair with ripped fabric.

"Welcome to my home," Emma said. "Can I get you something to drink? You look hungry; are you hungry?"

Olivia felt bad for asking Emma for anything since it didn't look like she had much but still nodded. She was starving and couldn't remember when she last ate.

"We have some leftover rice," Emma said and heated it in the microwave for Olivia. Olivia threw herself at it and ate it all down to the last grain.

"Thanks," she said when she was finally calming down and the adrenalin beginning to wear off.

"Who were those guys?" Olivia asked.

"My brother and his friends," Emma said. "We live here with my grandmother. My parents were both killed back in Haiti. We have to be quiet, so we won't wake her. My grandmother cleans houses for rich people. She has to get up really early."

"How do you afford your school?" Olivia asked, drinking the water Emma had served her.

"I got lucky. I got a scholarship. My brother isn't so lucky, and I worry about the friends he hangs out with. Lucky for you, I was out here tonight. My grandmother always throws us out when she goes to bed because she needs the house to be quiet. Normally, I'll go to bed with her, but I don't have to get up early tomorrow. School's out for the rest of the week at least because of what happened, so we were just hanging out when I saw you running down the street."

"That was my luck," Olivia said and looked at the plate, wishing there was more rice.

"You can sleep with me tonight," Emma said and grabbed her plate. "Tomorrow, I can take you to a shelter. They have food and a bed for you there. My Grams is going to kill me if she finds you here."

"Can I borrow your phone again? I need to call my mom," Olivia said with a sniffle.

Emma nodded and handed it to her from her pocket. Olivia fumbled with it nervously, then dialed her mother's number. She couldn't wait to hear her voice and speak to her again. It almost brought tears to her eyes.

One ring, two rings went by.

Come on, Mom. Pick up. Come on.

It went to voicemail, and Olivia looked at the screen of Emma's phone, then tried once more.

Voicemail again.

Shoot!

Olivia tried to remember her sister's number but couldn't get the last two numbers right. Maybe she was too tired. Besides, Christine would most definitely be asleep by now. Her phone would be turned off. And she didn't remember her dad's cell phone number, nor her grandmother's.

Emma looked at the clock on the wall. It was almost midnight.

"Maybe your mom is sleeping," she said. "You can try again in the morning."

Olivia nodded disappointedly. "Okay. Or maybe I should just turn myself in to the police."

Emma turned to look at her. "You can't do that. They're

searching for everyone involved in the attack. They'll take you to prison, Olivia."

"But… what I did was terrible," she said heavily. She was thinking about all those people on the train and at the church. There had been so many of them, so many faces. "Maybe I deserve to go to jail."

"No. It'll kill you," Emma said. "My brother's best friend went in, and once he came back, he was never the same guy again. Now, he's one of those crackheads you see lying in the streets, constantly looking for that same high they got the first time they shot up. You don't want that life, Olivia. The police aren't going to help you down here. They aren't your friends. You can't trust them."

Olivia didn't understand. She had never met anyone who feared the police before. It was so different from what she had known all her life. "But… but my mom is part of the police? I trust her."

"Do as you wish," Emma said, throwing out her arms. "I'm just trying to warn you. Now, let's get some sleep before Grams wakes up and throws you out."

Chapter 72

"What's going on?"

It was the next morning, and Matt had come in a little later, missing the morning briefing. He was holding a Starbucks coffee in his hand when he saw Carter coming toward him, face red in agitation.

"They raided the NYX headquarters this morning. A judge gave the warrant in the early morning hours," Carter said. "We need to go. Might wanna finish that coffee in a jiff or bring it with you. We're going out there."

"Why?" Matt asked.

"They found something that is of interest to us."

Matt followed Carter as they walked out to the cruisers in the back, and he got in. Matt took the passenger seat, coffee still in his hand.

"What did they find?" he said.

Carter took off and drove into the street in front of the Miami-Dade Police Department, tires screeching on the asphalt, putting on the siren. Matt held on for dear life while Carter rushed through downtown toward Coconut Grove. Carter wasn't exactly a good driver, and Matt preferred to be the one behind the wheel.

"Kelly Stone," he said. "She was found in one of the cottages."

Matt almost spat out his coffee. "Eva Rae Thomas's sister?"

Carter nodded. "They knew we were searching for her in connection with the murder of Lori Moore, so they called me. They're taking everyone in for questioning, but she'll be ours."

Matt leaned back in the seat as Miami rushed by his windows. Arresting Kelly Stone would definitely be all over the news and put a dent in her career.

"But we don't have anything that places her at the scene of the murder of Lori Moore," he concluded. "So, technically, we can't charge her with anything. We don't have any evidence placing her anywhere near any crime."

"True," Carter said. "But she doesn't know that. We just need to put enough pressure on her for her to give up her sister. It's her sister we want."

Matt felt his heart drop as they reached Coconut Grove and drove toward the blinking blue and red lights. Patrol cars had blocked the entrance. There was already a crowd outside, and a lot of TV crews. Three news choppers circled the area from above.

This was going to become a huge story.

"Lori Moore was a member of the cult too," Matt said as Carter parked the cruiser.

Carter looked at him.

"Defected a year ago. She wrote some pretty nasty articles about the cult afterward on her blog, and they tried to have her shut down, but without luck."

They both got out of the car, and walked up the driveway, showed their badges to the officer at the entrance, then continued underneath the crime scene tape.

"It doesn't add up," Matt said. "Why would Eva Rae Thomas murder Lori Moore? She barely knew her."

Carter stopped in his tracks. "And how do you know that? If her sister was a member of this cult, chances are Eva Rae was too. I think she plays an even bigger role in this than what we have thought up until now. And I intend to prove it."

He nodded toward a Mustang parked in the driveway. The

forensic team was all over it, taking samples and removing seats. Matt knew that Stang very well. It was the same that the hotel personnel at the Ritz-Carlton had shown them on the surveillance cameras from their parking lot. It was the one Eva Rae and Sydney had been driving while in Miami. If her sister was still here, then Eva Rae had to be somewhere close.

Chapter 73

I entered a small food mart and bought myself a hotdog, then ate it while still in there, enjoying the AC. Sydney had given me my purse with my gun back, along with a handful of cash to help me get by after I left the headquarters. We hugged each other and cried a little when realizing we had no idea when we would ever see one another again, but secretly praying that everything ended well for us.

Even though we both knew deep down that things weren't exactly shaping that way.

As I ate the hotdog, I watched several police cars rush by the windows, and I even heard a chopper. I walked back outside, realizing something big was going on. I had spent the night sleeping on a bench at a bus stop and felt exhausted still. I didn't dare check into a motel or even a shelter in case anyone turned me in.

I felt my gun strapped to my ankle and felt certain there was no one who could stop me now. Head bowed and my cap on my head, I rushed in the opposite direction of the patrol cars, then got on a bus and rode it to downtown. I got off close to Our Savior's Catholic School, where the attack had taken place the day before, and I approached it cautiously. I kept my distance since there were still several patrol cars present, and a crime scene unit with forensics was working the scene.

I didn't really know what I expected to find since I knew my daughter would no longer be here. But I just needed to go to the place where I knew she had been last.

Where are you now, baby girl?

Had she been taken in by the police? Had they arrested her? It was very likely.

I pulled away from the area, then jumped on another bus taking me a couple of stops and got out by the Miami Police Department's big building on Second Avenue. As the bus left, I stared at the building, my heart beating fast in my chest.

Was my girl in there somewhere? And if so, then how on Earth would I get to her?

I had an idea, but I wasn't sure I dared to follow through with it.

After minutes of contemplating it, going through it in my mind over and over again, I realized that I couldn't risk *not* to do it.

It was time to get radical.

Chapter 74

S he had never thought she'd find herself standing in line for a
soup kitchen. Olivia tried to blend in while among the homeless men, women, and even families surrounding her. She peered
down at her Converse and the shirt and ripped jeans that Emma
had given her and thought that if she just kept her head down and
her back slumped, then she wasn't doing too miserably. She actually
looked like a homeless person.

Olivia had tried again that morning to call her mother's
number, right when standing outside the soup kitchen where Emma
dropped her off. But once again, she received nothing but the voicemail. Olivia had left a message, telling her that she would be at the
soup kitchen and to come find her there. She had then hugged
Emma and thanked her for taking care of her and for saving her
life, then gotten herself in line. She was starving, and Emma didn't
have any food at her house that she could spare. Plus, her grandmother couldn't know that Olivia had spent the night there.

Now, she was looking around and wondered just how long she
would have to be in this place before her mother would find her. A
set of heavyset dark eyes lingered on her and made her feel uncomfortable. They belonged to a Hispanic looking man who was

standing further down the line. Olivia lowered her eyes again and kept her head down, then walked closer to the woman in front of her in the line, pretending to be with her, or at least to make sure she didn't look like she was there alone.

A flock of prostitutes stood on the corner and went to talk to the men in cars that drove up to them. One of them decided to get into a dark car, and they took off. Olivia felt her heart sink, thinking that the girl didn't look like she was much older than Olivia herself.

Please, hear my message, Mom. Please, come and find me.

The Hispanic man approached her, then grabbed her shoulder. Olivia gasped and looked up. He smiled and winked, then leaned forward and whispered, "Need money? I can help you get money. What are you? A runaway? Or did your parents throw you out? You know what? You don't have to tell me. I see girls like you come here all the time, and I can help. See those girls over there? They work for me. They make a thousand dollars a day. Do you want to make a thousand dollars a day? You won't have to eat soup anymore. You'll be able to go to real restaurants and have lobster. Do you want lobster, huh, little girl? Of course, you do."

Olivia breathed heavily. She felt his clammy hand on her shoulder and wanted to scream. Her heart was pounding in her chest with fear, and she tried to move away from the guy, but he held onto her tight with his big hands.

"Please, leave me alone," she said, but the words were barely a whisper as they left her lips.

The guy laughed and held onto her even tighter. She had no idea how to escape him when a van drove up on the pavement and made some of the waiting homeless people jump for their lives. The van came to a sudden halt, and the roller door on the side went up. Two men jumped out and ran toward Olivia. One of them swung a gun in the air, and suddenly, people surrounding them scattered without a sound. Even the Hispanic man was gone in a matter of seconds while the men grabbed Olivia by the arms and dragged her into the van, closed the roller door, and took off.

Chapter 75

"I knew it!"

Carter came to Matt's desk, smiling widely. He grabbed a chair and sat down. Matt exhaled and tried to seem excited, even though everything inside of him screamed with anxiety. That look on his face could only have to do with Eva Rae, and if Matt was honest, he could barely take any more bad news.

"What's going on?"

His voice was slightly shrill as he asked the question, and he sipped his coffee while trying to act calm.

"They found traces of the gas in the Mustang," Carter said, looking triumphant. He threw a file on the desk in front of Matt and opened the forensics report.

"See, here and here," he said and pointed. "Sarin gas. The same nerve gas used in all three attacks. All traces were found in the trunk."

Matt wrinkled his forehead. He couldn't believe any of this. "Nerve gas? In the Mustang that Eva Rae Thomas and her sister drove around?"

Carter snapped his fingers.

"Bingo."

Matt shook his head. Part of him wanted to laugh because it seemed so ridiculous, but unfortunately, it was no joke.

"But… this… I mean come on…" Matt said.

"What are you talking about?" Carter protested. "This speaks a very clear language. I think we're getting closer to a really big fish here. She is involved in these attacks somehow. I just haven't figured out her role in it yet. But she's involved with NYX and the attack; there's no doubt about it. She might even be in charge of it all. She's the only one there who fits the profile. My guess is that Lori Moore didn't want to be a part of it, that she wanted out, and that was why Eva Rae Thomas killed her. One of the men killed at the port was also NYX. Maybe all that was just about her getting rid of him, maybe because he wanted to talk as well. Who knows? Maybe it has all been about the attacks? Even the raids on the spas up north? Maybe they're all in it, and she's been cleaning out her ranks."

"Do you really seriously think that Eva Rae Thomas, honored FBI-profiler, mother of three children, is capable of murdering all these people, among them several children, and even using children to perform the task? You think she could do that?"

Carter shrugged. "Why not? She went through a bad divorce almost a year ago, and that's when things went downhill for her. It's been bad for a while; think about it. She feels guilty about not being able to save her partner's child; she is divorced; she quits her job and moves back to her hometown, where she finds out her father is a serial killer, and she loses it. She wants to send the world a message of some sort, so she starts planning these attacks and joins this cult who will believe anything, especially that the world is going under soon. Christopher Daniels and her plan it all together. Here, she can get the hands she needs to fulfill her plans, and the funds since the cult appeals to millionaires. But then her daughter disappears. My guess is the daughter ran away from her crazy mom, or maybe she was taken by some people who wanted to stop her, but Eva Rae uses it as an excuse to go rogue and get rid of anyone who might stand in her way. The first attack has already been done, but now some of them are getting cold feet when they realize what they have been a part of. These spas have been providing girls for her to train and use in the attacks, and they have threatened to reveal her, so she decides to rid herself of them under the pretense that she is searching for her daughter. Then she comes down here and hooks back up with NYX and helps with the last two attacks."

Carter looked at Matt like he expected applause, but Matt had no idea what to say to him. This was so far-fetched that it made him speechless.

"I know; I know," Carter said. "I don't have all the details yet, but I will soon. I'm sure I will. And once I crack this baby open, it will make my career. Just you wait and see."

Chapter 76

It was dark before he came out. I waited and kept my distance, while not letting my eyes look away from the entrance to the police department even for a second. I couldn't risk missing him.

As I finally spotted him walking out the glass doors, my heart dropped. He was standing under the streetlight, talking to someone, then they said their goodbyes, and he left.

I stared at the man I loved, feeling a deep punch in my heart as he got into a cab. I rushed to the cab parked right behind his and got in.

"Follow the one in front of you," I said. "But not too closely. Just make sure we get to the same destination."

The driver looked at me in the rearview mirror, then wrinkled his forehead. "Say, haven't I seen you somewhere around here before?"

"I don't know. Maybe," I said and pulled the cap further down my face. "I take taxis all the time."

"Are you famous or something? I feel like I've seen you on TV," he continued.

My eyes were fixated on the cab in front of us, and as they took a left, I feared my driver would lose them.

"They went left. Go left here."

"Easy there, lady. I've got this. You're not the first girlfriend in my cab trying to stalk their cheating boyfriend."

I wanted to tell him that Matt would never cheat on me, that he was the most honorable, most noble and loyal boyfriend anyone could have. And that I didn't deserve him. Because it was the truth, Matt was way too good for me.

But I didn't say anything. Instead, I just stared at the driver in the mirror, then turned to look at the cab in front of us.

"Is it the secretary?" he continued. "It often is. Or maybe an old high school sweetheart who came to town? Those are always tough to beat. There's something about that first love that just won't leave you."

"Sounds like you speak from experience," I said dryly.

The cab driver chuckled. "Touché."

"Yeah, well, I've been told I'm pretty good at reading people."

"You some kind of psychologist or somethin'?" he asked.

"You might say so. Go right. They're going right."

"I've got this."

He turned, and I stared at the cab with Matt in it as it came to a halt in front of a Marriott. I handed the driver a bill and told him to stop further down the road.

"Good luck with your cheating boyfriend," he said. "For what it's worth, I'm sure she ain't half as pretty as you are."

I gave him a wry smile, then left the car and walked up toward the hotel, where Matt soon disappeared inside. I stood on the stairs outside for a little while, contemplating my plan, feeling myself get cold feet for a second. Would Matt believe me? Would he help me? Or was he here to take me down? Had he lost his confidence in me because of what I had done? It wasn't well-received among law-enforcement to take the law in your own hands, especially not a cop. Had he turned his back on me for doing what I did? Did he resent me for it?

There was only one way to find out.

Chapter 77

"**D**o you have a Shock Top, please?"

Matt sat on a stool with a heavy sigh. The bar in the hotel was pretty much empty except for a woman sitting at the other end of the counter, sipping a cocktail. She looked to be in her mid-thirties, slim, and with long blonde hair reaching down by her shoulders. She smiled gently at him, then saluted him as his beer landed in front of him. Matt responded with half a smile, making sure she knew he wasn't there to pick up ladies. It was the last thing on his mind right now. He really just needed a beer after a very, very long day. Her eyes told him she understood. She looked like she had a long day as well. He wondered if she was on a business trip. She didn't look like a tourist in her skirt and white buttoned-up shirt.

Matt looked away and took a sip of his beer. He closed his eyes as the liquid slid into his throat, then put the glass back down. Matt rubbed his forehead in agitation like he'd been doing all day.

How was he supposed to solve this? How was he going to help Eva Rae?

Carter had set his heart on taking her down; heck, he was willing to risk his entire career for it. Yet none of it made any sense to Matt. Was he just being blind? Was he unable to see it for what it was, just because he loved her?

You've known her your entire life, Matt. Get a grip.

Matt shook his head and sipped his beer again, thinking about the necklace. He had been through the file from the findings at Lori Moore's kitchen. The necklace had been found there, and he couldn't for the life of him figure out how it would end up there. He knew that necklace; heck, he remembered toying with it between his fingers while kissing her.

What he wouldn't give to be able to kiss her again, to feel those lips pressed against his, to smell her hair, to... to...

"A glass of Chardonnay, please."

Matt opened his eyes with a small gasp. The woman sitting on the stool next to him smiled gently and instantly melted his heart.

"Put it on his tab," she said addressed to the bartender while nodding in Matt's direction.

"Eva Rae?"

"The one and only," she said as the bartender slid the glass of white wine toward her. She grabbed it and drank.

"Oh, boy. I needed that."

"What the heck are you doing here?" Matt asked, suddenly overwhelmed with fear that someone would see them together. "The entire police force is looking for you. Your face has been on every screen in this town. If anyone sees you here, they'll..."

Eva Rae gave him a look that made him shut up. He bit his lip as her eyes pierced into his. He didn't know what to say. There was so much he wanted to tell her, but no words seemed sufficient. He had dreamt of seeing her again for so long, and there she was, right in front of him, looking even more gorgeous than ever. It seemed impossible. She was out of this world.

"You're being investigated," he said quite unromantically. "Not just for the petty stuff you did up north at the spas, like impersonating a health inspector and beating up the spa-owners, or even for the murder of Lori Moore or the three men at the harbor. But also, as someone involved in the three nerve gas attacks around town. This is serious, Eva Rae. This is getting really serious."

Chapter 78

I felt like I was choking. I couldn't believe what I was hearing. Did they seriously think I had anything to do with the gas attacks? I stared at the man I loved, unable to speak a single word, unable to fathom what on Earth was going on.

"They found your necklace at Lori Moore's place," Matt continued. "They think you killed her because she wanted to reveal your plans since she defected from NYX. They think you're involved with NYX and Christopher Daniels, that... that you're the one pulling the strings."

My eyes grew wide, and I sipped more wine, then finished the glass and ordered a second one.

"And what do you think?" I asked when it arrived, and I could finally speak again. I waited for his response, scrutinizing his eyes, wondering if some part of him believed they were right, that I was capable of such a thing. He waited a little too long for my liking to give me his answer. The hesitation made me concerned.

"I think that it makes no sense, any of it," he said in almost a whisper. "But I don't know how to stop it. It's like lava coming toward you, and I can't prevent it from hitting you no matter how hard I try."

"You're darn right it makes no sense," I said with a snort.

"What were you doing at the estate?" he asked. "The NYX estate? They said you were there recently."

"I was hiding," I said and sipped my wine. "But then they wouldn't let me leave. They tried to force me to stay and locked me in. Sydney helped me escape. I thought I might find Olivia there, but she wasn't at the estate."

"We raided the place today," he said. "Took in everyone and interrogated them. They found your car, and it had traces of Sarin gas in it."

I wrinkled my forehead. "Why would there be Sarin gas in my car?"

He sighed and drank from his beer, his eyes avoiding mine. I didn't know what to make of him. He seemed confused, and it had me worried. I needed him to be on my side. No matter what happened, I needed him to know the truth. I placed a hand on his arm, and he looked up at me. I could tell he hadn't slept much lately. His eyes were red-rimmed, and he had deep furrows beneath them. This wasn't the healthy, always tanned and happy Matt that I knew so well. This had broken him.

"I am sorry," I said. "For dragging you into all this. It wasn't supposed to happen. I have made some bad choices along the way and gotten carried away emotionally, and I still haven't found my daughter. For a little while, I thought she might be at the NYX estate, but I couldn't find her there. Did they interrogate Christopher Daniels when they brought him in?"

Matt nodded heavily. "He's not talking. None of the cult members have said a word. Daniels doesn't even deny the accusations; he's just staring at us with a smug smile on his face. JTTF did the interrogation, but we watched it from the outside. You should have seen him, the way he thought it was all a joke. I want to punch him in that perfect face of his."

"That makes two of us," I said. "What about Sydney; was she brought in too?"

Matt nodded. "They want to use her to get to you. My partner Carter tried to work her all day. He is obsessed with getting you. But she has a good lawyer, and he will get her out tomorrow morning, just like the rest of the NYX members. They have some good lawyers and a lot of money. Sydney didn't say anything either, not even about NYX."

"Smart girl," I said. "The last thing she needs is them coming for her like they did to Lori Moore. There are some pretty powerful people in that cult. She could end up never working again, or worse."

Matt nodded and grew absent for a second, then looked at me again, affection in his eyes.

"I missed you, though," he said with a deep sigh. "I missed you a lot."

I swallowed and smiled back. "I was thinking about turning myself in. I need to tell my side of the story."

He nodded again but seemed hesitant. To my surprise, I realized that he didn't think it was a good idea. It was the right thing to do, in a perfect world where justice was served, but that wasn't our world, was it? By the look in his eyes, I sensed he didn't fully believe it was the right thing for me to do, yet he couldn't say so since it would go against everything he believed in, everything he stood for.

I sipped my wine again, a tear shaping in my eye, thinking about my poor Olivia. Was I ready to give up searching for her myself? Did I believe that she would be found if I left it to the police to look for her? The same police that believed I was a mass-murderer?

"I saw her, you know?" Matt said.

I almost choked on my white wine. "You saw Olivia? My Olivia?"

He nodded. His eyes weren't smiling, and he didn't seem happy to tell me, which scared me half to death.

"At the attack at the school. She was there. It was just for a brief moment, then she was gone, escaped somehow in the chaos." He grabbed my hand in his, then leaned over and whispered close to my ear. "I think she got away. She's alive, and she's out there somewhere."

I nodded, thinking about how I saw her on the footage from the chopper, but it felt good to have it confirmed. I wasn't just seeing things when I saw her on the surveillance footage from the train station either. She had been there, both times. But that also meant that my theory was correct. She was being used by unscrupulous people to perform these attacks along with other trafficked girls.

"They're using them for the attacks, right?" I said, hoping to get his confirmation.

Matt gave me a look. "You don't have it from me."

"Of course not."

"They haven't found any of the girls at the raid. They must be keeping them somewhere else, but who knows how long it might take to find them? By then, they'll probably be transported across the border and resold or maybe even killed."

I swallowed the rest of my wine while sensing the fear spreading like wildfire through my veins, engulfing everything on its way. He was right. If Olivia was still with these people, then they'd get rid of her soon, along with the others. If she wasn't and had actually escaped, then she was out there somewhere looking for me. No matter what, there was no time to waste. I knew what Matt was telling me to do, and I agreed.

Sometimes, you have to do the wrong things for the right reasons.

Chapter 79

His soft lips touching my skin made me shiver. I closed my eyes and moaned as he grew more insistent with each and every kiss. We had left the bar and gone to his hotel room, realizing this was our only chance, maybe for a long time, to be together. The thought was at once devastating and arousing. I just knew I needed to feel him close right now; I needed to have him.

"I missed the way you taste," he said between kisses. "I missed the way you smell, the way you look at me, even the way you breathe. I missed every part of you, Eva Rae."

I pulled him into a deep kiss, then wrapped my legs around him and pressed him closer. Neither of us wanted to think about the future in this instant, not even an hour from now. Still, it lurked in the back of our minds as he entered me. I felt tears roll down my cheeks as he pressed me back against the pillow.

We made love in silence, letting our desires overpower us and knock every thought of reality out of us.

Matt sank to the pillow next to me, moaning. His eyes were strained with sadness. I stroked his cheek, then kissed him again while he caught his breath. I forced a smile, but my tears revealed how I really felt.

I was terrified to the core. Scared that I was never going to see him again, that everything would go wrong after this and then we would never see each other again, and maybe I would never see my daughter again either.

It wasn't a result I was willing to live with. I had said this before, and I'd say it again. I was never going to give up looking for her. Ever. Not even if I had to continue my search from inside a prison cell. The people who had taken her were going to regret the hell that was being unleashed on them once I found them.

Matt mumbled something as he dozed off, and I realized he had once again told me he loved me.

I sat up in the bed, then looked at the clock. I couldn't stay the night. As soon as daylight came, it would be dangerous for me to try and leave the hotel.

I leaned over and kissed Matt on the lips, then whispered, "I love you too."

There, I had said it — the way I had wanted to for a long time. But then I realized Matt wasn't awake to hear it. He was in a deep, calm sleep, and I didn't want to wake him up. He needed his rest, and I wanted him to get a good night's sleep and for once not worry about me. At least not until he woke up and realized I wasn't there anymore.

As much as I hated to, I had to leave him once again. I felt another tear escape my eye, then wiped it away. I rose to my feet, found my clothes, and got dressed.

I stared at Matt from the edge of the bed, then leaned over, stroked his hair gently, and kissed him again. He mumbled my name, then smiled and turned to the side. I sniffled and chuckled, then smiled to myself, thinking about the hours we had spent together. I could still smell him on my skin, while leaving the room as silently as possible, closing the door carefully not to wake him up.

Chapter 80

I stood for a second by the door, a hand placed gently on it, the other holding my shoes and purse, while I let a tear escape my eye.

If only I could stay the night. If only I could make time stand still and stay in his arms forever.

I wiped the tear away with my sleeve, letting the images of us together in bed play like a movie in my mind, trying to savor the memory before I finally turned away and started to walk, my head slumped. I was so lost in my thoughts that I didn't even hear him approach me from behind. I walked down the carpeted hallway, then stopped to put my shoes back on.

"Well, well, well."

I jumped at the sound of his voice. I turned to see a small stubby man with sweaty patches on his light blue polo shirt. I immediately knew who he was. I had seen him with Matt in front of the Catholic church and coming out of my hotel.

It had to be Carter. Matt's partner.

"Eva Rae Thomas. We finally meet," he said and approached me. My eyes landed on the gun in his hand. Big drops of sweat lingered on his forehead, and I could hear his heavy breathing.

"I knew you two were involved. I sensed it," he almost snorted. "It was only a matter of time before you'd show up. And here you are."

"Please," I said. "Matt didn't…"

"Save it," he stopped me.

I felt my hands shaking as fear rushed through my body. The last thing I ever wanted was for Matt to get in trouble. First Sydney, now him? Was everyone that I loved going to have to pay for my decisions?

"Please…"

But he wouldn't listen. I could tell by the look in his eyes. He didn't care what I had to say. Instead, his lips pulled into a smile, and he raised the gun and fired.

Thank God for fast reflexes. As I heard the gun go off, I threw myself down. I dropped my purse on the floor. The shot whizzed over my head and ended up in the wall behind me. I screamed, got up on my feet, and jumped toward the emergency exit door in front of me. I pushed it open with all my weight as the gun was fired once again, this time aimed right at my back. Throwing myself out the door, the gun went off again, and the third shot hit me in the arm. I screamed, dropped my purse, and fell forward down the flight of stairs ahead of me, face first, the stabbing, throbbing pain in my arm making my entire torso shake. The door slammed shut behind me, and I scrambled to my feet while frantically staring at it, expecting it to open any second and him come out, shooting at me, this time to end me.

My purse had landed in the hallway, and I couldn't reach it. I felt the gun that I had strapped to my ankle and pulled it out so I could defend myself when he did come out after me.

I forced myself to move forward, even though the biting, burning pain in my arm made me want to give up. I somehow got myself down the next flight of stairs without my pursuer coming after me and, realizing this, I found the strength to get myself down one more. Seconds later, I was able to push open the door to the outside and, while leaving a trail of blood behind me, I staggered into the warm Miami night.

Chapter 81

M att woke up with a start. His eyes shot open, and he blinked to make sure he wasn't still dreaming. Had he heard right? Was that a shot being fired?

Hearing a scream, Matt jumped to his feet.

Eva Rae!

He bolted for the door, grabbed the handle, and pulled it open just in time to see Carter lift a gun and fire at Eva Rae. Eva Rae let out an ear-piercing scream and fell out the exit door. The door slammed shut, but Matt could hear her body as it fell down the stairs.

NO!

Carter was about to go after her and had his hand on the handle, when Matt leaped toward him, grabbed him around the neck, and pulled him back. Carter yelled in distress while Matt pulled him back and held him down, buying Eva Rae some valuable seconds to escape. Carter pushed the gun toward Matt's face and slammed it into his forehead. The pain made Matt lose his grip on Carter, and the small man jolted for the door, panting and agitated. He opened it, then ran down the stairs.

Please, be gone, Eva Rae; please, tell me you made it out.

Holding his breath, Matt waited. He listened anxiously and prayed that Carter wouldn't find her. Matt's eyes were fixated on the door in front of him, his hands shaking. He rose to his feet, then opened it and peeked out. It was eerily quiet out there, and all he could hear was his own ragged breath.

Where did they go?

Matt stood for a few seconds, feeling his knees go soft when he heard footsteps on the stairs below. He peeked down and spotted Carter coming back up, taking two steps at a time. He approached Matt on the plateau, sweat gushing from his face, his light blue shirt soaked. He spoke through gritted teeth.

"She got away. Because of you," he said, his voice growing louder and louder as he spoke like he was talking himself up, getting increasingly agitated the more he spoke. "Because of you, she got away. How do you explain that, *Detective*, huh? How are you planning on explaining what she was doing in your room, huh? Our main suspect in this town's biggest terrorism case, sleeping in your hotel room in the middle of our investigation. And then we add to it that you helped her escape? You know what that makes you? Do ya?"

Matt swallowed and stared at the angry little man in front of him. He knew it didn't matter what he said at this point. He knew how it looked. Still, he couldn't help but feel deep relief inside of him. Eva Rae had escaped. It was all that mattered at this point.

"That's right. You're now officially an accomplice," Carter continued and threw out his arms. "Congratulations."

Carter lifted the gun and placed it at Matt's forehead. He scrutinized him, his eyes oozing with anger.

"I knew there was something suspicious about you from the moment you set your feet in my police department. I have a brilliant nose for these things, you know. I'm glad I listened to my instincts and kept a close eye on you. Now, you're coming with me. I'm taking you in."

Chapter 82

They had beaten her up for running, and every fiber of her body was throbbing. She was back at the house with the rest of the girls but had been lying in a corner on the floor for most of the time since she got there, crying in pain.

Olivia looked around the room, and she realized that she didn't know any of the other girls anymore. She didn't know if the others had been killed or maybe sent away after the attack at the school, and she didn't allow herself to think about it. She hoped that they were arrested and maybe — *please let it be so* — sent back to their families.

Where are you, Mom? Why haven't you come for me yet? I need you, Mom. I need you more than ever.

Olivia smacked her lips and felt thirsty. She vaguely remembered someone helping her drink while she laid there, but she couldn't recall who it was. Deep down, she didn't want to know. If anyone had been kind to her, she was eternally grateful, but she didn't want to get to know any of the girls again. She knew too much to let herself get attached. The fact was, most of these girls would be killed in the next attack, and so would Olivia. It was only a matter of time.

Olivia curled herself into a ball and cried on the cold floor, her tears spilling on the tiles. She missed her family so much; it hurt her physically to think about. The guilt was eating her up. This was all her own fault. She deserved what happened to her. How could she have been so stupid as to meet with someone she barely knew? Why did she trust him? Because he said he could make her a model? How stupid was that? Her mother had warned her about this her entire life. After losing her own sister, she feared that her children would be kidnapped more than anything. Why hadn't Olivia listened? What made her think this guy was all right? That it wouldn't happen to her?

Olivia tried to imagine her siblings. Her sweet sister Christine and her annoying, yet so adorable, little brother, Alex. She pictured all three of them in the car, driving to the beach like they used to when she was younger. Back when her dad still lived with them, back when everything was all right, and life was worth living. But it was hard for her to picture them anymore. All the darkness and terror she had been through over the past months had altered the way she saw things. All her memories had turned gloomy.

"It's time to get up," a voice said.

Olivia felt a kick on her leg and lifted her head. She glanced at the man hovering above her, grinning from ear to ear.

"You. Get up now."

Fearing another beating, Olivia tried to push herself up using her arms, but the pain was terrible, and she fell back down. Seeing her struggle, the man laughed. He reached down and grabbed her by the collar, then pulled her to her feet. She gasped and felt like she was choking while the man grinned again.

"There. You're up. Now get in the line and follow the others. You have work to do."

Chapter 83

R yan Scott wasn't feeling well. He hadn't been for a while now. Not since the day he had been on the Metrorail during the gas attack. Lately, he was beginning to realize that maybe he needed help. Perhaps he couldn't deal with this on his own after all.

He stood in his kitchen and stared at the rat that had been living with him for the past few days, gnawing its way through the garbage that was piling up in his condo that he didn't dare to take out. The rat was munching on an old pepperoni pizza slice, making eerie squeaking sounds.

Ryan swallowed and looked at his phone; his only means of contact with the outside world. There were seven new messages from his mother, but he didn't want to hear them. She was worried about him; he got that, but there really wasn't much she could do to help him. She kept telling him to go see a doctor, and he would like to do just that, but the problem was that it meant he'd have to leave the safety of his apartment, and he didn't dare to do that. He didn't have to take the train or bus; he could just grab a taxi, she had said. His parents would gladly pay.

Grab a taxi? Did she have any idea how many people were killed in traffic every day?

"You have to leave the condo someday. You can't stay in there forever," she had told him.

Why not? He had thought to himself. But that wasn't what he had said to her. He had indulged her and told her he would go and see a doctor. That was why she had been calling him over and over again. To ask him how it went, if he went. But he didn't, and he didn't want to have to tell her that. So, now, he had stopped answering his phone at all. Maybe she would go away, just like everyone else had.

In the beginning, he had watched the news all day long to see if there was any development in the search for the terrorists that nearly killed him. But it had ended up driving him nuts and filling him with even more fear, so he had shut the TV off completely and pulled out the plug. He had stopped going on social media or even the Internet. He didn't want to know about all the dangers that were out there. He just wanted to sit inside, on his couch, and be safe. He didn't want to talk to anyone or see anyone.

Ryan rubbed his neck agitatedly. He felt the panic as it rose inside him like a burning fire, just at the thought of taking out the trash. His heart began beating rapidly, and he felt short of breath. The same thing had happened every time he had tried — trash bag clutched in his hand — to open the door and step out. An overwhelming force had hit him as the panic spread into every fiber of his body, and he was unable to get any further than the threshold. His heart was beating so fast, it became unbearable, and all he could do was shut the door again and put the trash down.

Ryan sat on his couch, flies buzzing around his leftover food, then stared at the black TV screen. Outside his windows, he could hear sirens wailing as usual, and it reminded him of how dangerous the world was. Ryan sniffled, then glanced at the bottle of sleeping pills given to him by the doctor who had examined him after the attack. To make sure he managed to sleep. He had never taken any, not yet.

Ryan picked up the orange bottle. He popped the lid open and poured them all out into his hand, thinking this was the only way he would be able to make it outside ever again.

Ryan lifted his hand to swallow all the pills at once when a rapid knock on the door startled him.

Chapter 84

W hen no one answered, I knocked again. This time even harder.

"Ryan!" I yelled, slamming my fist into his door. "I know you're in there. You don't dare to leave the condo. Open up!"

"W-who is it?"

"It's Eva Rae Thomas," I said, leaning my forehead against the door. I was so exhausted from dragging my hurt body across town all night; I could barely find the energy to speak. But I had to. It was my only chance. Ryan was the only one in Miami that I knew and trusted not to turn me in.

"Go away," he said. "I don't want any visitors."

"I know you don't," I yelled, sweat pouring down my chest, my shoulder throbbing. It felt like I had a fever, but maybe it was just the pain. "But I'm not here for your sake. I'm here for my own. I need your help. Please, just open the door, will you? I'm not trying to trick you here, Ryan. This is an emergency."

"I'm sorry. Could you come again later?"

I clutched my fingers, feeling my legs go wobbly underneath me. The room started spinning, and I could no longer stay on my feet. Instead, I sank to the floor with a loud thud, grasping in thin air for something to hold onto, to stop the fall, while desperately thinking: *This is it! It ends here!*

I sank into a sea of stars for what felt like an eternity, and when I came to, the door had been opened, and a set of hands was dragging me across the floor. I was placed on the ground, and the door slammed shut behind me. I blinked my eyes and spotted Ryan, who was locking it safely, then breathing heavily, leaning his back against it. I saw the panic in his eyes and realized that grabbing me and pulling me back in had taken all the strength he could muster.

"Are you okay?" Ryan asked. "I heard you fall."

"I'll be all right," I said and felt my sore arm, then winced in pain. "I'm just a little lightheaded. Say, what is that stench? It's even worse than when I was here last."

Ryan ignored me and knelt next to me, looking at my bloody wound. "W-what happened?"

"I was shot," I said. "It's a long story."

He stared at the wound. It was a deep graze. The bullet had entered right above my elbow and gone through the flesh. It didn't feel like it had hit anything vital or splintered any bone. But then again, I was no doctor.

"You'll need that bandaged," he said, suddenly sounding very determined, the fear in his eyes dissipating. "Let me see what I can do. I used to be a lifeguard, and I am a trained paramedic."

My eyes grew wide. "Really?"

"Yes. It helped me earn money during summer break and put me through college." He rose to his feet, his eyes scanning the area. "I have a first aid kit here somewhere. Give me just a sec to find it. Wait here."

"Where would I go?" I asked with a shrug, then wrinkled my nose at the trash bags piling up in the corners.

Chapter 85

I winced in pain as Ryan wrapped the bandage around my wound. I had told him everything while he cleaned it. He had asked me to talk about something else, so I wouldn't think about the pain, and it just spilled right out of me. I guess I needed to get it off my chest, even though I wasn't sure he would believe me.

"So, you're telling me this NYX cult is behind the attack that almost killed me?" he said.

My arm felt warm and numb, but I knew this wasn't the end. More pain would come later. I had been shot before, so I was prepared.

I laid my head back on the couch with a nod. "That's what they think."

"And they've been using the young girls like your daughter to perform them?" he asked, startled.

I sighed. "I'm afraid so, yes."

"But they've been arrested now? And the girls?"

"A few of them were arrested during the attack at the school, but most escaped as far as I know. The thing is, most of them don't even speak English, so it's a mess, as you can imagine. Even finding out who they are and where they're from is going to take some time.

Matt told me there was one woman, though, who had told the police everything. She was a member of the cult. She said they forced her to be in the attack. No one else has dared to speak up against the cult leader. One woman died after doing so. I just pray that they protect this woman properly, so she won't be killed like Lori Moore was. These cult people don't joke around."

I stared at Ryan, who looked at my bandage, then smiled. "There. You're as good as new. Well, almost. Now you must rest."

I smiled back. "Thank you. You're a lifesaver." I glanced toward his TV. "Do you mind if I watch the news while resting?"

He shook his head but seemed concerned. "No. No, of course not. Let me just plug it in."

Ryan rose to his feet, then walked to the TV and plugged it in the wall. He then handed me the remote. I turned it on, and Ryan sat down to keep me company. As expected, my face was all over the broadcast, and there were no limits to how dangerous they believed I was, especially after almost killing a detective at the hotel while escaping the night before.

"I didn't even pull out my gun," I grumbled like I could argue my way out of this with the TV.

We watched the next few segments that were also about me and my connections with the cult, and apparently a long-term friendship with the leader Christopher Daniels, and how it was believed that I was the one planning the attacks, the big mastermind behind it all. Because my daughter had been kidnapped and because my stepfather was a serial killer, I had gone rogue and lost it, was the explanation.

"She's extremely irrational and, frankly, we don't know what she might do next," said detective Carter in an interview, where he was wearing a sling on his arm.

I sat up straight on the couch and leaned forward in anger. "Look at this? I didn't even touch him! He shot at me while I tried to talk sense into him. Can you believe this guy?"

Ryan gave me an uncertain look, and I forced myself to calm down. I didn't know the kid very well, and for all I knew, he might not fully trust me or my story. The last thing I needed right now was for him to be suspicious or even afraid of me.

Next, they showed pictures of Christopher Daniels leaving the Miami-Dade Police Department with his lawyer, and suddenly, my blood was boiling again.

"They're letting him go? He's been released, that bastard? After what he did to those girls and to… to my daughter? I can't believe this; can you believe it?"

Ryan shook his head nervously. "He posted bail, they say."

"I still can't believe they'd let him even get bail with what he has done. It makes me so mad! Don't they know what he did to my daughter?"

I sat up, my fist clenched, and yelled at the TV through gritted teeth. "That means he's going to be out there instead of being interrogated about where my daughter is. God knows what he might be up to next, what his plans are. Olivia's life is in serious danger. If he finds her, he will kill her. I can't believe this."

I felt the gun in my ankle holster when touching it from the outside of my pants. Christopher Daniels, alias the Iron Fist, was on the loose once again, but so was I. He wouldn't be able to hurt my daughter anymore, not if I got to him first.

I took in a couple of deep breaths and controlled myself when the anchor showed up on the screen again. Under a severe expression, he presented a breaking news story about the arrest of someone who the police believed had been handing me inside information into the police investigation.

I held my breath as I watched this person be taken out of the police car and transported through the crowd of journalists, head bowed.

Then my heart dropped.

It was Matt.

Chapter 86

"Come on, Detective Miller. You might as well tell us everything."

Carter looked at him from across the table. Next to him sat Agent Patrick Albertson from the FBI. Matt had never been on this side of the table in an interrogation room and had to admit he was beginning to understand why so many became aggressive when sitting there. They kept asking the same darn questions over and over again until they got what they wanted. But Matt couldn't give them that since he didn't have it.

"We just need to know where she's hiding," Patrick Albertson said. "We know you've been in contact with her."

He threw a stack of papers in front of Matt. "Phone records show anonymous calls in the middle of the night from different phones, burner phones. We assume they came from her. Here and here."

He pointed at the underlined numbers, but Matt didn't even want to look at them.

"I told you; I haven't seen her or spoken to her until she showed up last night. It was totally unexpected."

"Yet the two of you went to your room and had sex," Carter said. "Was that unexpected too?"

Matt swallowed. He thought about the intimacy they had shared and felt a warmth spread throughout his body. It had been intense. The fact that they didn't know when or if they'd ever see each other again had added to the intensity. He wasn't sad that it had happened or even that he had been caught. He was just sad that it was over, that he couldn't be with her longer. He was happy that he had managed to help her escape. Now, he just prayed that she would find Olivia before it was too late. No matter if she was still in the hands of those NYX people or if she had escaped and was walking the streets, she was in great danger.

"Didn't you?" Carter said.

"Yes, we had sex. We love each other; there. Is that what you want to hear? I love her. I love Eva Rae Thomas, and I know that she hasn't done any of what you accuse her of. All she wants is to find her daughter. That's it. Her daughter was in those attacks."

Carter burst into laughter. "But that's exactly it. Don't you see it? She's even using her own daughter in this. That's how unscrupulous she is. She's got you completely fooled; doesn't she? She comes here batting her eyelashes at you, and you just believe everything she tells you, don't you?"

"I'd believe her over you any day," Matt said, knowing that the smirk on his face wasn't doing him any favors. But in all fairness, he was just stating the truth.

Patrick Albertson gave him a look, then wrote on his notepad. "How much have you told her about our investigation?" he asked.

Matt exhaled. "I just told her that she was now being investigated as part of the terrorist group, that it was believed she killed Lori Moore and that we found the necklace, and that they found the traces of gas in her trunk. She said she wanted to turn herself in. She wanted to tell her side of the story, clear her name."

"But she didn't, did she?" Carter said. "She ran in the middle of the night after getting what she wanted from you. She fooled you again. Tricked you into telling her these things because she knew you couldn't say no to her. She's been using you, Miller."

Carter rose to his feet and gathered his papers. Patrick Albertson followed him to the door.

"But we're gathering lots of evidence against her now, and the fact is that the ground is burning underneath your little girlfriend," Carter said. "You better start talking soon, or she'll drag you right down with her, Detective."

Chapter 87

I wasn't feeling better, nor was I able to rest. I couldn't sit still on that stupid couch when the man I loved was in trouble, and the man who caused it all was still on the loose. Christopher Daniels had caused so much suffering, and several lives were on the line now. Not just my daughter's, but also the other girls and that woman, Helen Wellington, who was the only former member who had stood up to him and told the truth. Christopher Daniels would come for her in one way or another like he had come for Lori Moore. I was certain of it and obsessed with the thought of stopping him.

But how? How would I find him? He would most certainly want to go into hiding now, and he had plenty of devoted very rich followers to help him do just that.

After turning off the TV in anger, I had borrowed Ryan's computer and flipped through news stories, reading about the case. It was all they wrote about, and the rest of the day, all I could do was flip through news sites, going through each and every article I could find, anger rising inside of me more and more as I realized the many lies that were being said.

Ryan was being sweet to me and made me chicken noodle soup from a can and made sure I was comfortable. I sensed that he was worried about having me there and maybe even a little scared of me, and so I wondered how long I would be able to stay. How long before he gave into that fear in him and called the police? On the other hand, I got the feeling that he believed my story when I told it and that he genuinely wanted to help.

And there really wasn't anywhere else I could go right now. Also, Ryan was right. I needed rest to feel better, to regain my strength. I was stuck here. At least for now.

I sipped my water and opened an article from the *New York Times* dated a few days back. Luckily, Ryan was a member, so I could read the entire thing as it proved to be increasingly interesting. As I finished it, I Googled a name from the article and opened a few pages, then read through it, learning more and more about NYX.

I asked Ryan for a notepad and started to scribble a few things down, then frantically did another search and then another, taking a closer look at the NYX's members and who they were.

Day became evening, and Ryan served more soup and ate with me, his eyes continually lingering on my every move like he was scared I'd suddenly attack him.

I ignored him completely and stayed immersed in my research about NYX. I was hoping to find out if they had other places besides the estate in Miami where they might keep the girls they bought. A few hours later, Ryan announced that he was going to bed.

"Will you be okay on the couch?" he asked. "I'm sorry about the smell."

I lifted my glance from the screen, then smiled. "It's no problem. I'll be fine. And don't worry about the smell; I hardly notice anymore," I lied.

"Okay," he said and disappeared into his room.

Meanwhile, I had no intention of going to sleep. Instead, I stayed up all night, researching, and when the sun was about to rise, I suddenly felt better, good enough to get back on my feet. A gazillion thoughts still rushed through my mind, and I was frustrated that

I still had no clue as to where those girls might be kept. I kept tapping on the computer when suddenly I stopped. I stared at a picture for a very long time, then went into Ryan's room.

"Wake up," I said.

He blinked and looked at me groggily. Outside the windows, the sun was beginning to rise, but it was still dark.

"Do you have any means of transportation? No, of course, you don't, or you wouldn't have taken the train to work on that morning. Does your neighbor have a car or anything we can borrow? It's urgent."

Ryan looked confused, then scratched his bed head. "My neighbor keeps his motorbike parked in my garage because he has his car in his."

"A bike, you say?" I answered. "You might want to show me where that is."

"I...I can't," he said and sat up in the bed.

"Why not?"

"I...I can't leave the apartment."

I walked out of his room, looked around, then spotted a set of keys hanging on a hook in the kitchen. I grabbed them and dangled them in the air. Ryan came up behind me, still looking sleepy, but now wearing pants and a shirt.

"I bet it's one of these; am I right? I'm guessing this one is for the garage, and this one is for the bike."

"Y-you can't do this," Ryan said and stepped forward. "He'll kill me."

I shrugged. "Well, better him than me, right?"

I held the keys tightly, then opened the front door.

"Stop," Ryan said and came after me.

I was out on the doormat now, and he was still standing inside, but one more step would take him out across the threshold. He stared at it, like crossing it meant apocalypse now.

"I don't have time for this," I said and shook my head. "There is someone I need to find. Now. My daughter's life is in danger. If you want to stop me, then you'll have to follow me."

With that, I turned around and rushed down the stairs. Ryan

stayed behind and yelled for me to stop one more time, but I didn't have the time even to slow down.

I had reached the second set of stairs when I heard his tapping steps behind me.

Chapter 88

The garage door squeaked eerily as it opened. Ryan turned on the light nervously. His hands were shaking, and he was breathing raggedly.

"H-here it is."

The Harley gleamed in the light from above it. I whistled and ran my finger across the fuel tank. She was a beauty. I couldn't blame the neighbor for being protective of her.

I wheeled the bike around and threw my leg over it, then revved it and let the noise echo in the parking garage underneath the building. I had been a bike rider in my younger days when everything was new and exciting with Chad.

"This will do just fine."

"You can't just take it," Ryan said. "What do I tell my neighbor?"

I shrugged and put on the helmet that was hanging from the handle. I snapped it shut, then gave him a look.

"Tell him we borrowed it."

"You can't do that."

"Yes, I can if you're with me," I said. "Come on."

Fear struck Ryan's eyes. Drops of sweat appeared on his upper lip. He shook his head.

"But... I... can't."

"Suit yourself," I said. "I'm going now."

"No!"

I stopped and looked at him.

He grunted nervously. "Okay. I'll come."

I smiled and revved the bike a few times. "Then what are you waiting for? Jump on but grab a helmet first."

Ryan found the other helmet and put it on, then whimpered lightly when he climbed onto the bike behind me before we rode out of the garage and into the dawning day. Ryan held onto me tightly from behind, and I could hear him moan loudly even above the noise coming from the bike below us.

What I didn't tell him was that I was very pleased to have him come along, since the police were looking for a single woman on foot and not a couple on a bike. The way I saw it, if we stayed clear of the roadblocks, we had an actual chance of making it through town unnoticed.

Chapter 89

Olivia felt her pulse quickening as she approached the line in front of her. She stood close to a family of four and stared at the two children in their light summer clothes. In front of them, the line moved slowly toward the breakfast buffet.

They had given them new clothes and taken the girls there to spend the night, pretending to be several families on vacation. Not because of their generosity or because they wanted them to have a nice bed to sleep in for once. No, it was so they wouldn't stand out, so they would be able to get into the restaurant in the morning without anyone paying attention to them. After all, they looked just like the rest of the tourists and happy families in the hotel. The only difference was the bags of liquid gas that had been strapped to their stomachs, the same bags they were instructed to poke with forks as soon as they reached the buffet.

Two other girls had taken their seats in the restaurants by the exits and were waiting for their signal before they would do the same.

Olivia felt the bag under her loose white shirt with her finger. Once she poked a hole in it, she was going to die along with the people standing close to her. She knew this was to be her fate. They had told her so. She had been chosen to be one of those that didn't make it out. They had guards placed both inside and outside the hotel, ready to shoot her if she didn't do as told or if she tried to make contact with anyone.

There was no way she'd get out of this alive.

The little girl in front of her grabbed a fork and a plate from the pile and Olivia did the same, fighting to keep her hand from shaking so badly she risked dropping the plate on the floor and causing a spectacle. It was important that she didn't draw any attention to herself, were the instructions when she was sent down in the elevator with the three other girls. Olivia considered dropping the plate on purpose and maybe creating a diversion, but she didn't dare to. From the other end of the restaurant, a set of eyes followed her every move. A tall guy dressed in swim shorts and a Hawaiian shirt stared at her from behind the sunglasses, his hand clutched on the gun in his pocket. He was standing by the door, so he would be the first to get out once the gas was released.

Olivia exhaled nervously and held out the plate in front of her, while the girl next to her whined because she wanted to have a soda, but the buffet only had juice.

"You can have soda for lunch, okay?" her mother said.

"I don't wanna have soda for lunch. I want it now," the girl said and pulled her hand out of her mother's grip.

Olivia felt her heart race while thinking about her siblings and her own parents. She knew in this instant that she was never going to see any of them again, and it tormented her so deeply she felt tears pile up in her eyes. She wished that she'd at least get to say goodbye.

I miss you, Mom. I miss you so much. You would know what to do!

"Are you okay?" a man standing behind her suddenly asked.

Olivia gasped and bit her lip to stifle her crying. She glanced toward the guy by the door. His eyes were fixated on her, his hand on the gun.

"I'm fine," she said and looked up at him.

The man smiled comfortably. "Say, are you here alone?"

Olivia glanced briefly at the guard by the door again while

contemplating telling the man the truth, just spilling it all, but once again, she didn't dare.

"No. I'm with my parents. They're over there," she said and nodded in the direction of a couple that sat at the other end of the restaurant.

"Ah, I see. You on vacation?"

She nodded as the line moved forward. She was supposed to poke the bag as soon as she reached the front of the line by the fruit. That way, she'd hit the densest area of people in the entire restaurant. The liquid would run out onto the floor, and she'd breathe in the gas, which would kill her slowly and painfully.

"Where from?" he asked as they took another step forward.

"I'm sorry; what?"

"Where are you visiting from?"

"Oh. Wisconsin."

"Wisconsin, huh? I'm from Texas."

"I hear it's nice there too," she said, her voice shaking.

But you'll never get to see it again if you don't run far away from me now. Run, you idiot, and take all the children with you.

"And hot," he said. "It's a different kind of hot than here, though."

"Because of the drier air," she said and took yet another step forward. There were about three steps left until she reached her target. She held the fork tightly in her sweaty hand. The two children in front of her were laughing, the girl holding her mother's hand tightly in hers again, having forgotten everything about the soda she wanted a few seconds ago. They were dressed in swimsuits underneath their thin shirts, ready to jump in the pool as soon as breakfast was devoured, while their parents were looking forward to spending an entire day just resting poolside while the kids played and had the time of their lives. They had probably been looking forward to this piece of heaven for months, maybe even years.

Olivia's eyes met those of the other girl that had come here with her, standing in the back of the line. She too was sweating heavily, and her eyes were struck with deep fear. She was supposed to die today as well, while the two other girls sitting at the tables by the exits would be able to make it out in time. They had already placed their bags on the floor and were ready to poke them as soon as it was time. Then they would leave while Olivia and the other girl in the line would never be able to make it out in time. They were too far from the doors, even if they threw the bags and ran.

The closer Olivia came to the fruit, the closer the man kept an eye on her, and the more strained his face got. The fork almost slipped out of Olivia's sweaty hand as she took another step forward, and now only stood a few feet away. She took in another deep breath as the line moved again, and she now stood right in front of the fruit.

She turned her head with a light gasp and looked at the man by the door. He nodded to let her know that it was time.

Olivia felt the fork in her hand and turned it a couple of times before she lifted it in the air.

Chapter 90

"Oh, boy. I'm going to die!"

Ryan had his arms wrapped tightly around my waist while I zigzagged between cars through morning traffic. He was yelling and screaming behind me, but I chose to ignore him.

Cars honked at us, and someone flipped us off, but we had no time to waste on an idiot like him. As we came up toward a roadblock ahead, I turned around and went back. I found another way and raced through the smaller neighborhoods as fast as possible. At one point, I even drove off the road and over a hill to avoid a roadblock.

"Where are we going?" he yelled, his voice shivering as we came to a red light and I stopped for a few seconds.

"I told you; I'm going to find my daughter," I said. "And there is only one person who knows where she is."

"Do you know where this person is?"

"I have a hunch, yes."

"I'm risking my life on a hunch?" Ryan asked.

"You and me both, baby," I said and revved the machine as the light turned green again. "Hold on. This might get a little bumpy."

Ryan let out another shriek as I raced down a small street and soon reached downtown. I made a left turn and ran a red light when a patrol car caught my tail and put his siren on.

"Shoot."

Seeing this, I sped up, and he tried to follow, but I was way faster than him and able to zigzag between cars. Soon, he had called for backup, and three police cruisers were following us, racing across town toward Coconut Grove.

I could see the big, tall buildings as they rose in front of us and, soon, I raced the bike up in front of one of them. I threw the bike just as the patrol cars came up behind me, tires screeching. There was a lot of yelling, and Ryan screamed and stood with his hands over his head.

"Don't shoot. Don't shoot."

Guns were pointed at us, and the yelling continued.

"STOP, or we'll shoot! Hands where we can see them!"

I put my hands above my head while more patrol cars came driving up. Ryan whimpered and fell to his knees, while I stared at the entrance to the building, feeling my heart pound uncontrollably in my chest.

If they take you in now, it's over. You're so close, Eva Rae.

I sensed they were coming closer, guns pointed at me.

"I said down on your knees! Hands behind your head," someone yelled.

I contemplated this for a few seconds and was about to do as I was told; I really was. But then something came over me; I can't exactly explain what it was. A stubbornness, you might call it. Maybe stupidity. Whatever it was, it empowered me just enough to stop midway, then lower my hands and make a run for it.

I stormed toward the front entrance, while the police officers yelled behind me and a shot was fired. The doors slid open in front of me, and I threw myself into the lobby of the building.

Chapter 91

"More salmon, sweetie?"

Helen shook her head. She had never liked salmon, but of course, her mother didn't know that.

Her mother's Botox-face tried to smile but was unsuccessful. It barely moved. She was sitting on the couch with the views over Biscayne Bay from everywhere you looked. It was a gorgeous place, and most people would love to be sitting where she was right now, but not Helen. She loathed this place more than anywhere in this world. She couldn't believe she had ended up back here again.

"It's just so good to have you back," her mother said and sipped her Champagne. It was still only eight in the morning but never too early for her mother to drink alcohol.

Helen's father shoveled in scrambled eggs and salmon while grumbling loudly.

"Don't you think, Jack?" her mother said. "That it is wonderful to have Helen back again? I'm just so glad that you finally were able to break free from that awful cult. And now we don't have to talk more about that. Just that we're happy that nightmare is finally over. Now, we can begin a new chapter."

Her mother moved a lock of hair from Helen's face, and she

pulled away, annoyed, then sipped her coffee. Her sister Aubrey was standing by the window, looking out over the bay. She had barely spoken a word to Helen since she came back to them. Helen had disappointed them. She could tell by how they looked at her.

Helen's father drank from his cup, then put it down hard on the table, causing all the plates to jump. Helen's mother gasped, and they all looked at him.

"I just don't get how she could have been so stupid," he said with that low growl that had always frightened Helen so. He hadn't looked at her since she got back, and he wasn't looking at her now either. He still spoke about her like she wasn't even in the room.

"She gave them millions of our hard-earned money, for Christ's sake. Of the family's savings. Money I have worked to be able to give to her. Couldn't she see that it was a trap? How could anyone be so stupid?"

"Jack!" her mother exclaimed with a light snort. "You promised me. We need to put this behind us. Besides, I have read that this leader was very persuasive and charming. Lots of people fell for his schemes. Respectable people like our family. Helen is the victim here."

Her father grunted and rose to his feet, then began pacing. "But becoming a terrorist? Killing people? For what? Because she loved him? Because he was so attractive and charming, she couldn't say no to him? Explain this to me because I don't understand it. She did this willingly. She gave him money of her own free will; she took nerve gas into a high school intending to kill hundreds of children. They forced young kids, young girls that had been trafficked and held hostage by the cult to do these awful things. But you, Helen. You went to them. You chose to be in this cult. You were there because you wanted to be there. You could have walked out of it long ago before it got this far."

"She was brainwashed, Jack," her mother said. "The therapist told us so, remember?"

"The way I see it, you always have a choice," her sister said without turning around and looking at Helen.

Helen shook her head with a sniffle. "I couldn't get out of it," she said. "It was too late. I was in too deep. They would have locked me up if I refused to participate in this. That's what they do to people. One woman spent an entire year locked up, being abused by the leader. Haven't you read the stories that they have written, the interviews I have given where I tell everything?"

"Yes, we read those awful articles," her mother said, shaking her head. "I really wish you hadn't gone public with it that way. It is… terribly embarrassing."

Helen shook her head in disbelief. Here she thought she had done the right thing, telling the world about Christopher Daniels and the bastard he was, and still, her family resented her for it. She couldn't win with those people, could she?

It didn't matter what she did. It was simply never enough. *She* was never good enough.

Chapter 92

"Where are we going?"

Somehow without me realizing it, Ryan had managed to follow me inside. He was pale as a ghost, staring at me while the commotion continued inside. The police had barricaded the exit with their cruisers and were running for the door.

My nostrils were flaring, my mind going in circles because of fear, but luckily, I was one of those people who thought best under pressure. I knew exactly where we were going.

"The elevator," I said and ran for it and pressed the button excessively. It dinged, and we entered just as four officers came through the sliding doors into the lobby. It took them one second to spot us inside the elevator.

"STOP!"

The doors weren't closing even though I kept slamming the button. Ryan whimpered next to me and, as the officers approached us, I knew the doors wouldn't close in time. I looked up at Ryan while the angry footsteps approached us, then said: "I'm sorry. I didn't want to have to do this."

"W-what do you mean?" he asked, holding his hands above his

head. Meanwhile, I reached down to my ankle and pulled out my gun. The police yelled. One of them reached the elevator door and placed a hand in it so it couldn't close.

"I am sorry," I whispered, pulled out the gun, and placed it against Ryan's head.

"GUN!" one of the officers yelled, and I knew just what that word meant to them in a situation like this. Fear and adrenaline would rush through their minds while remembering all the colleagues they had lost and stories they had heard about situations escalating with a mad shooter.

This was serious now. The minute I pulled the gun, I had crossed a line. From now on, I knew they'd shoot me the second they got the chance.

"Step back, or he gets it," I said, pressing the gun against Ryan's temple. I was screaming like a madman, trying to sound convincing.

"I'm not joking here. Stand back, or I'll shoot!"

It worked. The officers took a few steps back, enough for the doors to close, and soon, the elevator was lifting us up. My heart rate was in a frenzy, and I could barely breathe. Ryan stood like he was frozen, his hands shaking, but not making a sound. I removed the gun, then bent forward to breathe better.

"That was close. I'm sorry, Ryan. That I had to do this to you. Are you okay?"

I looked up at him, and he breathed raggedly.

"You knew I wasn't going to shoot you, right?"

He finally nodded as the elevator reached its stop. "S-sure."

"Good because I wouldn't have. Not in a million years. I was only buying us some time. Now that they think I've kidnapped you, they'll have to call for the hostage taskforce. It'll take a while, and they'll stay away. Besides, once we are finally caught, they'll think you were a victim, not my accomplice, and you won't get in trouble. You're welcome, by the way."

We stopped by a door, and I took in a deep breath, then felt the Colt in my hand. This was it. It was time to face the music.

I knocked, and soon the door opened.

"You?" the person said, startled.

I nodded, making sure Christopher Daniels could see the gun in my hand. "Yes, me. You and I need to have a little chat."

Chapter 93

"How did you find me?" Christopher Daniels grumbled as he closed the door behind us. I made sure the gun was visible still as I sat down in a recliner by the window. Ryan looked nervously around, then stood by the window, staying a few steps away from both of us. Christopher Daniels sat down too, right across from me, folding his hands in his lap, looking at me with a smirk. He looked relaxed in his white loose linen clothes and, as usual, annoyingly handsome.

"Some punk took a picture of you entering this building and posted it on Instagram last night," I said. "I'm surprised to see that the place isn't already crawling with journalists, but the day is still young. They'll be here soon. It wasn't hard for me to find out that one of your inner circle cult members, Giselle Hovers, whom I had the pleasure of meeting while staying at the NYX estate, owned one of the top floor apartments here, and, of course, that was where you were staying."

He answered with a smile. "I always believed you were very bright. You could have made it far in NYX if you had cared to stay long enough for us to show you what we can offer."

"I know what you have to offer," I said. "And I am not interested."

He shrugged and leaned back. It bothered me that he didn't seem the least bit afraid of me or the gun in my hand. I had to control myself. I wanted to hurt this guy so terribly, but so far, he was the only one who could help me find my daughter.

"Suit yourself."

"I want my daughter back," I said.

"I'm sure you do," he answered.

I lifted the gun. "Where is she?"

He stretched out his hands. "I don't know."

"What do you mean you don't know? Don't mess with me," I said and rose to my feet. "I will hurt you and take great pleasure in doing so. Starting by shooting you in the right kneecap, then the left one, and moving my way up until you talk. The one in the crotch should make you scream. A lot."

He chuckled and leaned forward in the chair, hands clasped against one another.

"You can do all you want to me, but it won't help. I don't have your daughter. I never had her. Not her. Not any of those other girls that the police are accusing me of kidnapping."

I stared at him, my hands growing sweaty. "B-but... you used them. For the attacks. You're the Iron Fist."

He shook his head gently. "That's what everyone keeps telling me, but I am not him. I never was. I don't even know what an Iron Fist is. And I had nothing to do with those attacks."

"But... but the cult leader in Japan. You were inspired by him. You were just like him; you did what he did because you..."

He shook his head. "Never."

"You're bluffing. You do this. You mess with people's minds. You're the mad cult leader."

He sighed.

"That might be, but I would never do any of those things. I'm not a violent person. I believe in higher enlightenment. I believe you and I can reach a higher level of understanding ourselves, not by violence, but by reaching inside ourselves and stripping ourselves from our former nature. I believe in the releasing powers of the sexual act. Of submitting yourself to another human being, one who has obtained greater enlightenment than you."

I stared at him, unable to speak.

"B-but that can't be," I said. "If you're not behind this, then who is? And where is my daughter? No, it has to be you. You're just trying to trick me. Unless… Oh, dear Lord."

Could it be? No, it can't be… could it?

A huge piece of the puzzle suddenly fell into place, and I stared at Christopher Daniels, then placed the gun to his head. "We're leaving, and you're coming with us."

"That might be a little difficult," Ryan said and glared out the window. "The place is surrounded by cops and reporters."

"I might have a solution for that," I said and gave Christopher Daniels elevator eyes.

Chapter 94

"Get out."

Matt did as he was told and got out of the patrol car. Carter grabbed him by the arm and pulled him up toward the condominium. Matt's hands were cuffed in front of him as he was being led to the scene. He didn't know exactly what was going on, only that it had to do with Eva Rae, and that terrified him.

"Your little lady has kidnapped someone and taken him into this building," Carter said as they walked up toward the many parked police cruisers and the group of officers waiting for them. Their nervous eyes were lingering on him. None of these officers would hesitate to shoot Eva Rae if they got the chance. That's how dangerous they believed she was. It was written all over their faces.

"What is this place?" Matt asked and looked up at the tall building. "Why did she choose this place?"

Carter sighed. "Her little friend, Christopher Daniels, is hiding from the press in one of the top condos. My guess is she came to pay him a visit. Maybe make sure he didn't talk to us and rat her out. Maybe she came to kill him. Who knows? The lady has gone nuts. Who knows what her next move is? But today, it ends. Today, we're taking her in, and you're going to help."

"There really isn't much I can do," Matt said, exhausted. He had been so worried about Eva Rae all night while pacing in his cell. He had seen the blood on the stairwell of the hotel and knew she was hurt. Now, she was apparently trapped inside of that building and, by the looks of it, there was no way out. All exits were blocked by heavily armed cops. A Hostage Rescue Team had just arrived, and a SWAT team was on the way.

"The thing is," Carter said. "Our boss is really keen on getting her alive, so we need to at least try our best to do so. But you need to work with us here, Miller. You are her last resort. Either you talk her out of the building, with none of her hostages getting hurt, or we go in and take her down. It's up to you how this ends. Either way, we're getting her today. Do you understand what I'm saying?"

He did. But he just wasn't very sure that Eva Rae would listen to anything he had to say. When it came to getting her daughter back, she would stop at nothing. When it came down to choosing between Matt and her children, Matt knew he was her last priority. That was just the way she was wired.

"Now, the HRT is trying to establish contact and, as soon as they do, I need you to start talking to her. I'll give you one shot at getting her out of that building alive. If it doesn't work, then that's too bad. SWAT will go in on my orders."

Matt swallowed hard, then nodded to let Carter know he understood. He prepared himself for what he would say when an officer suddenly yelled.

"Someone is coming out!"

All the officers on the scene turned, guns pointing at the front door just as someone approached it. It was a man. He was wearing loose white clothes and walked with his head bowed.

"It's Christopher Daniels," Carter said. "Careful! He might be armed."

All the officers surrounding the building left their posts and ran to assist. Daniels walked out the sliding doors, then knelt on the ground, placing his hands behind his neck. Carter let go of Matt and ran to Daniels, along with the rest of the police force. They were yelling at the guy to stay down, not to move a muscle. As they slowly dared to come close enough, the man lifted his head and looked up at them. He spoke, his voice shivering.

"Don't shoot. Please, don't shoot me."

"It's not him," Carter yelled. "This is not Christopher Daniels."

Just as he realized this, Carter turned around. He then ran to the back of the building, yelling: "It's a diversion. It's a diversion!"

But he got there too late. As he reached the side of the building, the gate leading to the underground garage opened, and a Jaguar roared out, so close to Carter that he had to throw himself to the side not to get hit.

"STOP!" Carter yelled, then lifted his gun. Matt watched, holding his breath.

Step on it, Eva Rae. Floor that thing and get out of here!

Carter fired a shot at the car, but it was already too far away, and he missed. Soon, the black Jaguar was on the street, disappearing between the palm trees.

"That son of a gun!"

Carter cursed loudly, then stomped his foot like a child. He rushed to Matt and placed the gun to his head.

"Where are they going?"

Matt shrugged.

Carter gave Matt an angry look, then turned to address his officers.

"I'm not letting her get away. Not today, people. Track that Jaguar down. Get a chopper in the air if need be. She's not getting away this time. Not today, people. Do you hear me? Not today!"

Chapter 95

The fork swirled through the air, spiraling down toward the bag underneath Olivia's shirt. But just as it was supposed to poke the bag like you'd pierce a microwavable bag of beans, Olivia turned her hand, and it missed.

Olivia couldn't breathe. She stared down at the fork in her hand. The children in front of her were still chatting, holding the hands of their parents, the restaurant still buzzing with happy voices.

I can't do it. I simply can't do it.

Olivia lifted her gaze, and she stared at the tall man with the sunglasses leaning against the door. He mouthed something that looked like a threat, his nostrils flaring aggressively. His hand on the gun in his pants moved, and she knew it was her last chance.

"Do it now," his lips said. "Or your family will die too. Not just you."

Olivia felt a ripple of fear rush through her body, and she could barely hold the fork between her fingers anymore. Her torso was shaking, her lips quivering, and soon she could no longer hold her tears back. They rolled down her cheeks as she — hands trembling — lifted the fork once again.

Just do it, Olivia. You'll die, no matter what. Poke a hole in the bag, take in a deep breath, and it'll be all over. The gas will make you pass out, and you won't feel death coming. Soon, you won't feel anything anymore.

Olivia took in a deep breath to steady her hand between sobs. The man behind her noticed her struggle.

"Say, are you okay?" he asked and put a hand on her shoulder.

That made her lose it completely. Olivia bent forward, crying.

"Hey… hey, are you okay?" the man continued nervously.

Olivia was sobbing now and didn't even see the tall man as he pulled out the gun and sprang forward.

"I… I can't do it," Olivia said and dropped the fork on the floor. *It's all over now.*

The tall man approached her, and now she saw the gun. She readied herself for what was about to become her fate and decided to embrace it. It was out of her hands now. At least she wouldn't take anyone else with her when she went down. At least the kids in the line in front of her were safe.

Olivia stepped out of the line and staggered toward the tall man, who now held the gun up toward her. Seeing this made panic erupt in the restaurant, and it swept rapidly through the crowd. Someone screamed.

"GUN! He's got a gun!"

The tall man stood in front of her, blocking her way, gun pointed at her. Olivia stopped moving. She stared at the gun pointed at her, then closed her eyes, blocking out the world. Meanwhile, people ran for the exits, screaming. Olivia barely noticed them anymore. She was ready for this.

She was no longer afraid.

When the gun went off, she thought about her family and how she hoped they all knew how much she loved them.

Chapter 96

I wasn't breathing. Everything inside of me had stopped. I stood in the middle of the restaurant at the Bayside Hotel, my gun clenched between my hands.

In front of me, a tall man in a Hawaiian shirt and sunglasses had his back turned to me. He was facing my daughter, gun lifted in his hand and pointed at her. On his back, the flamingoes on his shirt were being colored red as the blood gushed from his wound, where I had shot him.

He spurted, then tried to turn and see what had hit him, but he never made it that far. Instead — halfway turned — he dropped the gun from his hand and fell to the floor with a thud.

The restaurant had been emptied, and people had run outside. It was just us left.

Me and my daughter.

She still had her eyes closed, but soon opened them and blinked.

"M-mom?" Her voice grew shrill and loud as she repeated it, realizing I was truly there.

"Mom? Mo-om?"

I could hardly breathe, let alone speak, so instead of replying, I simply ran to her and grabbed her in my arms. I sobbed loudly as I felt her body close to mine. Our bodies shook violently as we held each other, crying. I kissed her face, stroked her hair, looked into her eyes, and still couldn't believe she was really there, that I had finally found her.

"H-how?" she finally said. "How did you know where I was?"

I sniffled and wiped my cheek with my arm. "I didn't. I came for someone else. I saw you and then the guy who was running for you, pointing his gun at you. I can't believe it's really you. I'm never letting you out of my sight again; you hear me?"

She chuckled, relieved. "Please, don't."

I felt something on her stomach and lifted her shirt to have a look. Olivia grew serious as I saw the bag attached to her. It was strapped around her waist. My heart stopped as I saw the green liquid inside of it.

"Careful," she whispered.

I turned and looked around us. Other bags just like it were placed on the floors. The green liquid was already leaking out.

"We need to get out of here," I said.

Christopher Daniels was standing behind me and helped me get the bag off of Olivia and leave it on the ground. We walked fast toward the exit of the restaurant, staying clear of the other bags. Luckily, the restaurant was in a big room, and we hadn't been close to any of the leaking bags. With some luck, we hadn't been exposed.

As we left the restaurant and closed the doors, I grabbed a couple of bottled waters, and we flushed our eyes with it, just in case. Outside, behind the sliding doors, we could hear sirens. The area was probably blocked off by now while the police tried to talk to the many people that had run outside. It would take a while for them to get the SWAT team ready, especially if they knew that gas had been released. They'd need to get hazmat suits. That bought us a little time.

"So, what do we do now?" Christopher Daniels asked.

I looked around me, then walked to the front desk in the lobby. I tapped on the computer and found the number I was looking for.

"The penthouse, of course. I should have guessed that. Now, how do we gain access to that?"

The doors opened, and a young bellboy came rushing out. He looked confused and probably had no idea what was going on. I smiled and lifted my gun.

"Hello there, young friend. You sure are a sight for sore eyes. How about we take a little ride in the elevator?"

Chapter 97

The bellboy used his keycard to get the elevator to the penthouse floor. As soon as it dinged and opened, we stepped out and let the boy go down again. The elevator opened straight into the penthouse apartment and, seconds later, we were standing in the living room of the owner of the hotel.

Jack Wellington was a big man, despite his seventy years of age. In his raging eyes, you could tell he wasn't someone who was used to being defied. And that was exactly what I was doing right now — defying him. I was standing in his living room, interrupting what seemed like a family brunch.

The man rose to his feet when he saw us. I had asked Christopher to stay behind me with Olivia.

"What in the…?"

His voice was hoarse and furious. I felt intimidated as he approached me with wrathful steps.

"Who are you people, and what are you doing in my home?" He paused when seeing me properly. "Wait. You're that woman. The one they're all searching for."

All eyes in the room were on me now. Jack Wellington's fell on Christopher behind me.

"And you… you… what are you doing here?" he spat. "You have some nerve to come here after all you've done to my family."

"I'm calling security," a small nervous-looking woman, who I could only assume was his wife, said. I remembered having seen pictures of both of them in magazines before, dressed for premieres or gallery openings.

"I wouldn't do that," I said and lifted the gun to stop her.

Mrs. Wellington put the phone down.

"What do you want?" Jack Wellington asked, addressed to Christopher. "More of my money? Huh? You haven't taken enough?"

Christopher shook his head. "I have never asked your daughter for any money. She came to me because she wanted my help; she was unhappy with her life, and I tried to help her, but… it went wrong."

"You're darn right it went wrong," Jack Wellington said.

"I might have done a lot of things wrong, but I never asked for a penny from your daughter."

"You're lying," Jack Wellington said. "I know your type. You're an embezzler; that's all you are. A maniac who thinks he can use our money to pay for his terrorist acts. But it's over, buddy. You're not getting one cent more from us."

"Christopher Daniels wasn't the man behind the attacks," I said. I turned my head and looked at Helen Wellington, sitting on a couch, her purse clutched between her hands. I turned the gun toward her.

"She was."

Mrs. Wellington huffed. Mr. Wellington grumbled. "Oh, you people are insane."

Christopher stepped forward. "Tell them, Helen. Clear your conscience and free your soul."

"Will you listen to him?" Jack Wellington snorted. "Trying to blame my daughter… for what? A terrorist attack? Will you look at her? She can barely even tie her own shoes."

Helen stood to her feet, her purse still in her hand, her eyes blazing.

"That's right, Daddy Dearest. I never could do anything, could I? But guess what? They're right. I did do something. Something no one would ever think I was capable of, least of all you. I killed all those people. In the Metrorail, in the church, at the school, and now here at your beloved hotel. I. Killed. Them. All."

Chapter 98

"I'd do it all over again any day if I got the chance, Daddy Dear."
Helen stared at her father, who, for once in his life, had become speechless. "There. I finally have your attention, don't I?"

Helen turned to look at me. "How on Earth did you know?"

"It struck me when I read an interview about you in the *New York Times*," I said. "After your arrest, you told your story to every media outlet who would listen, didn't you? You spoke about NYX and said they had forced you to carry the gas into the school. You told the reporter in detail how they chose you among the members and that you had to go in with a bunch of trafficked girls that Christopher had bought online and that were dispensable. You spoke about NYX like you came straight from the house, but I never saw you there. And then there was something else that made me suspect you. I couldn't figure out why you were so open with the police and the press about the cult and what had been going on when every other member who was arrested stayed silent. But now I know why. You wanted them to go down. You wanted NYX to take the blame for the attacks. I wondered about these things while still thinking that Christopher was behind the attacks. It wasn't until I spoke to Christopher and asked about this that I fully understood what was going on. He told me what you had been through — about your past. And once he did, it all suddenly made sense."

"He was on the train, wasn't he?" Christopher said and stepped forward toward Helen. "Brian? Your ex-husband? He took the Metrorail every day to one of the courthouses where he worked, always getting out at Government Center."

"You wanted him hurt for what he did to you because he left you," I said. "He abandoned you when he realized you couldn't have children. And then he married someone else and had a family, leaving you all alone."

"You're right. I won't deny it," Helen said. "Daddy always thought I couldn't do anything, but I did this. Under the username the Iron Fist, I bought the girls in a chatroom on the Dark Web," she said. "I hired a guy to do it for me, someone who knew the Dark Web very well. It was so easy; you wouldn't believe it. A few others that had decided to leave NYX and I planned this together. We gathered a group of girls and kept them at my family's farm outside of town that my dad had put me in charge of, thinking I couldn't mess things up too badly all the way out there. He blamed me for the divorce, thinking I had ruined my marriage just like everything else. I used the girls at the chicken factory at night, breaking them until they obeyed my every word, making them my soldiers. No one would miss these girls who had already been trafficked across the country, some of them across half of the world, and they most certainly could never be traced back to me once their bodies showed up at the scene of the attacks. They were the perfect little soldiers."

My heart sank when hearing the brutal coldness to her voice when talking about these young girls, some of them just children. It was beyond cruel.

"It was because of the abuse; wasn't it?" I asked, my voice cracking slightly when thinking about Olivia in this woman's hands. "That you couldn't have children? You were abused when you were just a young child by a priest at the Catholic church your family attended and where you sang in the choir, at St. Mary's Cathedral, the second place you attacked. You were abused again and again, and no one would listen when you tried to tell them. Not even the

nuns at the Catholic school you went to. And once it started showing, once it became evident that you were pregnant at the age of
only fourteen, you were the one who was punished. It was reported
to your father, and instead of punishing the priest, you were sent
away to a place where they could perform an abortion, even though
you were so far along that it was illegal."

"They killed my baby," she said, spitting. "They poked something up inside of me and murdered my child. Then they pulled out
my baby. I saw him when they did it. I could have taken care of
him. I wanted to, but my father wouldn't let me."

"And because of the procedure, you were unable to become
pregnant again," I said. "They robbed you of that."

"There was scarring," the doctors told me later when Brian and
I went to the fertility clinic, and they examined me. Brian became
furious at me for having never told him about the abortion or the
fact that I couldn't have children, and so he left. Our marriage was
based on a lie, he said. I thought I was going to be alone for the rest
of my life when Brian left me. I thought I'd never survive it."

"But then you met Christopher, and you fell in love all over
again," I said, glancing at him standing by the window.

Chapter 99
THEN

Helen stared at the barren wall in front of her. She was sitting on her bed in the bedroom at the NYX house, a room that she shared with another girl. She had been there a year and a half now and had never felt so alive. Especially not back when she had been married to Brian.

"My God, I think I'm in love," she mumbled with a giggle into the empty room.

Just the very thought of Christopher Daniels and being with him filled her with butterflies of expectation.

The sex between them was intense. It wasn't often, only like once a month or so, but that was enough. She actually kind of liked having to wait for him to call on her to come to his room. She never knew when it would happen, and that made it all the more exciting. Everything about this man was so exhilarating; it made her blush just to think about it. She had no idea love could be this way. She had no idea life could be this way.

Helen smiled secretively. It amazed her how much better her life was now that she was at the NYX house and didn't have to deal with her family and their disappointment in her. Her father had given her the farm to take care of after the divorce, but she didn't have to actually be there to run it. It was just a way of keeping her busy; she knew that much. There were caretakers to handle the day-to-day stuff.

Helen stared at the stick in her hand. No one knew that she was taking the test; she had kept everything a secret. She had been disappointed so many times before in her life. But now, as she stared at the two lines, she could hardly contain herself.

Pregnant? It's really true? I am pregnant? But… but they said it was impossible? That it could never happen?

Stick still in her hand, Helen rose to her feet, almost bubbling over with excitement.

"Christopher is going to be so thrilled when he hears this. He's gonna be so happy. And then we can be together forever and ever. Oh, I can't wait to tell him."

Helen rushed out of her room, then hurried toward the stairs leading to Christopher's chambers on the top floor of the house. Normally, she wasn't allowed to go up there until she was called, but today was a special day. He would want to know right away.

Of course, he would.

Helen grabbed the railing and walked up the wooden stairs, butterflies fluttering in her stomach.

What shall we name the child? I know. Annie if it is a girl and Robert if it is a boy. I've always loved those names. Brian never liked those names, especially not Robert because it reminded him of a kid from his school who picked his nose in class and smelled bad. But screw him. I am calling my child — our child — Robert if it is a boy.

"Christopher?"

Helen reached the top of the stairs, then walked to the door. Behind it lay Christopher's private rooms. Not many were allowed up here. She felt another tickle in her stomach as she lifted her hand to knock. But no one answered. She tried again. Still, no answer. She then grabbed the handle and opened the door carefully.

"Christopher?"

She entered his reading quarters and office. This was where he wrote his books, where he came when he needed quiet.

He wasn't in there.

Could he be somewhere else in the house?

She was about to walk back out when she heard a noise coming from behind the next door, the one leading to the bedroom.

Ah, he's in there.

"Christopher?" she said, then walked to the door and pushed it open.

Helen stopped. In there, on the bed, she found Christopher, surrounded by several women. All naked.

"C-Christopher?" she said, perplexed. He lifted his head from between the breasts of a woman, and their eyes met across the room.

"Helen?"

She shook her head in disbelief. "But... I thought... I thought... you made me believe that I was someone special."

He approached her, reaching out his arms. His naked body suddenly repulsed her where it used to be so exhilarating.

"You *are* special, Helen. I have told you this over and over again. You are truly special. We all are."

He stood there, smiling like it was the most natural thing in the world that he was having sex with an entire group of women like it couldn't possibly hurt her in any way.

Helen took a step backward. As she did, Christopher spotted the stick in her hand, and his expression changed.

"No. No. No."

She nodded. "Yes, Christopher. We're having a child. Together."

He lifted his finger and walked closer. "No, we're not. I don't have children. I never wanted children, Helen. You must have it removed. Do you hear me? I can't have children. I simply won't."

Helen stared at the man she had loved so dearly until a few seconds ago. Suddenly, all she could see was her father's face as he told her she was going to have the baby removed, and she begged him to not do this to her. All she could see and hear were her own screams as she saw the dead baby be pulled out of her body. It overwhelmed her so violently that she started to shake.

Seeing this, Christopher stepped forward again. "Helen, it'll be okay. We'll find a solution for this, okay? It doesn't have to be like what happened last time. We can do it properly. There are ways. You're still not very far along. The baby is barely a baby yet. We can see a doctor and he'll…"

But Helen wasn't listening anymore. Tears streamed across her cheeks, and she stepped backward, shaking her head and crying heavily.

"Helen, let's talk about this…" he tried, but she was gone.

Helen turned around and ran out of the room, heart pounding in her chest, hearing nothing but the screams of her dead, unborn baby.

Chapter 100

"You were pregnant and wanted to keep the baby, but Christopher didn't," I said. "That's when it all came back, everything you had fought to keep down, tried to forget. It stared you directly in the face once again. The abuse, the people who didn't protect you when they should have, the forced abortion, and following infertility. Everything that had destroyed your life, you were reliving once again, and so you ran."

Helen was crying now. She was biting her lip, staring at Christopher, who shook his head.

"It wasn't my fault, Helen," he said. "You need to understand this. It was an accident. You fell down those stairs. You lost the baby, yes, you lost *our* baby, but it was an accident."

Helen swallowed hard. Her lip was quivering. "You killed our baby, Christopher. You killed him."

Christopher clasped his mouth, and I could tell he was fighting his tears. It was the first time I had seen genuine emotion in the man.

"I am sorry," he said. "I never got to tell you how sorry I am. I should have known this would break you. I knew your past. You had told me everything in our therapy sessions. I should have seen this coming. But you wouldn't talk to me. You left our group in anger, and I thought you needed your space — that it was for the best. I should have known it was you when the attacks occurred, especially when you hit the church and your old school. But I just never thought… it's no excuse, I know. I should have seen it. You did all these things to get back at those that had hurt you over the years. Your ex, the church and the priest, the school, and now… your family."

"By buying Sarin gas, which is also easily found on the Dark Web, on sites by chemists who earn a lot of money producing it and selling it, you made it look like the attacks in Japan back in 1995," I said. "Their leaders had just been executed recently, and their ways could be compared to those of NYX. It would easily be perceived that their leader, Christopher, was obsessed with the Japanese leader and wanted to be like him. To make sure the public understood, you told that about Christopher over and over again in the many interviews you did afterward. You described in detail how he talked about the Japanese leader Shoko Asahara constantly and how he even dressed like him and spoke of creating a utopian society. You ganged up with other former members of NYX, who were also angry or disappointed with Christopher, and wanted to hurt him. As it turned out, he had made a lot of enemies over the years. One of those you contacted was Lori Moore, who was very angry with NYX, but she didn't want to be a part of your plan, and she threatened to reveal it all, didn't she? So, you got rid of her and continued your plans with the others. Because they bore the brand when helping you perform the attacks, you made sure all suspicion turned in NYX's direction. Witnesses would see the burn marks, the brands, like Ryan Scott did in the Metrorail. You made it look like NYX was behind it, so you'd take Christopher down in the process. And then you planned an attack on your father's hotel, in the same place he lived, so that when you killed your family, it would look like it was just a part of the terrorist attack on the hotel. No one would ever suspect you, the daughter who had been a victim of NYX. They would think it was a way to get back at you because you had spoken up against NYX. With Christopher released from prison on bail, this morning was the perfect moment to strike. While the guests were eating their breakfast in peace and quiet, not suspecting to be exposed to a deathly gas."

Helen's parents turned their heads to look at her, mouths gaping. Her sister, Aubrey, came closer too.

"Is this true?" her father asked. "Tell me, Helen. Is this true?"

I walked up to Helen and grabbed her purse from her hand. She held onto it, but I pulled it out of her grip. I opened it and then showed its contents to her family. Inside was a clear bag with green liquid in it.

"Sarin gas," I said. "My guess is she was planning on appearing upset, then leaving this brunch prematurely and accidentally forgetting her purse, with the bag that had been punctured still inside of it. She'd then take the elevator down and use a back exit to get out of here. The police would arrive when it was too late and assume you had all died as a part of a terrorist attack, planned by NYX. Very clever."

Mrs. Wellington cupped her mouth. Her eyes lingered on her daughter. "I can't believe this. Helen? Please, tell me this isn't true?"

Chapter 101

J ack Wellington sat down in a chair, then hid his face between his hands. His wife stared at their daughter. She stood like she was frozen, like she was still waiting for her to say that it wasn't true.

"Don't you even have anything to say?" her mother asked, her voice cracking.

Helen Wellington's eyes lingered on me and the gun in my hand.

"It's over, Helen," I said.

I stared at the woman in front of me and didn't even notice her sister went for her purse. Not until it was too late, and she too had pulled out a gun. As I turned to look, it was pointed at my daughter, at Olivia's head. Aubrey's hand was shaking.

"I am sorry," she said. "For having to do this. But I can't let you destroy my family. Now, please lower your gun, or I will shoot."

"She's bluffing, Mom," Olivia said. "Don't do it."

I stared at my daughter, unable to believe her. There was no way I'd risk her life like that. Are you kidding me? I had just gotten her back.

I raised my hand with the gun in the air, then placed it on the ground and kicked it to Aubrey, who picked it up.

"Now what?" I asked. "You're gonna let your sister get away with this?"

"Actually," Helen said as she approached her sister and grabbed one of the guns. "My sister has been helping me all the way."

"Aubrey!" Mrs. Wellington exclaimed. "Why? I have never... I didn't raise you to..."

Aubrey took two steps forward. She lifted the arm that held the gun and shot her mother point-blank in the face.

Olivia screamed and turned her face away. I watched Mrs. Wellington jolt before she crumpled to the floor, her red blood gushing onto the white carpet below.

My heart pounded in my chest as Helen walked to her father and placed the gun on his forehead and pressed it against the skin until he was forced to look up at her.

"How does that feel, Daddy, huh? How does it feel that your fate is in someone else's hands? Huh? How does it feel to have someone completely ruin your entire life, everything you've dreamt about and worked for? Huh? How does it feel to be betrayed by your own flesh and blood? By the very ones that are supposed to care for you?"

He just stared at her, his steel-grey eyes overflowing with menace.

"Answer me!" Helen snorted. "How does it feel to be betrayed by your own daughter?"

Jack Wellington's eyes grew stale. He spoke with calmness.

"You weren't even worthy of my name. Not since the day you let that priest defile you. Since then, you were nothing but a dirty whore to me. A useless dirty who..."

With a loud scream, Helen fired the gun. Jack Wellington fell backward in the chair, while Helen fired another shot at his chest, then another, still while screaming.

"I HATE YOU. I HATE YOU. I HATE YOU!"

Aubrey came up behind her sister and pulled her into a hug.

"He isn't worth it, sis. He isn't worth it."

Helen sobbed and held her sister tight while my eyes met Christopher's. Knowing these sisters' level of anger and capability, especially toward men, I believed he would be next. Christopher knew it too. He turned around, then bolted for the elevator while the sisters were still hugging.

Chapter 102

He almost made it. Almost. Christopher was by the door, and it was open when the sisters let go of one another, then cocked both of their guns and pointed them at him.

"Stop," Aubrey said.

Christopher paused for a second, but then realizing that they were at the other end of the living room, out of range, he continued into the elevator. He turned around and pushed the buttons, hard, frantically, while the sisters rushed toward him, soon getting close enough to shoot. I didn't know how well they shot, but I had a feeling it was something they had trained at since childhood, by the way they held the guns with confidence. It was customary for especially rich families in Florida to train their children in shooting guns. I myself had been trained by the man who I had believed was my father back then. At least once a month, he would take me to a shooting range, and we would spend the day there together.

Close the doors. Close the darn doors.

The doors began to move, and my heart raced while watching it. Olivia held onto me tightly while the sisters came closer and now both fired at Christopher. Three shots were fired before the elevator doors closed.

I held my breath.

Did he make it?

Seconds went by, while Aubrey pushed the button to get the elevator to come back up. I scanned the apartment, searching for an emergency exit when the elevator dinged again, and the doors opened.

I probably shouldn't have, but I couldn't help myself. I stretched my neck to see, and then I saw it. I saw him. I saw Christopher lying inside the elevator, on the floor, in a pool of his own blood.

Oh, dear God.

Seeing this, Olivia turned her face away and hid in my arms. I held her tightly, trying to calm myself down.

In that second, the sisters turned to look at the two of us.

Chapter 103

They tied us up. Backs leaned against one another, Olivia and I were tied up with duct tape and placed on the floor. Then, Helen grabbed her purse and pulled out the plastic bag with the Sarin gas in it. My heart dropped as she placed it next to us.

"I am so sad not to be here to watch you die slowly because it would give me such deep joy," she said with a tilted head. "But we need to go down and talk to the police. We'll tell them how you came up here with the gas and then shot and killed my entire family. Then we'll tell them how Christopher backstabbed you and tried to kill you as well, then tied you up and released the gas, trying to kill us all. But, of course, my sister and I managed to escape and shot Christopher, then ran for the emergency exit, just in time for us not to be exposed to the gas. Unfortunately, we were the only ones to survive. Now, it might take us a while to tell the story properly since we are in such a deep state of shock, so you'll have to excuse us if it takes a little while before anyone comes up here. But you won't mind because, after about a few minutes of breathing this gas, you'll be so sick you'll hardly be able to speak anyway. Some people experience symptoms within as little as thirty seconds of having been exposed to it. Others take a few minutes. You'll probably die from respiratory paralysis pretty fast I'd assume when being this close to the contamination device. You know how they train for these types of events, how they prepare to approach a gas attack? They actually tell the first responders to resist the urge to rush to help. You wanna know why? Because if the patient is so incapacitated by the nerve agent, to the point where they are incapable of self-evacuation, it is highly likely they'll die despite any intervention the first responders might be able to provide. Isn't it nice? They'll simply leave you to die. Because there is nothing they can really do to prevent it. No one will come for you, Eva Rae Thomas. No one."

"You're sick," I said. "Do you know that? I'll come after you. I'll hunt you down and kill you. You hear me?"

I yelled at the top of my lungs, but it was too late. Helen stared at me, then took in a deep breath and held it, while lifting a small knife in the air and poking it through the plastic bag. I whimpered as I watched the hole grow, and the liquid inside of it start to move. For days, I had read about this type of gas and just what it did to the body. I knew this was definitely going to kill us both if I didn't act fast.

"Bastards!" I screamed as the two women rushed to the emergency exit at the other end of the room and left.

Chapter 104

"What are we going to do, Mom? What do we do?"
The panic in my daughter's voice didn't help make me calmer. I was struggling with the duct tape while trying to not breathe in too deeply. Meanwhile, the liquid had reached the carpet now, and it was beginning to sting my eyes. So far, only a small amount of the gas had made it out of the hole. I didn't know how much of the liquid it took to kill us, and I wasn't planning on sticking around to find out.

I moved my hands back and forth, getting the tape loose, and soon pulled my hands out. I removed the tape from my feet then rushed to Olivia and started pulling at hers.

"How did you do that?" she asked. "How did you get your hands out?"

"When they tied me up, I made sure there was a good gap between my wrists, so they didn't fully touch," I said. "They didn't notice, luckily, since they were so busy talking. Once they left, it was easy to pull off since it was so loose. Here. Now, you're free too."

We sprang to our feet, and I pulled my daughter away from the gas. It was stinging my eyes severely now, and I felt like my throat was closing up. It had to be the worst feeling in the world, not to be able to breathe properly. Panic erupted in me as we rushed across the room.

"Mom," Olivia said. "I don't feel so good."

"I know, sweetie. We just need to get to the emergency exit. Hurry."

We tried to run, but it was hard when we couldn't breathe properly. I gasped for air and felt like my lungs were collapsing.

We reached the door to the emergency exit, then tried to open it, but it wouldn't budge.

"Mom? What's happening?" Olivia said. "Why won't it open?"

"They must have... blocked it somehow," I said and tried again, pushing it hard.

It didn't move.

"What do we do?" Olivia said.

"We'll try the elevator," I said and pulled her by the hand. We reached the elevator, where Christopher's dead body lay on the floor. I stepped in some of his blood and felt like I had to throw up. Olivia came inside with me, whimpering as she tried not to look at him. I pressed the button, but nothing happened.

"Mom?" Olivia said. "Why doesn't it do anything?"

I pressed again, then again and again. Nothing.

I stared into the apartment and realized there was no light on in any of the lamps. I couldn't hear the AC running either. I walked out and flipped a switch, but nothing happened.

"What's going on, Mom? Mom?" my daughter shrieked.

"They turned the power off. So, we couldn't get down in case we escaped somehow. They're smarter than I thought."

"But... but if the emergency exit is blocked and the elevator doesn't work, then what do we do?" Olivia said. "How do we get out of here before the gas kills us?"

Chapter 105

"We've been told she's holding the entire Wellington family captive in the penthouse apartment," Carter said.

He looked at Matt, who was standing next to him. Matt held his cuffed hands in front of him. He folded his hands and mumbled a prayer under his breath. He was worried about Eva Rae more than anything.

"You still believe in her innocence? She's up there with him, with Christopher Daniels. The bellboy over there told us he helped them get up there, that Eva Rae Thomas put a gun to his head and forced him to take them up there. And you still want to defend her? I'm beginning to think that either you're very stupid or maybe very blinded by your love for her, or maybe you really are in it with her. But there is no way she's coming out of that building without us getting her. I have guards at every exit, and the entire area is surrounded. This time, we'll get her. I just know we will. Her reign of terror is over."

Matt swallowed hard and looked up toward the penthouse. He felt a pinch in his heart. How was this ever going to end well for her? Carter had told him that they believed Olivia was there too. The bellboy had said that a young girl was in the elevator with them, and when they showed him a picture of Olivia, he had said it looked like her, only she had shorter hair.

Matt breathed to calm himself down. At least Eva Rae had finally found her daughter. That provided Matt with some level of comfort. But would they make it out alive?

"Someone's coming out," a voice yelled.

Please, let it be Eva Rae; please, let it be Eva Rae.

Carter approached the entrance, escorting Matt with him. There was movement behind the sliding doors, and soon they opened. Two women came out, but it wasn't Eva Rae or Olivia.

Dang it.

"It's the Wellington sisters!" A reporter yelled, and they all threw themselves forward but were stopped by the police barrier they had put up. Officers rushed to the women. Both looked to be in great distress. Tears were rolling from their eyes.

"We need paramedics over here!" an officer yelled. "Fast!"

"It's was horrible," one of the sisters said. "She tried to kill us."

"Eva Rae Thomas did?" Carter asked when approaching them.

One of the sisters, who Matt recognized as Helen Wellington, lifted her head and nodded. "Her and Christopher Daniels. Christopher killed our parents, and then he killed her too."

"Eva Rae Thomas?" Matt asked, his pulse quickening.

Helen nodded. She struggled to get the words past her lips.

"Yes. And her daughter. Using nerve gas."

Matt didn't hear anything after that. He gasped for air and stepped backward, hearing only his own heartbeat.

Eva Rae is dead? She's dead?

He could barely breathe and felt dizzy. Carter was busy taking the sisters' statements, so he didn't notice him as he stepped out of the crowd to gather himself. He bent forward, squatting down, his cuffed hands held up in front of him and started to cry.

Carter came up behind him and placed a hand on his shoulder.

"It's time to go, buddy. I'm taking you back to the station. You're of no use to me anymore since Eva Rae is dead."

Matt nodded, still sobbing heavily, then rose to his feet. As he did, he threw a glance toward the top floor of the building in front of him. Up there, on the seventy-fifth floor, he could see something moving.

Was it someone waving?

No, it couldn't be.

Matt squinted his eyes. He always had hawk-like vision, but this was far away. Still, he couldn't help thinking that someone had opened the window and was waving.

Could he hear them screaming too?

"Wait a second," he said. He stepped forward, while Carter grabbed his shoulder.

"We need to go."

Matt stood still for a few seconds more, staring into the air, then turned to face Carter.

"I'm sorry," he said, "But I can't go right now."

Matt then lifted his knee and slammed it into Carter's crotch, causing him to bend over in deep pain.

Then, Matt turned around and made a run for it. It took a few seconds before Carter was able to speak and yell to his colleagues, and by the time he did, Matt was already approaching the sliding doors. They took off after him, but he was faster than them, and soon he stormed inside.

He knew they wouldn't follow him in, not when they knew there was gas inside of the building and, just as he thought, they stopped their pursuit at the doors.

Matt ran to the elevator, but nothing happened when he pressed the button. He found the exit sign, then ran down a hallway and soon reached the stairs.

Then, he started climbing.

The first steps went smooth and easy, and he took them two, sometimes three at a time, eager to get up to the penthouse before it was too late. He was certain it was Eva Rae he had seen in the window, waving at him. He might be mad, and it might end up killing him, going up there to the nerve gas without proper protection, but he had to do it. He simply had to.

As he reached the fortieth floor, he began slowing down, feeling his heart pumping in his chest, and as he reached the fiftieth floor, he had to stop and catch his breath before continuing.

It took forever to climb this many stairs, especially with no AC, and by the time he finally reached the seventy-fifth floor, he was completely drenched in sweat and out of breath. But it didn't matter. All that mattered was getting to her. Matt refused to believe she was dead. It simply couldn't be true.

He had to at least see it with his own eyes. Even if it meant he died while trying.

Matt reached the plateau and saw the door. He took in a couple of breaths, then approached it.

When he stood close to it, his blood froze to ice. The door had been blocked by several big, heavy boxes. The rest of them rested on a pallet against the wall next to it. It was obvious someone had just grabbed them to block it purposely.

Creating a deathtrap.

The thought made Matt's heart race even faster. This meant the two women had blocked the exit so no one else could follow them. No one else could make it out.

Matt raised his fists and hammered on the door with his cuffed hands.

"Eva Rae? Eva Rae? Are you in there?"

When no answer came, Matt started pulling the boxes to the side, frantically carrying them one at a time. It wasn't easy with his hands cuffed, and them being very heavy, but soon he had pushed them away. He grabbed for the handle, only to realize that there was none.

"Oh, dear God," he cried out in desperation. "The door only opens one way!"

Matt used both his fists to hammer on the door once more.

"Eva Rae! You need to open it from the inside. Come on, Eva Rae; come on!"

Matt slammed his fists against the door until his knuckles started to bleed. He cried and leaned against the door.

"Come on, Eva Rae. Push the door open."

He had almost given up hope when a small voice came from somewhere behind the door.

"M-Matt? Is that you?"

"Olivia?" he said, his voice shrill. "Olivia? Where's your mom?"

"She's passed out. She couldn't breathe and fell to the floor by the window. I'm not sure... I don't... my lungs are burning, Matt. It hurts. My eyes too."

"Olivia, I need you to push the door open. I've removed the boxes that blocked it, but you need to push it open from the inside. Can you do that for me?"

A heartbeat went by, and nothing happened. There was a fumbling behind the door, and then it clicked and slowly opened, but only a little. Matt put his fingers in the crack and pulled it all the way open. Olivia fell out in the hallway, her body shaking like she was having a seizure. Eva Rae lay utterly still on the floor by the window.

"My God," Matt exclaimed, then looked from one to the other. He stared at the stairs behind him, leading down. There were seventy-five floors. How was he supposed to carry two bodies down all those stairs? How was he supposed to make it in time? With both hands cuffed?

Matt turned to look at Eva Rae.

There was only one solution. He'd have to choose between them. He could only carry one at a time. The question was, should he take the woman he loved or her daughter?

Chances were only one of them would survive.

Chapter 106

Matt made it halfway before he tripped and dropped Olivia's lifeless body. He hit face-first into the ground and screamed with anger and frustration. Olivia's body slid across the floor.

He had chosen the daughter. Not that it was an easy choice, but he knew that Eva Rae would kill him if he took her over Olivia. She would want it this way, and he'd have to respect that.

Matt got up, grabbed Olivia by the arms, and tried to sling her back onto his shoulder. He made a grimace when his back hurt, then was about to take another step, when suddenly the lights in the hallway were turned back on. Matt gasped and looked up at the lamp above him.

The power is back on! That means the elevator is running again.

Matt found the door leading to the floor he was on, then carried Olivia inside and down the hallway. He found the elevator, then pushed the button, and soon it arrived. He gasped when seeing the dead body inside of it, but carried Olivia inside, then pushed the button to go down before running out of it and letting it leave without him. He knew that if he came downstairs with her, he'd get taken away and they would never look for Eva Rae. He had to get back up and take her down as well.

Before it was too late.

So, he did. He ran back up the many stairs, praying that the first responders would find Olivia and get her the help she needed. Turning the electricity on again meant they were inside the building. Matt guessed there were still many people trapped in their hotel rooms all over the building that they came to get out.

He had left Eva Rae on the plateau, so she wouldn't be exposed to any more of the gas, and she was still there as he came back. She was lying on her side, motionless, but she had a pulse when he felt for it.

He grabbed her by the waist and swung her above his shoulders, then — energized by fear of losing her, he started the climb back down again.

He made it two-thirds of the way down when he couldn't walk anymore. He fought to take another step, then another, before he felt like he couldn't walk anymore. His legs were getting wobbly beneath him, and he was getting dizzy.

You've got to make it, Matt. Just a few more steps.

At first, he thought he was just imagining things when he heard voices coming from below him, but he peeked down to see the first responders arriving wearing their hazmat suits, breathing heavily inside of them.

"Sir? Are you all right, sir? Have you been exposed to the gas?" the one who came up to him first asked.

Matt shook his head, breathing hard and tearing up. He was almost out of strength and hope. They had come at the right time. One more minute and he would have caved in.

"No, but she has. Please, help. This woman needs medical care right away."

THREE DAYS LATER

Chapter 107

"When it all comes down to it, you're in deep trouble."

I coughed behind the oxygen mask and fought to breathe. It was happening over and over again. My respiratory system had been damaged, and they didn't know how badly yet. But I was alive, and so was my daughter. I had been in the hospital for days, and they had given me a reversal agent to save my life. Now, Carter had come to visit and stood by my bed, telling me how much trouble I was in.

My arms were cuffed to the bed, so I had no way of actually doing it, but I wanted to punch the man in the face.

"But..." I said between heavy breaths. "But I told you that Helen and Aubrey Wellington..." I lost my breath and wheezed, then took in a couple of deep breaths through my oxygen mask.

"I know, I know. You stick to that story, but no one believes it. Detective Miller keeps saying the same thing, but frankly, it's a little too far out to be true, don't you think?"

I coughed again, then shook my head. "Not more far out than me being the great mastermind."

Carter shrugged. "Well, that's just too bad, isn't it? Because that's what I think. And I have the evidence to prove it."

I wheezed again before being able to speak. "You planted that evidence. Don't you think I know you did?"

Carter came closer, then leaned over me and spoke with a low voice. "Between you and me, yes, I did. I took the necklace from your hotel room when we searched it and placed it in Lori Moore's kitchen. I also used a cloth with the nerve gas that I took from the evidence room, sealed in a bag, and placed it in the trunk of your car. Just to help the case go a little smoother. But you'll never be able to prove it. It'll be your word against mine, and who do you think they'll believe? I'm guessing not the woman who is known as a fraud and who we have on surveillance video assaulting spa owners."

"Maybe you should try and guess again," a voice said coming from behind Carter.

A large woman stepped inside my room, gliding comfortably in her high heels and tight skirt.

"Oh, Detective Carter," I said. "Meet my former boss, FBI-director, Isabella Horne. She was in here earlier, and I had the chance to tell her the entire story. I told her I was certain I could get you to admit your guilt on tape, but she wasn't sure I could. You owe me five bucks, Isabella."

"I sure do," she said, then reached over and removed my phone from the table next to me.

"It's so simple these days," I said. "Can you believe how easy it is? Back in the day, we'd have to wear a wire and everything. It was a lot of trouble. But today, it's different. You can simply use your phone to record sensitive material without anyone knowing it."

"But… but…"

Matt came in behind Isabella, flanked by Chief Annie and a local officer from Miami. The officer removed my cuffs and placed them on Carter instead.

"See, the thing is," Chief Annie said, "it was actually the FBI who sent out Eva Rae on a mission, in cooperation with our department, to find the Iron Fist. He had long been under suspicion for the trafficking of girls in south Florida, and we saw no one better to do the job of finding him than Eva Rae."

"So, she was actually working for us all this time," Isabella said.

"Undercover and top-secret, naturally, so we couldn't tell anyone — not even when you started to chase her. All we could do was to send Matt in to keep an eye on your investigation and make sure she wasn't harmed. But then we caught ourselves a corrupt cop along the way too, which isn't half bad. Helen Wellington and her sister have been taken into our custody now, and will not see daylight for a very, very long time. Lots of trials will follow in the coming years when the sisters and their helpers will have to answer for their actions. Finding the girls at the farm helped us a lot in putting the pieces together, and they will serve as excellent witnesses after they have been reunited with their families. We have even set up a group of investigators to look into NYX to see if there are others who will need to be prosecuted for what happened there before the leader was killed. So, all in all, a very successful mission. Meanwhile, you should probably prepare yourself to spend some time in the darkness as well. Nothing worse than a criminal cop, in my opinion, taking the law into his own hands."

Isabella nodded at the officer, who grabbed Carter and took him away. Chief Annie and Director Isabella Horne left as well, and Matt and I were alone. I asked Matt to come closer to me and wrapped my arms around him, then held him very tight.

"How are you feeling today?" he asked.

I smiled, relieved. "Better. Slowly getting there day by day. Now that we got Carter in custody, I have to say I feel a little like dancing. But not yet, though. My lungs aren't ready for that kind of activity. At least not yet."

"But are you maybe ready for a visit?" Matt asked.

Olivia stepped inside, and I couldn't help smiling through my tears. "Oh, my baby girl. Come here."

She walked up to me and threw her arms around my neck. I kissed her frantically and eventually she told me to stop.

"Never," I said. "I am never letting you out of my sight again; do you hear me?"

She leaned over and kissed my forehead. The doctors had told me she had been very lucky and that her lungs seemed fine. Her eyes were still bothered by the gas they had been exposed to, but it would get better in time.

As I looked at my beautiful daughter, I suddenly heard a set of voices coming up behind her. The sound made my heart run amok.

"Christine? Alex?"

"Mo-o-om! Alex won't stop talking about bunnies. It's all he ever talks about, and it is driving me nuts!" Christine exclaimed. "He's been reading everything on the Internet about them."

"Dad promised me we could get bunnies," Alex said with that glint in his eyes.

My mom and Chad came in with them. Chad held Alex by the shoulders. He shrugged while I hugged my mom.

"You look awful, dear," she said and corrected my hair like that would help. I chose to ignore her.

"You did what?" I asked Chad, suddenly thrown back to reality. "You promised them bunnies? And just who is supposed to take care of them?"

"I will," Alex said. "I love bunnies; they're so CUTE!"

"What can I say?" Chad said. "I felt bad for the kids. We didn't know when you'd be home, and I gave in. I was weak; forgive me."

I took in a deep breath of oxygen through the mask.

"I guess we're getting bunnies then."

"YEAH!" Alex exclaimed, then gave me a warm hug. I coughed again and had to take another couple of deep breaths with the oxygen when I realized someone else had arrived in the room too.

She was standing a little behind the others, looking shy. She was wearing a hat and sunglasses, even though we were indoors. Not to be recognized, I guessed, but someone had to tell her that wearing a hat and sunglasses only made people look at her even more.

"Sydney," I said with a sigh. I reached out my hands and grabbed hers in mine. "Thank you. For all your help. I couldn't have done this without you."

She shrugged. "What are sisters for, right? You could have told me you were on an FBI mission, though. Would have made me feel a whole lot better."

"It had to seem real," I said. "From now on, I'll tell you every-thing. I promise."

Sydney hugged me and held me tight, then whispered. "There was no mission, was there? It's something you have all come up with afterward, isn't it?"

I chuckled, then smiled. "On second thought, you don't need to know everything. There should be room for a little mystery between sisters."

I shared a glance with Matt, and he smiled. I then saw him look nervously at Chad. He was surrounded by our children, who seemed to be exhilarated to have their father back in their lives. I couldn't blame them, but I couldn't blame Matt either for feeling a little threatened by the presence of my ex.

I reached out my hand and grabbed Matt's in mine, then took a deep breath from the oxygen mask before I removed it and looked deeply into his eyes.

"Matt?"

"Yeah?"

"I love you," I said and touched his lips gently. "Gosh, how I love you."

THE END

Want do know what happens next?
Get Book 4 in the Eva Rae Thomas Mystery Series,
SAY YOU LOVE ME here:
https://readerlinks.com/l/704695

Afterword

Dear Reader,

Thank you for purchasing *Never Ever (Eva Rae Thomas #3)*. It was a thrill to write this book, and I hope you had just as much fun reading it as I had writing it. Now, you might be thinking '*what a crazy ride; I'm glad these things didn't happen in real life.*' But a lot of it actually has happened, I am afraid. When writing this book, I have picked things from real life, amazing as it sounds. Three of the stories came from real actual events.

A little while ago, a story broke down here in Florida about a health inspector. The inspector had been to several massage parlors and spas during routine checks and discovered that they were harboring trafficked girls. The story became very big and ended up involving celebrities who had been to these places.

The shocking part — to me at least — was that we see these places in strip malls everywhere. To think that they are keeping young girls as sex slaves in places like that, in areas I pass by every day, right under our noses, is so scary to me.

If you haven't heard about it, then you can read more here:

https://www.tcpalm.com/story/news/crime/2019/03/15/
trafficking-spa-inspection-records-show-red-flags/3079435002/

https://www.bostonherald.com/2019/04/30/health-inspector-
testified-she-felt-uneasy-in-florida-spa/

In the book, we meet a young woman who joins a cult called NYX, encouraged by a friend who thinks it will be good for her. What happens to her was highly inspired by the current real-life drama of the cult NXIVM. This story has so much fascination; I knew I had to write about it. How the celebrities and billionaires fell into this leader's claws - and how he preyed on their vulnerabilities. The things he got away with doing to them, like branding them and having sex with them. It is truly gripping.

If interested, you can read more here:

https://www.rollingstone.com/culture/culture-news/nxivm-
what-we-know-about-alleged-sex-trafficking-forced-labor-204958/

The book begins with a nerve gas attack on the Metrorail in Miami. This was inspired by the gas attacks in Japan in 1995, where a cult brought in bags of nerve gas and released it. None of the passengers suspected that anything was going on, till it was too late and they had trouble breathing. Here's a link if you want to know more:

https://www.bbc.com/news/world-asia-35975069

Thanks again for all your support. Don't forget to grab the next book in the series, called *Say You Love Me*, and don't forget to leave a review if you can. It means so much to me.

Take care,

Willow

To be the first to hear about new releases and bargains from Willow Rose, sign up below to be on the VIP List. (I promise not to share your email with anyone else, and I won't clutter your inbox.)

- GO HERE TO SIGN UP TO BE ON THE VIP LIST :
http://readerlinks.com/l/415254

Tired of too many emails? Text the word: "willowrose" to 31996 to sign up to Willow's VIP text List to get a text alert with news about New Releases, Giveaways, Bargains and Free books from Willow.

FOLLOW WILLOW ROSE ON BOOKBUB:
https://www.bookbub.com/authors/willow-rose

Connect with Willow online:
https://www.amazon.com/Willow-Rose/e/B004X2WHBQ
https://www.facebook.com/willowredrose/
https://twitter.com/madamwillowrose
http://www.goodreads.com/author/show/
4804769.Willow_Rose
Http://www.willow-rose.net
madamewillowrose@gmail.com

About the Author

Willow Rose is a multi-million-copy best-selling Author and an Amazon ALL-star Author of more than 80 novels. Her books are sold all over the world.

She writes Mystery, Thriller, Paranormal, Romance, Suspense, Horror, Supernatural thrillers, and Fantasy.

Willow's books are fast-paced, nail-biting page-turners with twists you won't see coming. That's why her fans call her The Queen of Plot Twists.

Several of her books have reached the Kindle top 10 of ALL books in the US, UK, and Canada. She has sold more than three million books all over the world.

Willow lives on Florida's Space Coast with her husband and two daughters. When she is not writing or reading, you will find her surfing and watch the dolphins play in the waves of the Atlantic Ocean.

Tired of too many emails? Text the word: "willowrose" to 31996 to sign up to Willow's VIP Text List to get a text alert with news about New Releases, Giveaways, Bargains and Free books from Willow.

Cover design by Juan Villar Padron,
https://www.juanjpadron.com

Special thanks to my editor Janell Parque
http://janellparque.blogspot.com/

**To be the first to hear about new releases and bargains
from Willow Rose, sign up below to be on the VIP List.** (I
promise not to share your email with anyone else, and I won't clutter
your inbox.)

- GO HERE TO SIGN UP TO BE ON THE VIP LIST :
http://readerlinks.com/l/415254

Tired of too many emails? Text the word: "willowrose" to
31996 to sign up to Willow's VIP text List to get a text alert with
news about New Releases, Giveaways, Bargains and Free books
from Willow.

CPSIA information can be obtained
at www.ICGtesting.com
Printed in the USA
LVHW101525080223
739004LV00019B/610/J

9 781954 139732